I0598244

THE MISSING THREAD

SACRED KNIGHT: LEGEND #5

DAWN BLAIR

MORNING SKY STUDIOS

Copyright © 2021 by Dawn Blair

All rights reserved.

ISBN: 978-0-9985441-5-1

No part of this book may be reproduced in any form or by any electronic or mechanical means, including information storage and retrieval systems, without written permission from the author, except for the use of brief quotations in a book review.

The story and characters are entirely fictional. Any resemblance to actual events, persons (living or dead), or locales is purely coincidental.

Cover and layout copyright © 2021 by Morning Sky Studios
Cover design by Dawn Blair/Morning Sky Studios
Cover art copyright © Kriscole | Dreamstime.com,
© Alona Stepaniuk | Dreamstime.com, © Sonyakamoz | Dreamstime.com,
© Photowitch | Dreamstime.com

Torch image © Kreatiw | Dreamstime.com

Morning Sky Studios
PO Box 5422
Twin Falls, ID 83303
Visit us at www.morningskystudios.com

ALSO BY DAWN BLAIR:

Onesong

Tangled Magic

Walk the Path

Sacred Knight

Quest for the Three Books

Manifest the Magic

To Birth a Destiny

History of a Dead Man (companion novella)

Prince of the Ruined Land

The Unicorn and the Secret (companion novella)

The Loki Adventures

1-800-CallLoki (Omnibus of novellas 1-5)

1 800 IceBaby

Help Wanted, Call Loki

Wells of the Onesong

The Doorway Prince

Stardust

Mystery of the Stardust Monk

Alexander's Den

And many more!

To Gordon K.

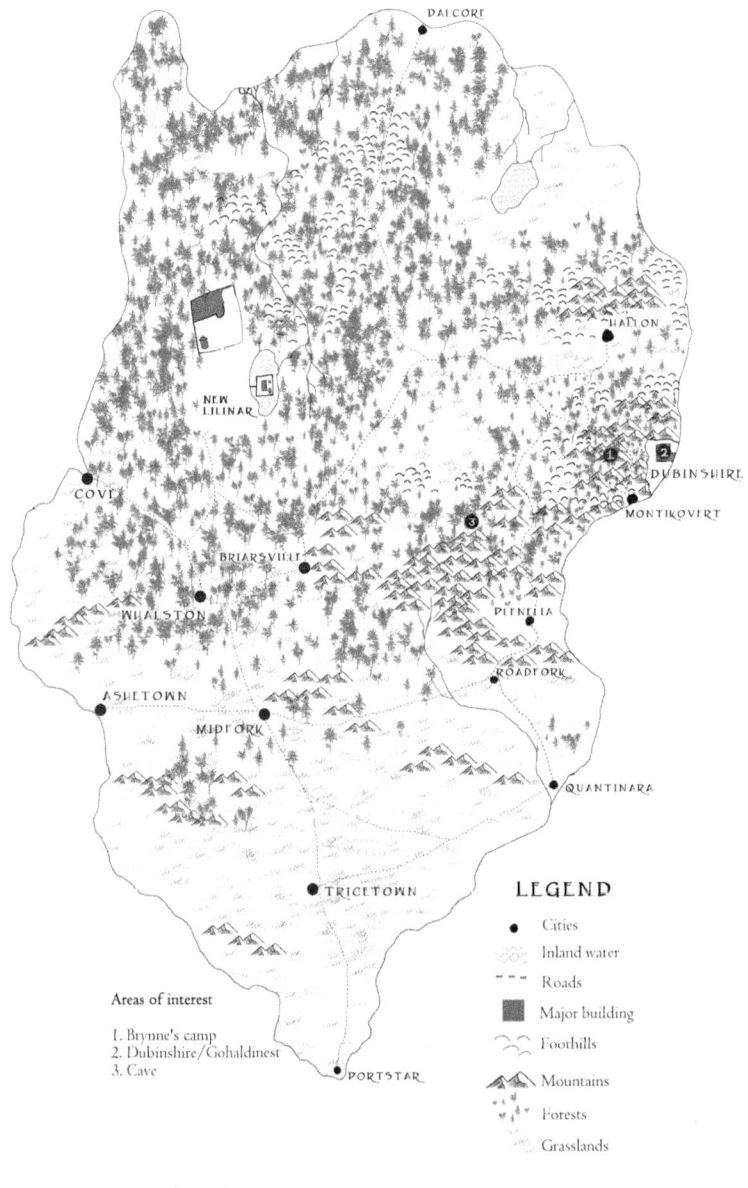

DALCORE

IZY

NEW
LILINAR

COVE

HADLON

1 DUBINSHIRE
2

3 MONTIKOVERT

BRIARSVILLE

PLENELA

WHALSTON

ROADFORK

ASHETOWN

MIDFORK

QUANTINARA

TRICETOWN

LEGEND

•   Cities

   Inland water

– – –   Roads

   Major building

   Foothills

   Mountains

   Forests

   Grasslands

Areas of interest

1. Brynne's camp
2. Dubinshire/Gohaldinest
3. Cave

PORTSTAR

Main characters

Steigan – Our hero of the tale
Aeribela – Princess of Dubinshire and daughter of Lord Irragon
Alityka – the first Dominari and the Goddess, Steigan's woman in white
Arlyn – Steigan's friend and mentor
Cirvel – Lord of Gohaldinest and the Destroyer of Civilization
Dragzel – Ellis' pet cahaster
Ellis – son of Tethys and Greytas
Ithanes Selmik – former Lord of Dubinshire
Keteria – last Queen of Lilinar who cast a spell to withhold magic from the world, Tanold's twin sister
Laurient de Santz – former sapere and longtime friend to Steigan
Martias Pendorian (Martias-na) – once Steigan's best friend, -na designation refers to his title of Necroatheling
Rivic Taburath – Founded the city of Lilinar and a relative to Steigan
Valic Tymerrianon – a dominus for the Temple and member of the Onim

Other characters

Adonid – prior Holy Sapere
Brynne – a dominus for the Temple
Cetty – Brynne's daughter and Rue's wife
Epious – Ithane's father
Galault – guardian and watcher of worlds
Greytas – a dominus for the Temple
Irragon – Lord of Dubinshire and Aeribela's father

Kalis – Brynne's grandson
Norsis – Brynne's son
Phyn – Quin's late wife
Quin – Brynne's son
Rue – Kalis' father
Tigma – a unicorn
Torsep – a man from Hallon leading several magic sick people toward Dubinshire
Verna – Brynne's wife

Cameo/Mentions

Annae (Bytherhourn) Chitanik – Searn and Centhya's daughter raised by Steigan in the life of his former timeline
Centhya Bytherhourn – Searn's wife
Cirello Taburath – king of Lilinar and Steigan's father
Corina Taburath – queen of Lilinar and Steigan's mother
Ellonia – daughter and tribal healer for Chief Krithstand, Rivic's love
Freygorio (Frey) – son of Lord Ithanes
Jepssa Pendorian – Martias older brother and chief of one of the centaur tribes
Krithstand – tribal chief during the time of Gohaldinest, father to Alityka and Ellonia
Leloran – High Maege of Dubinshire for Lord Ithanes
Lucinia Balas – Sim's wife and Steigan's adopted mother
Matoline (Lihn Harvestendale) – mistress to Lord Cirvel, she is mother to Keteria and Tanold
Nyree Taburath – Rivic's twin sister
Searn Bytherhourn – Steigan's uncle
Sim Balas – Lucinia's husband and Steigan's adopted father
Tanold – Keteria's twin brother
Tethys – Ellis' mother
Tyana – Steigan's unicorn

CHAPTER 1

"The life of man is like a game with dice; if you don't get the throw you want, you must show your skill in making the best of the throw you get."

— TERENCE (ROMAN PLAYWRIGHT)

---

*M*orning light filtered through the dense pine trees, scattering broken shadows over criss crossing ruts in the dirt mountain road. The colors in the cloud-streaked sky, which had started off pink, now drifted to a burning orange. Soon, they would blaze silver for just a moment before draining to white.

The exertion of the ascending climb kept the chill from Steigan's skin, but he had already noticed the weather's change brought from the difference in altitude from yesterday. Among the evergreen trees, the aspens here were losing their leaves. Already, a colorful blanket formed over the ground, preparing for all the plants to seep their energy back to their roots to sleep through the coming snow season.

Steigan found himself breathing deeper, relaxing even, and that disturbed him. He needed to be focusing on solving the problems at hand, not languishing in a carefree moment. Yet his thoughts wouldn't stay where he wanted them directed. Rather, he wished to enjoy the outdoors and the scent of the campfire still lingering on him. It reminded him of better times.

Yet, it would be nice when they were in Dubinshire and he could have a bath and wash the constant taste of grit from his mouth.

"Nothing like a long uphill hike," Lord Ithanes groaned as he looked at the mountain before him. "Lovely way to start the day."

"Are you going to complain about going home?" Steigan asked, stretching out his stride a little so he could come up alongside Ithanes. He let his gaze drift up the trail set before them and travel all the way up to the sky. It would be another day or so before they caught sight of Dubinshire, the city Ithanes once ruled.

"You probably have considered these last few days great fun, haven't you?" Ithanes said, grimacing at Steigan. "Sleeping out in the woods, rocks beneath you, not only as a pillow, but to continuously jab you in the ribs or in your side every time you move."

Steigan shrugged, enjoying the crisp morning air against his face. "While I won't say these past days in the forest hasn't reminded me of many fond memories of time I spent with Arlyn while growing up," he said, with a quick look back at the others following him up the mountain trail, "there is something to be said about returning home after being away so long."

He didn't realize how much the words affected him until

after he'd said them. In some ways, Steigan was going home too, yet that wasn't quite correct. He'd resided in Dubinshire for many cycles. But he was pretending to be Searn and very few people had known his true identity. He had never settled there. Even now, his heart wanted to be back at Whalston. Or Lilinar. With a sorrowful pang, he realized that New Lilinar wasn't his home and it never had been. It made him feel even more like a traitor to the Temple. He didn't feel like he fit with these people traveling up the mountain with him. He sure wasn't certain where he belonged in this world.

"Your thoughts are a bit far off, Dominari." Ithanes' usual, steady, insightful tone had returned.

"I have too much to think about these days. Two lifetimes' worth."

Ithanes nodded and glanced back toward the trail, which he followed toward the top of the mountain. It was impossible to see Dubinshire from here, but it wouldn't stop them from trying anyway.

"What's he like?" Ithanes asked.

"Who?" Steigan asked.

"The current Lord of Dubinshire. Or is it a Lady of Dubinshire."

It took Steigan a moment to decipher the information that Ithanes really wanted. Dubinshire had always used Lord and Lady to designate their rulers rather than the title of King or Queen as Lilinar did, but both had called the heirs as Prince or Princess. "It is lord, but I don't know Irragon," Steigan commented. He couldn't recall if Aeribela had ever mentioned her mother.

Ithanes drew in a tight breath. "Lord Irragon." For a moment, he said nothing further, as if his thoughts centered on the name.

The pause gave Steigan another moment to look back at the weary group on the slope behind them. Arlyn and Valic hauled a stretcher carrying Rivic while Aeribela walked beside as if she were a funeral's Honor Guard. Laurient pulled a travois bearing Keteria while Ellis and Dragzel followed behind watching for signs that they were being followed or tracked.

"I have not had much chance to speak with her. What is she like?" Ithanes made a jerking motion with his head to indicate someone behind them.

"Do you mean Princess Aeribela?"

Ithanes nodded. "Princess Aeribela," he confirmed more slowly as if letting the name and title lock firmly in his mind. "Tell me about her."

Steigan's mind went blank and he shook his head. "She's the princess of Dubinshire. She put herself in serious jeopardy in coming to New Lilinar to find the books which sent me back in time. What is it that you want to know?"

"Does she have any siblings?"

"She had a sister," Steigan said. "She died in one of the magic pulses."

A sorrowful looked pressed across Ithanes' face. "Is that it?"

"I believe so."

"How about cousins?"

Steigan realized how sadly little he knew about Aeribela. "In this timeline, I haven't been friends with her for very long." He glanced at her again, noticing her bouncing ringlets had wilted into straggly curls. She walked, dirty faced, with her gaze on the ground and a tired sag to her shoulders.

Steigan saw something off the path and quickly realized that if he hadn't been looking back at the rest of the group, he would have missed this entirely. Reaching toward Ithanes, but not quite touching him, Steigan veered around to the other side as he whispered, "Move to the far side of the road. Quietly. Draw the others with you and stay together."

"What?" Ithanes asked, spinning around.

But Steigan bolted toward the sign he'd seen in a scrawny tree just off the road. As he went, he caught Arlyn's questioning gaze. Steigan gestured toward his eyes, pointed, then held up the index finger of his left hand and bent it with the right to indicate a snapped branch. Arlyn nodded with understanding as his hand went to his hilt. He whispered something to the others, but Steigan couldn't hear it, only saw the fear rise in Aeribela's eyes as she started moving toward where Ithanes stood. As the group gathered, Valic moved with Arlyn over to where Steigan examined the oddly twisted and knotted branch he'd found.

"Someone's been here. It's a couple days old."

"At least," Arlyn said. "We have no idea who or why."

Steigan could tell Arlyn was trying to dismiss this as if it weren't important. Maybe it wasn't. Or, it could mean trouble. "Martias has been this way."

"Why would he leave a sign for you?" Valic asked. "Wouldn't he rather that you didn't know he'd been here and take you by surprise?"

"I agree," Arlyn said. "We shouldn't go making assumptions."

Steigan acquiesced. "All right, but we should check it out, make certain."

"Steigan, the Onim of Dubinshire might just have been out here doing some training or patrolling. They do that. Remember, my grandfather taught me, so there's quite a few people who use the same signals. We don't want to stumble upon any Onim members out here. It'd be hard to explain what we're doing."

"Then we don't let them sneak up behind us. And if we find them first, we leave them alone. Agreed?

"I'll tell Laurient," Valic said. "You two start. I'll catch up."

As Steigan and Arlyn stepped off the path into the forest,

Arlyn growled, "Why would you think that Martias was here already?"

"We don't know if he's been traveling by magic. We spent several days with the centaurs and we've been traveling encumbered since then. Martias could be ahead of us."

"If we can't use magic, then why would you think that they can?"

"I don't know what fuels the Destroyer's magic, but he still is using it. I have to wait for mine to catch up, but I don't assume that his is the same. And Martias, he's had magic for a while, as you well know. I don't think any of us knows what the rules are here, so let's quit presuming that we do."

Steigan went several more paces, trying to get a little ahead and hoping that Arlyn would remain quiet, knowing the possible dangers that could be around them. Steigan just didn't want to continue the argument. However, he saw another marker and pointed it out to Arlyn, "Look, here's another."

The rich, forest undergrowth squished and snapped beneath their feet as Arlyn moved over to study the break. "I don't think this is the Onim. They would never use the same one twice."

"Neither would Martias."

The statement fell with a quiet stare between them. Then Steigan looked back out into the forest.

"Found something?" Valic asked, coming up to them.

Arlyn was the one to answer him. "Only a bigger mystery of who is out here." Arlyn pointed at the twisted branch and received Valic's muttered acknowledgement in response.

Steigan turned and walked away, searching the ground rather than the branches. "Here!"

He knelt as the others came closer. Steigan used his fingertips to gently probe the soft outline of a footprint on the undergrowth. "Hard to tell for certain, but I think it's the boot of a dominus."

Arlyn's knees creaked as he joined Steigan to examine the print.

"Here's another," Valic called out.

Steigan didn't wait for Arlyn to rise but went to check out what Valic had found. "Two prints," Steigan reported to Arlyn, "spaced closely together. More pressure on the outside of the right foot. He was hobbling."

"Come on. Let's see if we can find some more of the trail." Arlyn's face held a worried concern that now played out through his hurried movements.

Going in the direction of the footprints, Steigan, Arlyn, and Valic spread out to follow a path which they soon found to be clumsy and obvious. Whoever had come this way had no skills at tracking or covering their trail. The single twisted branch was used over and over more like bread-crumbs to follow. Steigan started to worry if they had intentionally been pulled away from the others.

"Valic, go check on the others please," Steigan said in hushed tones. He really didn't want Arlyn to hear and sense the fears going through him right now.

Valic merely nodded and turned away. Steigan quickly lost sight of him through the trees and soon the movements of Valic's retreat diminished to silence.

"Why haven't we found him?" Arlyn turned in a circle to do a blind search of the forest. "Certainly, he's lame or injured. He can't have gone far."

Apparently Arlyn had someone already in mind. "This trail is a couple days old. Maybe he just needed to find his way off the road far enough to have a safe camp, then he went back to the road and continued for Dubinshire. We might find him along the way."

"Have you seen any retreating footsteps?"

Steigan flinched at the harsh question. It had been a long time since Arlyn had used that chiding tone with him, indicating that he'd stated a blunderously naïve opinion. He found himself at a loss for words.

"I'm sorry. It's been a long journey." Arlyn rubbed his hands over his face. "You've hardly said two words to anyone other than that Ithanes fellow since leaving the centaurs, and he has said less than that to us. He treats us like peasants."

"Ithanes treats everyone like that. Do not take offense by it."

"What makes you so sure that we should trust him?"

"What makes you think I can't?"

Arlyn turned his gaze away. "I'm sorry. Maybe I just feel left out of the plans."

"Left out? We're making this up as we go along. We're out here running for our lives, knowing that if Cirvel and Martias catch up to us, it's over. And now we're out here fighting over this trail."

"You're right; these markers are days old. Maybe someone set them in case he didn't locate what he was looking for and wanted to find his way back."

Steigan took Arlyn's words under advisement. What was located out here that someone could possibly be going to? He couldn't think of a single thing. Still, Arlyn's theory was a likelihood.

"Some people need to know when to break away," Arlyn said, his words slowed with thoughtfulness. "Maybe now that Aeribela is with you and you're on your way to Dubinshire with Lord Ithanes, I should head back to Whalston. Sim and Lucinia could probably use my help."

"What's really going on with you?" Steigan stepped back and assessed Arlyn for a moment.

Tears gathered in Arlyn's eyes and he blinked rapidly as he tried to hide them away. "I'm feeling old, Steigan. When I gave up the life of a dominus, it's like my body was done. Blacksmithing hasn't been easy either."

That Steigan knew all too well. "I know."

"I don't even have the forge house to return to. I don't know what I'm going to do."

"Your forge house is gone?"

A single breath broke from Arlyn's lips. He drew in another quick breath, then let out a ragged sigh and nodded.

"So, what you really need is a mission to keep your mind off of what you've lost?"

"No! I can't start over again. This was fine for a while, but I don't have the endurance for it anymore. I'm tired."

"We're all tired. It'll all look better when we get to Dubinshire and we've had a meal and some sleep." Steigan reached out and grasped Arlyn's arm. "Come on, you're with us. We're heading to Dubinshire. Forward, not backwards."

Tears spilled over Arlyn's cheeks and he wiped them away with both hands at once. "Forward."

Steigan turned Arlyn away from the path they'd found and started to guide him back toward the road. Meanwhile it was hard not to touch the armor he wore, even though the armor he'd made in Arlyn's forge house rested on Searn's corpse beneath the Temple in New Lilinar. He had so many memories. To think of Whalston gone made him want to cry out in agony. Arlyn's tears weren't helping. He wanted to tell Arlyn that he was sorry, but the words wouldn't issue from his tight throat.

"Well, if this isn't a first," a voice cracked behind them. "The two of you caught both unaware and speechless."

Steigan's first reaction to the familiar contempt rising within him was to draw his sword, but he only got his hand to his hilt before realizing that Arlyn stood between him and Dominus Brynne.

"Got your wits about you and come to join the domini, I hope," Brynne stated.

Arlyn moved forward to grasp Brynne's arm in a firm, friendly greeting. "I wondered if it might be you out here. Long way from home, aren't you?"

Brynne's cold eyes glanced Steigan over. "Not sure I should be saying. Our present company is a traitor."

"No more than I am," Arlyn defended.

"Then you aren't here to join the domini?"

Now more than ever, Steigan wanted to get back to the group on the road and get them far up the mountain until they were behind the large, locked gates of Dubinshire.

Arlyn continued with caution, "There are other domini here, in the forest?"

"No, they're going to Dubinshire."

"Why?" Steigan asked.

"To destroy the city." Brynne pointed at Steigan and started to laugh. "You are still in leagues with those superstitious evildoers, aren't you?"

Arlyn didn't look happy that Steigan had jumped in and thrown diplomacy to the wind. "Brynne, what are you doing out here? If there are domini here, why aren't you with the rest of them?"

Brynne's face took on the same saddened look Arlyn's had had only moments ago. The older dominus wrapped his arms around himself and turned away. "My grandson... I couldn't let them see."

"You couldn't let who see what?" Arlyn asked with a cautious step forward. He put his hand on Brynne's shoulder.

Brynne shook his head as vigorously as he could and he nearly fell over from the effort of it. He ran his hand over his head, shrinking into himself. His fingers plowed through his whitened hair. "Goddess, why is this happening?"

Arlyn caught Brynne before the older man fell over.

Holding Brynne by his upper arms, Arlyn shook him gently. "Dominus Brynne, tell me what's going on?"

Brynne started to rock, gasping. "He's with Verna. Why doesn't Adonid come back?" He covered his face with his hands. "He can appease the Goddess."

"Brynne, take us to your grandson. Maybe we can help."

Steigan once more found himself under the scrutiny of the older dominus. Brynne stepped closer, but he was still shaking. "Are you Saint Steigan returned?"

Wishing he could weigh the answer he could give with what the old man wanted, Steigan felt the unicorn magic pressing the answer from him. "I am Saint Steigan and I have returned."

Brynne limped over to him and reached out unsurely to grasp Steigan's hand. "Then I certainly don't want to ask, and I don't have the right to, but will you please help me?"

The domini were on the road somewhere out there and Steigan's friends might very well be falling into a trap set for them. Did the domini know they would be going to Dubinshire and figured they only had to wait? Was this a distraction, or a trap?

Steigan wished he could feel anything beyond this quiet spot in the forest.

Brynne's wizened fingers tightened around his.

The dominus had never been kind to Steigan. He wanted nothing more than to turn Brynne away, but the warmth of the old man's hands on his convinced Steigan that Brynne had never meant to be cold. Right now, Brynne pleaded with the champion of the unicorns, not with the young, impressionable boy Steigan had once been.

"I will help. Where is your grandson?"

CHAPTER 2

Through the forest trees, the sight of several people gathered around a central bonfire came into view. A couple, a man and a woman, stood separated from the others in a worried huddle. The man raised the woman's hands in his and held them tightly against his chest. She slowly leaned in toward him.

Brynne entered their camp first with Steigan and Arlyn following behind. Many of the family members turned and stared, their eyes going wide at the sight of the newcomers. A woman matching Brynne's age stood and approached Brynne as he reached the campfire at the center, then she flung her arms around him to hug him. Her gray hair was pulled back into a bun and Steigan couldn't help the emotional pang he felt at thinking of Lucinia.

"You remember my wife, Verna?" Brynne said.

Steigan couldn't say that he did.

Verna turned from Brynne and bowed to Arlyn. "Dominus Arlyn, Dominus Steigan, welcome."

Arlyn tipped his head forward. "Please, you don't need to

use the titles. Chances are good that we don't have them anymore."

"I officially don't," Steigan said nonchalantly. If all these people were family or friends of Brynne, he would not let any of them see his aggravation over losing his title. He'd worked hard for it in two lifetimes. On the other hand, he would easily sacrifice being a dominus for being a Dominari. So, in truth, he didn't much mind losing his title after all. He smiled at himself for the recognition of his own growth.

"Come, my grandson is this way?" Brynne stated, motioning for Steigan to follow.

"Brynne?" Verna asked, putting a hand out to Brynne's chest.

He smiled back at her. "He's here to help."

Steigan felt the surge of magic and spotted the boy's location. He started to move in that direction. "I see him. I'll go."

The couple at the camp's perimeter started to move to intercept, but Steigan suspected that Brynne waved them off as they stopped. The man draped his arms around the woman, embracing her with strength. Steigan gave them a glance, glad that they had each other to cling to in this uncertain time. Then he continued forward.

A sweat-drenched child of four cycles lay curled up on his side, thumb in his mouth while blue webbing covered the exposed skin. A coarse blanket shrouded the full terrifying sight of his body encased in the magic sickness.

Steigan knelt beside the boy, who gave no acknowledgement of Steigan's presence. "How long has he been like this?"

"Three days," Brynne answered, still standing back.

Steigan started to reach out for the boy, but at the sounds of struggle, noticed the woman break from the man's embrace and come rushing forward. "What are you going to do?" she asked.

13

"If I take a little bit of the magic from him, it'll clear his head." Steigan kept a calm voice.

She nodded.

Steigan reached down and swept two fingers across the child's feverish brow, taking in a layer of the child's magic. Rather than the wisps floating away, they absorbed into Steigan's skin and he felt the uplift of his own magic like it had been recharged.

The boy moaned and his eyes fluttered.

"Kalis!" The woman dashed over and dropped down beside him. She tried to gather him in her arms as he started to open his eyes, but Steigan stopped her.

"He still has a ways to go," Steigan said.

"Yes, but you've given us hope!" She glanced up to her husband now coming to stand beside them, then she reached up to take ahold of his hand as she smiled brightly.

"Cetty, let him work," the man said to her.

Kalis opened his eyes. He tried to speak, seeing his mother and father there, but he couldn't make the words in his weakness.

"Let me help you with that. Watch." Steigan touched a finger to the boy's brow and pulled a thin line of the blue magic away from him. He held it up and circled it in the air. A bird of the same color as the webbing took flight into the night sky.

The child giggled.

Steigan gathered another wisp from the boy and let it take wing.

"How are you doing this?" Cetty asked, a mixture of fear and awe.

The unicorn magic pressed him to answer, but her husband leaned forward. "Cetty, don't ask him how he does it; just be glad that he does."

She smiled with a soft sigh and nodded. It brought release to Steigan.

"Do it again," Kalis whispered around his thumb, his voice a frail, muffled rasp.

Steigan shook his head. "You do it. Take the magic and blow it away into the wind."

"Don't encourage him," Cetty's husband growled. "Take it all from him."

Steigan looked up, feeling anger hardening in his face. "I won't do that."

The boy pulled his thumb from his mouth and looked at the webbing surrounding his hand. He puffed against it. The tiniest of birds flew away and vanished like the first. The child giggled again.

"You can control this magic. This is your power." Steigan placed a hand on Kalis' shoulder. "I hope you understand that."

Kalis sat up. As he did so, the sweat evaporated from his forehead. Some of the webbing fell from him. "It's going away," the child cried out fearfully.

"No, it will always be within you."

"No," Cetty gasped as she realized the meaning of Steigan's words. He cut her off with a sharp glare.

"You need to walk around, shake off being magic spun. Then you need rest," Steigan told Kalis.

The boy stood up and hugged his mother, then ran to his father and hugged him as well. As his father released Kalis from a tight embrace, Kalis blew more birds from his hand. The webbing continued to dissolve as Kalis ran to the other people in camp, delighting them with the creatures he created.

Tears puffed in Brynne's eyes. "Thank you." Brynne turned and walked away to follow his grandson.

Cetty's husband approached Steigan, his hand out. "I am

Rue." After a quick handshake, Rue put his arm around Steigan and drew him away from the others. "While I am grateful for what you have done for my boy, I hope you haven't created a monster. This goes against the Goddess."

"Your son has magic. That is the way the Goddess has created him. And She decided for me, someone with magic, to be nearby and directed me to help. If you see fault with that, then you have a problem with what you have learned of the Goddess' teachings. The mistake lies with your misguided understanding, not with the nature of what is."

"Steigan, come," Brynne waved to him. "I wish you to meet the rest of my family."

Steigan stepped away from Rue and Kalis rushed over and took Steigan's hand, pulling him toward the rest of the family. "These are my uncles, Norsis and Quin!"

Steigan recognized Norsis as one of the merchants in New Lilinar. His hair was the same color as Steigan remembered Brynne's had once been. Had Steigan ever seen the two of them together, Steigan would have realized they were father and son.

The younger man who acknowledged the name Quin looked pale and weak.

"May I see your hands," Steigan asked Quin, who shook his head.

Brynne came over. "Son, are you all right?"

"I'm fine," Quin insisted, but there was a flash of bright blue in his eyes.

"You're magic spun too, aren't you?" Steigan said.

Quin trembled as he raised his hands and uncurled his fingers from around his palm.

Kalis drew in a long, excited breath. "Uncle Quin, you can make birds too!"

"I don't want this," Quin hissed. He pressed his hands

together, attempting to wipe away the blue webbing collecting on his palms.

Norsis shook his brother. "You watched my wife die. Do you want the same thing to happen to you? Let Dominus Steigan help you like he did Kalis."

"Dominari Steigan. I no longer hold the title of dominus." Steigan reached out, waiting to see if Quin would pull away. When Quin didn't, Steigan tugged a thread of magic. It evaporated, but Steigan felt the rush of power.

"I get it. I understand," Quin muttered as he studied his hands.

Kalis jumped up and down trying to reach Quin's arm. "Make birds with me!"

Quin sat down on a log and held out his palm. Kalis climbed up beside him and pulled some of the sticky webbing from Quin, then made it fly away as a bird. Quin took another and turned it into a horse which galloped around between his family members before dissipating.

Verna pressed her hands over her face. Arlyn stood nearby, trying to comfort her.

"Your wife died from this?" Steigan asked Norsis.

"Yes, a couple days after we left New Lilinar. When she first showed signs like Quin, I went out to fetch my father, to tell him that we needed to bring our brother back, and I found out my wife wasn't the only one ill. Many of the people were getting sick and dying. We decided to catch the domini to get them to return home. We all left the city together, but Phyn didn't make it across the flatlands. Then Kalis fell sick. Is the Goddess angry with us for the Holy Sapere's actions? You were the one that gathered the signs. Why does she turn her favor from him now?"

Rue charged forward until he came face to face with Steigan. "She is angry because a dominus once again betrayed Her saperes! Strange that you carry the same name as the Bloody Saint!"

Brynne came over and shoved Rue, surprisingly forcing the man back. "How dare you? He is Saint Steigan and he saved your son as well as my own. Do you not clearly see that Holy Sapere Martias is the one who has betrayed everyone?" Brynne stepped over to Steigan and put his hands on Steigan's upper arms, squeezing with probably as much force as the old man could muster. "I have been a wretched fool. It's not easy for me to admit that I've been wrong."

"It's fine. I get it." Steigan tried to pull away, but Brynne wouldn't let him go.

"No. You saved my grandson after I have never shown you any kindness. I realize you did this for him, not for me. You are a better man than me and I want you to know this. I mocked you and poured hate onto you. I said things that were unforgivable. I wanted you to fail so that I could laugh at you." He raised his head to look at Steigan. "But if you had failed, my grandson would not be recovering now. That makes me a foolish man. I planted no seed of kindness, yet now I reap a harvest not my own. The Goddess will not clear such a debt. I owe you. I will help you defeat Martias."

"Your family needs you. You are their only guardian. I won't take you from them. There is no debt; I merely did what was right. Pettiness, jealousy, and superstition don't serve people. If I have made you understand that, then you should now understand that the Goddess doesn't keep score and hold you in liability. Only you can do that to yourself. Even I hold no claim over you. There is no repayment to be made."

Once again on the edge of tears, Brynne hugged Steigan. "Arlyn is a lucky man, getting to call you son."

"Are you hungry? Would you like something to eat or drink" Verna asked.

"We have friends waiting for us," Arlyn said. "But, Dominus Brynne, you said the domini were heading toward Dubinshire and Norsis mentioned he'd gone to get you to bring Adonid back. Can you explain what all that is about?"

Steigan remembered Norsis saying that he wanted Brynne to fetch his brother back. Did that mean that Adonid was Norsis' brother and Brynne's son?

Brynne nodded his head. "Adonid leads the domini toward Dubinshire. He intends on starting a war. But if his own family holds magic, then what he is doing is wrong."

Quin rose from his seat on the log and approached Steigan. "Can I talk to you?"

"Of course." Steigan replied, then followed Quin as he led the two of them away from the group. "What's on your mind?"

"I want to go with you."

"I'm not sure that's a good idea."

"But I need to learn about the magic. You can't go around to everyone who has this magic sickness and assist them. You can teach me, then I can help." His gaze moved faster as he surveyed Steigan's face and Steigan saw the desperation growing in his eyes. "I can then instruct Kalis. He'll need to know how to use his magic."

"I'm sorry. I have no time to help you. At any moment, I could be facing enemies I don't want to face myself, let alone watch out for someone else. I'm sorry, but you just can't come with us." Steigan started to turn away.

"I can talk to Adonid for you."

"He's the least of my concerns."

Quin grabbed Steigan's tunic sleeve. "Please. The only think I have ever done is help Norsis in his shop. I've never had anything different or special about me." He held out his hands, palms upward. "This could have killed me, like it did Norsis' wife, like I saw it doing to Kalis. I had kept it at bay for days, terrified that someone would notice. I don't know if you still believe in the Goddess or not, but I believe in Her and I have faith that this means something. If it didn't, you wouldn't have noticed me after helping Kalis. You did and when you pulled that thread of magic from me, I saw my place so clearly. That place is at your side."

"Look, your father and I have never been on the best of terms. I don't know how he's going to feel about you leaving with me."

"My father can be harsh, but he is a good man. Right now, he is very grateful to you. He will approve of me going with you especially if I can talk to Adonid. I can be the proof that magic runs in our family."

"And what if he wants to put you to death? That is the price of treason and your magic will be seen as just that."

Quin stepped closer and lowered his voice. "Adonid and Rue had quite a few interesting discussions about the superstitions of magic. A few cycles ago, they became more heated rather than their typical friendly discussions. Adonid had shifted his position. But then something else happened about the time Holy Sapere Martias was inducted. I don't know what it was, but Adonid was angry."

Steigan could only wonder if it was his own actions which infuriated Adonid so.

"If you think Rue is against magic, you should see Adonid now. I've never seen him so charged and ready to go to war, even during the Palin Wars."

If he hadn't been so young and naïve, Steigan might have paid more attention to why the domini had gone off to the Palin Wars. He remembered the Plenelians claiming that New Lilinar was hiding magic. They had tried to get Dubinshire to raise arms with them, but that never happened. The people of Dubinshire kept to their own superstitious beliefs about magic.

Steigan nearly whipped around. "The Bloody Saint!"

"What?" Quin asked.

"Rue knew that I had the same name as the Bloody Saint, but that's a myth that grew from Dubinshire. How did he hear about it?" He knew that somehow the legend of the Bloody Saint had reached Martias in New Lilinar, but how had it spread to someone who wasn't even a dominus... unless Brynne had heard it too. Had Adonid? Had anyone yet made the connection between St. Steigan and the Bloody Saint?

The Plenelians had.

No wonder when Arlyn had left for battle, he'd been so adamant about Steigan remaining in New Lilinar, and why he'd been so furious when Steigan had followed anyway.

Steigan realized that Quin still stood before him, but now Quin bore a confused look on his face. "I'm sorry. You can't go with us," Steigan said. He strode back into the camp with determination. "Arlyn, we need to be leaving."

Arlyn made some awkward goodbyes as Steigan continued through their camp and headed out into the woods. Steigan kept a moderate pace until Arlyn caught up to him, then he tried to speed it up, but Arlyn was too out of breath and kept falling behind.

When Steigan figured they were far enough away from Brynne's camp, he asked, "Was I the reason for the Palin Wars?"

"What? You? No!"

"What was it then? They obviously suspected that someone had magic and that New Lilinar was harboring it. So, they didn't make the connection between me and Saint Steigan?"

Arlyn huffed a deep breath. "No. It wasn't you."

"But then it was someone?"

"Yeah."

"Who, Arlyn?"

"Who was brought to the human so his tribe wouldn't put him to death?"

"Martias," Steigan sighed. "The Palin Wars were because of Martias?"

Arlyn shrugged as he continued to walk along with his head down, his feet dragging in the undergrowth as if he didn't care if he left a trail or not. He kicked a rock from its place, letting it skip along before them. "Ever since the time of Sapere Tanold, when he married a Plenelian princess, New Lilinar and Plenelia were against magic. The two countries always figure that if magic returned, they could stand together against Dubinshire."

"Wait, Tanold married a Plenelian?" Even though the question came out with shock, Steigan wasn't really that surprised that Keteria's magicless twin brother had taken an oath with someone from Plenelia. Tanold had never liked magic.

"Yes, but I don't understand why all this matters now." Arlyn stopped and doubled over, putting his hands on his knees.

At the distressed sounds of Arlyn panting and seeing the sweat forming on his brow, Steigan put his hand on Arlyn's shoulder. Even through the tunic, Arlyn was warm to Steigan's touch. "Are you sick?"

Arlyn waved him off. "Just tired. I told you, I'm getting too old for this."

Steigan needed to make Arlyn's journey easier. Maybe he needed to make everyone's traveling simpler. He disliked the thought of using his limited magic to flash everyone to Dubinshire even though it might be the quickest thing to do.

Was there another way? The unicorns possibly? They had frequently come to check up on him through the cycles when he'd been living in Dubinshire. They'd often come to his call, even though he'd felt anything but heroic and pure during those cycles of his other life. The unicorns had constantly been around him ever since he'd found Tyana, but since leaving the centaur tribe, he hadn't seen any hint of them. Were they around, watching him from a distance? Or were they unhappy about how he'd used their magic to travel through time once more? Maybe he'd drained them as much as he was, and they were resting and recuperating.

"Come on. Let's continue," Arlyn said, dragging Steigan from his thoughts. Arlyn's next few uncoordinated steps were lumbering and Steigan realized that Arlyn had been leaving a trail behind them, not because he didn't care about covering his tracks, but because the very act of walking took all his energy.

Steigan whistled, hoping that any unicorn strong enough to bear Arlyn would hear him. He repeated the sound, finding himself desperate now. If this didn't work, he'd have no choice but to flash them back to the road. He wished he hadn't sent Valic back to stay with the others. Steigan probably could carry Arlyn out if he had to, but if there were domini ahead, he needed to save his strength for that potential battle.

Had he done the right thing in leaving Quin behind? It would be handy to have someone here to help him with Arlyn now. Why had he refused Quin, especially since the argument to talk to Adonid had been so logical?

Because the boy had magic and Steigan didn't.

He knew the truth of it as soon as it flittered through his mind. Why did some people have magic and he still experienced being so drained? Was he losing it?

Was that why the unicorns never showed up? Did they feel he was unworthy of being their champion since he had wiped out all his magic? Surely that couldn't be the case.

He whistled again.

"Stop already," Arlyn grumbled.

Steigan proceeded after Arlyn, pretending like he wasn't disappointed by the lack of appearance of a unicorn. Knowing he needed to turn his thoughts, he reflected on the question Ithanes had asked him and realized that maybe Arlyn knew. "When you were captured and brought to Dubinshire, did you meet Lord Irragon? What's he like?"

"You asking because you want to know how Aeribela's father is going to react to you?" Arlyn asked with a chuckle.

"No. I've had a long time to think about my relationship with Aeribela and I've known other women. I'm a hard man to put up with. She needs someone better than me, someone who can focus on her rather than a mission."

Once again, Arlyn chortled. "At least you no longer are convinced that you're going to die in battle."

"If you can retire, so can I."

"May you do a better job of it than I did."

Steigan thought about being a blacksmith in Dubinshire, trying to take care of Annae and Centhya. He'd messed that up so badly. The amends he'd finally been able to make had never felt as if they were quite enough.

"Your thoughts always turn to that time, don't they?" Arlyn asked.

"My head is so full of things that I wish I could dump it out sometimes," Steigan answered.

"You'll have time soon enough."

Steigan wished he could share Arlyn's belief that this would all be over the moment magic returned, but Steigan knew differently. Martias-na and the Destroyer of Civilizations were out there somewhere making plans. Steigan didn't even know what their agenda was other than to get into Gohaldinest, the seat of Cirvel's power. But what made the old city so special?

"Steigan!" Valic called out, jogging toward them.

Steigan and Arlyn were coming out onto the road a little downhill from the rest of the party. Relief came over Steigan at seeing everyone together and safe.

"No signs of Adonid?" Steigan checked with Valic anyway.

Valic shook his head. "Been quiet. How about you?"

Steigan turned and faced downhill so that his voice wouldn't carry back to the party. "We ran into Dominus Brynne and his family. One of his sons and a grandson were magic spun."

"Magic spun?"

Steigan nodded. "Keteria's spell is breaking."

"There are going to be a lot of scared people out there."

"I'm afraid people are already dying. I don't know why, but so far the victims seem random."

"Brynne's family will be safe, right?"

"I can only hope," Steigan replied before turning and finishing the walk toward the rest of the party. "We ready to get to Dubinshire?" Once again, he took the lead up the road.

CHAPTER 3

*D*ictated*

Steigan wasn't prepared for the sight of Dubinshire as the closed gates came into view. It made his heart pound with emotions and turmoil. He had to stop and catch his breath.

"Second thoughts, Dominari?" Ithanes asked.

"I always seem to end up here when my own home is disavowed me."

"Maybe you should quit trying to call anywhere else home and end your own heart ache."

Arlyn approached. "We should let Aeribela take the lead. The guards may not take too kindly to us otherwise."

Once again, Steigan remembered he wasn't going home. This was, in fact, enemy territory for him in this lifetime. Arlyn's counsel was very wise all considering. If he'd approached and just announced himself as Searn Byther-hourn as he had so many times in the past, the guards would have no concept of who he was. He stopped, waiting for the rest of the group and more specifically for Aeribela to come forward. When she stopped a little prematurely, he caught her attention and motioned her forward. "I need you to talk to the guards and get us inside."

She smiled. "I can do that." She stepped forward to pull the bell cord to alert the gatemen to the presence of someone outside.

No one answered.

Ithanes made a disgruntled sound and reached around Arlyn to pull the rope again. When the gates didn't instantly open, he repeated the noise as he turned away. "Maybe my wish came true."

"Wish?" Steigan asked, moving off with Ithanes.

"If I thought it would help, or that you would do it, I would have asked you to place a sleep spell on Dubinshire to keep her people safe. Maybe we are too late and Cirvel has already come. Perhaps he showed mercy." Ithanes looked toward the forest.

"Maybe we should try pulling it open. The gate isn't barred during the days," Aeribela offered.

Ithanes stormed back toward the gate. "Then why is there no one guarding? Perhaps the rulership here has gotten slack since my day."

Steigan, Arlyn, Valic, and Ellis grabbed onto the edges of the wood. The gates dragged open, swinging freely on their hinges now as the chains rattled. Steigan, Arlyn, and Valic pressed forward to check the gatehouse.

"Over here," Valic said in a loud whisper. He motioned them over to a walled off section of the room. Beyond was an older man sound asleep on a mat. Snoring indicated he was alive.

"Out cold and didn't hear the bell," Steigan said to those standing in the gatehouse. The domini all shared an amused smirk, which Ithanes caught and rolled his eyes. As they left, Steigan once again caught up with Ithanes. "Nothing evil here. Just a guard too old for duty sleeping on the job."

"We shall see. I did say a sleep spell, didn't I?"

Quiet followed them up the streets as they headed toward the castle. Steigan searched for landmarks he knew only to find everything so different to how he remembered it and yet a ghostly cast of how it had once been at the same time.

Ithanes stiffened at Steigan's side, possibly having the same experience.

As they reached the street Steigan knew by heart, he looked down it for the house where he and Centhya had lived. He wondered what had happened to the garden where he'd planted the strickleberry bushes. He didn't quite have a view of it.

Steigan thought about running down the street with Annae when she'd been a little girl and so excited to spring through the streets. Catching sight of the building where the baker had been, he thought about all those times he had limped painfully down the street to get there. Nothing had ever quite been the same after Annae had reinjured his knee, and though he no longer suffered the infliction now that he was back, the memory of it nearly made him start limping again. So many things had become infinitely harder after she had slammed his leg in anger and even standing became agonizing.

"I tried not to blame her."

At his mutterings, Ithanes looked over and asked, "What did you say?"

"Nothing. Just thinking out loud to myself." He wanted to tell Ithanes that he wasn't ready to be here in Dubinshire. What if nothing he had done here had lasted? Just because there were a few members of the Onim in New Lilinar didn't mean that it had survived here. Yes, he knew that the people of Dubinshire clung to what those around him had always called superstitions, but that didn't mean that his work had anything to do with it. He knew the toward the end of his life here and they had started to understand what he was starting to do trying to do, but it all could've easily been undone. Especially, if the truth had ever been revealed about his identity had been revealed beyond his family.

Yet Arlyn had said that members of the Onim had captured him during the Palin Wars. It still didn't mean that they would be happy about following him now. His true name had become hated by many who didn't understand why he'd done some of the things he'd needed to do, like the destruction of the Cauldron of Life after it had been fouled by the gargaxes.

"I tell you, Dominari, this is too eerie. Someone should be about. Anyone," Ithanes commented.

"Lord Ithanes is correct," Arlyn agreed.

Steigan didn't understand what they wanted him to do about it, or how they expected him to be able to explain the strangeness. Maybe Ithanes was hoping that Steigan would confess to putting a spell on the town if and when the Destroyer ever got loose from the painting. That seemed more plausible for Ithanes to have done than himself. At any rate, Steigan could make no such admission. Instead, he kept his steady pace up the streets.

Eventually they reached the tall staircase leading into the castle. At this point, they encountered guards who recognized Aeribela and allowed them entrance inside. One of the younger men ran ahead as an escort toward the main halls, alerting others of their approach.

Aside from new tapestries and artwork, Dubinshire castle looked little different. Then, up the interior staircase to the hallway where they took a right, they weaved through the halls until they came to the short staircase that led into the great hall.

Two armored guards standing at the entrance of the grand hall opened the wooden double doors.

A bearded man in long black and gold robes much like Ithanes' currently stood just inside the room.

"Father," Aeribela cried out, dashing down the stairs toward him.

Hopeful anticipation, supplanted by happiness, passed over his face as he rushed to hug her. He looked to Arlyn and gave a broad, thankful smile. He released his embrace from Aeribela long enough to guide them into the great hall.

Several other royal guards entered and closed the door behind them.

Once at the dais on the far side of the room, Aeribela's father greeted her with a second, big hug. He squeezed her tightly and closed his eyes hard. There was a sad smile, which Steigan could barely see behind Aeribela's bedraggled ringlets.

"Dominus Arlyn," the man said. "It is good to see you again."

"Father, there is someone I'm excited for you to meet," Aeribela said after she had pulled way. She returned to Steigan, took his wrist, and led him to stand before the dais as her father sat down upon a throne of gold, a second one empty beside him. "This is my father, Lord Irragon." But before she had a chance to introduce him, Steigan dropped down on bent knee and bowed his head.

"Rise, young man," Lord Irragon said. "What is your name?"

"I am Dominari Steigan," he said, rising off his knee.

Irragon didn't really seem to want to take his gaze off of Ithanes, who stood slightly behind Steigan, but did so in order to acknowledge his daughter's introduction. "Like Arlyn, you are a dominus from New Lilinar?"

"I am." Or at least he was. Easier to just give the affirmative than explain the whole story.

Irragon looked Steigan over. "You are certainly not what I

expected. I had thought you would be older. But then, Arlyn had said that he'd taken you in as a baby."

Aeribela took a hold of Steigan's arm, drawing herself close to him as she did so.

"I see my daughter has taken a fancy to you," Lord Irragon said.

"You should have seen him, Father," Aeribela said. "He's taken on gargaxes, found the books, saved my life, and even bested Braccus a couple of times. He was trained by Arlyn."

"Saved my daughter's life, did you?"

Steigan realized the loaded depth of that single question. To admit that he had helped a princess of Dubinshire confirmed his treason against New Lilinar. But to side with the Temple as he should would make Irragon distrust him, which could lead to the events that Ithanes feared happening. And yet, he had long ago forsaken the title of dominus. "As a Dominari, I am a champion for the world, not merely one side. I will shield those within my power to protect."

"Speaking of Braccus, what happened to him and the rest of the guard detail I sent with Aeribela? Arlyn? Would that be the reason that you are returning her to me?"

"I have no knowledge of what happened. I was not in New Lilinar," Arlyn answered.

Valic stepped forward, put his hand over his heart in the customary salute of a dominus, and bowed his head. "I regret to report that four were captured. Three were put to death, and only one escaped with his life but not before divulging a great deal of information."

"Information?"

"Of Aeribela's mission within New Lilinar's territory, of the Onim," Valic said. He paused, straightening and meeting Irragon's gaze. "Of Dubinshire's plans."

Steigan felt Ithanes stiffen.

"Who are you?" Irragon asked, not letting the façade fall from his face. "We have yet to be introduced."

"Valic Tymerrianon, member of the Onim of New Lilinar."

Irragon nodded. "Tymerrianon… I am well acquainted with your family here in in Dubinshire. Well met."

Valic seemed pleased that Irragon knew his family name.

Emotion powered through Steigan and he wobbled slightly on his feet as he realized that he too now had a family name. Taburath. He was Dominari Steigan Taburath. Tears flooded his eyes and he blinked them back. Dominari Steigan Taburath, prince of Lilinar.

"Well, that leaves one introduction left." Irragon looked directly at Ithanes now. "Who do you claim to be, as if I did not know?"

Aeribela moved around toward Ithanes. "This is Lord Ithanes."

"Ithanes Selmik, Lord of Dubinshire and Gohaldinest," Steigan added, feeling it important to point out exactly who Ithanes was.

Irragon glared at him, as if Steigan had spoken out of turn and making him feel like shrinking back. Compared to Ithanes, Irragon was like a bear of a man. Irragon's face, covered with his thick beard, showed a kingdom with many years of prosperity behind him. He seemed nearly twice the size of Ithanes.

Raising a pointing figure toward a wall behind them, Irragon said, "I realize full well who someone of his resemblance would claim to be, but a man lost and dead for a thousand cycles does not walk again."

Ithanes didn't turn to look, but Steigan did. There, hanging on the wall among several others, was a portrait of Ithanes.

"A golden king can open any door," Ithanes said, making Irragon's eyes widen. "Are you such a golden king?"

Irragon's fists slammed against the arms of his throne. "How dare you!" He rose from his chair.

Valic glanced at Steigan and mouthed, "Golden king?"

Steigan pointed to the gold trim on Ithanes' robes and shrugged. Maybe it had something to do with the difference in colors on the robes: Dubinshire had gold and Gohaldinest had silver. But Steigan felt like he only made a wild guess at that.

"I dare," Ithanes continued, "because I know you cannot while I can."

"Guards!"

Irragon made to step around Steigan and Valic, but Ithanes moved with him and blocked Irragon's path.

Ithanes put a hand up near to Irragon's chest. "I cannot allow you to put us in the dungeons, nor do I have the time to prove to you that I am who I say I am. But I know you wear a false crown."

"You bring your own lies and falsehoods. What fabrications did you use to ensnare my daughter in your games?" Irragon growled. He turned to Valic. "You say the domini of New Lilinar have learned the plans of Dubinshire. Is this your way of countering those intentions?"

"Come now, you know I am who I claim to be," Ithanes said, stepping back and lowering his head a little. "How many times have you sought my council? More times than I can count."

Irragon spun toward Aeribela. "This is really Lord Ithanes from the portrait?"

"It is, Father," she confirmed. "He was freed when the Destroyer escaped from the painting."

Irragon's blue eyes turned toward Steigan. "Then it is

time. You are Saint Steigan returned, possibly the reincarnation of Rivic as well?"

Steigan raised his palm to show the silver birthmark to Irragon, but he shook his head and answered the Lord's questioning glance, "It is not me; I am not the reincarnation. I am merely one of Rivic's lineage."

"But you say the time is upon us?"

"Yes, it is," Ithanes responded.

Irragon looked like he wasn't really sure what was happening and half scared to be there. "You're right. I have sought your council many times," he said to Ithanes. The sadness in Irragon's eyes deepened, rooting far into their dark depths. He looked suddenly older as well. "I suppose I should be grateful you are here to council me in person."

Steigan moved behind Ithanes and Aeribela came up beside him and took his arm.

"Aeribela, come here," Irragon commanded. He glanced toward the portrait of Lord Ithanes hanging on the wall while he reached out for Aeribela's hand as she came closer.

Aeribela sat down on the empty throne next to her father. Even as dirty and disheveled as she was, she looked at ease as if she had every right to be there.

Ithanes had taken a slow survey of the room and now he rounded back to Irragon. "My good lord of Dubinshire," Ithanes began in a tone which made Steigan flinch. What would follow would not be favorable. "I have but a humble question for you. The city seemed to be barren when we entered. Where have all your people gone?"

For a moment, Irragon looked ashamed and he cast a sidelong glance at Aeribela. He struggled for the words enough that Steigan wondered if the ruler was affected by the unicorn magic, but Steigan knew he stood too far away for that to be the case. "With all that has been going on, with the possibility of our city being under attack by the domini of New Lilinar and withstanding a siege being nearly impossible with our current resources, I sent as many of the people as I could to Hallon."

Ithanes approached the dais. "Resources unable to withstand a siege?"

This enflamed Irragon's face. His hands curled around the ends of his chair's arms as he leaned forward. "I don't know how you ran things, but do not pass judgement on me for the way the world has become."

Steigan jumped in, standing close to Ithanes, but putting a hand out toward Irragon. "Please, we're tired from our journey. I'm certain Ithanes will see things more clearly after he's had a meal and a good night's sleep."

"Father?" Aeribela whispered, clutching onto his arm with a look pleading for clemency.

This seemed to make Irragon relax a bit. "Would you have left the people here? They don't have the knowledge or skills they need to defeat someone who is a ruthless master of magic with an army of Necroathelings. Don't you see that we don't stand a chance without magic ourselves?" Legends say that the Destroyer will sail his ships into the bay at Montikovert, so there is not safe. Would you send them fleeing to Plenelia? Or further, to lands where they will be persecuted for their 'superstitious beliefs?' The snow season is upon us and could begin any day. I had to decide. Many would be trapped in the mountains if I delayed sending them out. Would you have their lives upon your head for letting them freeze?"

"I think a man fighting for his home is a dangerous enemy. Why not let them stay and defend the city that is theirs?" Ithanes paced a few steps away, putting his back to Irragon.

"He cares nothing for anyone's home or the people that

live there. All that matters is that he gets back to Gohaldinest. He will wipe out Dubinshire."

"Dubinshire was built from the bones of Gohaldinest."

"Yes, it was. But that doesn't mean it can't be razed just the same."

"The people of Dubinshire are safe. I guess I should be thankful for that." With a nod of agreement, Ithanes pivoted around and decided almost as an afterthought to give a half bow. "Forgive me. As previously stated, I am tired from my journey. Sleeping on the ground does not suit me. Yet it is also hard to give up caring for the city I once ruled, even if that leadership is over."

"Over? As you stated, I am a false king, and you claim to be the true one. Do you not wish your birthright?"

"I submit that there cannot be two of us as Lord of Dubinshire, not in a time such as this. I propose I hand my title as Lord of Dubinshire over to you."

Irragon looked genuinely shocked by the suggestion. "You believe that to be the best?"

"I do. I will, however, retain my title as Lord of Gohaldinest." Ithanes robes changed to black and silver. "I believe it time to split the kingdoms and divide the power."

CHAPTER 4

*A*t Ithanes' mention of splitting the powers of Gohaldinest and Dubinshire, the main hall fell silent. Irragon stared long at Ithanes.

"You've seen the beasts, the gargaxes, have you not?" Irragon asked finally as if trying to recreate a friendly bridge between them.

Ithanes nodded. "We have."

"I heard New Lilinar had refugees heading to Cove and Briarsville. Please understand that we had no idea what had overtaken them, only that people were fleeing. I had to assume that New Lilinar had been possessed and I didn't know by what evil. Caution and sending the citizens of Dubinshire to the safety of Hallon seemed like the best course of action."

"I believe you did what was best and I support your decision. My harsh questions were meant to discover what kind of ruler you are. I have to be sure that leaving Dubinshire in your hands is the proper resolution."

"Yet I must still approve it as well. My father always told me to examine deals carefully," Irragon said finally.

"He said that even in the best of offers, the one making the arrangement is always watching out for his own best interest."

"Your father would be a wise man," Ithanes conceded. "His words are true even here."

"Then why do you wish to give up the powers of Dubinshire and keep those of Gohaldinest to yourself?"

"It is not my desire that I give up Dubinshire. Dubinshire is my land, my home. But I have to let it pass on."

"How do I know this isn't some plan you concocted with the Destroyer during your captivity? A way to usurp my throne?"

"I assure you it is not. Did you know, Lord Irragon, that people cannot lie when they are in the presence of the Dominari? As such, everything I have told you is the truth." Ithanes removed his crown. He looked at the blue teardrop gem swinging from it. "This stone belonged to Dominari Alityka. It is said that she was born with it in her mouth, and that she would not breathe until the midwife fished it out from where Alityka had nearly swallowed it. That, of course, is the legend."

As Ithanes stepped up on the dais. "In wearing this crown, you accept the rulership and magic of Dubinshire and all that Lady Alityka stood for when she fought for freedom from the Destroyer and his beasts. Do you accept this?" Ithanes asked.

"Yes," Irragon answered hungrily, removing his crown and setting it up on the empty chair to his left.

"Hear me now, stones of Dubinshire. I, Lord Ithanes of Dubinshire, do hereby pass all my magic onto Lord Irragon of Dubinshire for now and all time. He stands ready to serve the return of Dominari Alityka with bravery and loyalty." Ithanes placed the crown on Irragon's head. "All hail Lord Irragon of Dubinshire."

"All hail Lord Irragon," Steigan repeated, surprised that he heard others around him saying it as well.

Ithanes stepped down from the dais and folded his hands humbly before for him. "What I have now come to realize is that even though I handed everything over to my son and relinquished my throne to him, my true succession of Dubinshire never occurred. I never handed over the magical reins before I sealed myself in the painting with the Destroyer. This error is my oversight. I still have every claim to the magic of this land, Dubinshire and Gohaldinest alike. To release this, I must go into the fallen city."

Lord Irragon looked worried. "You cannot do that."

"Dubinshire's magic is peaceful, calm, and in tune with the natural laws. Gohaldinest is another matter. For as learned as you and your daughter are about magic, you are unpracticed and untested. One does not wield the powers of Gohaldinest lightly. I must stay in command of them if we are to keep them from returning to Lord Cirvel. That is why I refused the Destroyer every oath with my son. It was never my intention that the magicks of Gohaldinest leave me."

"We should not be speaking of this. You do not under-stand," Irragon insisted, slapping his hands against the arms of his throne.

Ithanes stepped closer to the dais and folded his hands together before him. He looked down, then slowly raised his gaze thoughtfully to Irragon. "There is only one way to prevent the downfall of Dubinshire. I must erase my line in the sand. Therefore, I must go into Gohaldinest."

"I say we should let him," came a familiar voice from behind them.

Steigan turned to see Adonid along with several saperes and domini having entered the room.

When Steigan reached for his sword, it was Greytas who moved forward. "I wouldn't, boy. Negotiations have been reached with Dubinshire and you'd find yourself on the wrong end rather fast."

Glancing to see if Arlyn would back him up, Steigan saw Arlyn shake his head. Steigan wished he hadn't looked as it had made him once again feel like a naïve and unschooled child.

"Negotiations?" Aeribela asked. "Father, what does he mean by that?"

"The Holy Sapere came here to forge a peace treaty between our countries," Irragon explained.

Steigan turned to the Lord of Dubinshire. "Prior Holy Sapere. He is merely a member of the Council of Elders now and has no right to make treaties."

"On the contrary, New Lilinar is without a Holy Sapere at the moment, as our newly elected seems to have galloped off with his tail between his legs."

Several of the domini snickered at the jest aimed at Martias. Steigan watched the smirk play on Adonid's lips while waiting for a reaction. When the prior Holy Sapere saw that none would be coming, his demeanor straightened right back to business.

"In his absence, the Council of Elders has requested my reinstatement until another contest can be held," Adonid continued. "However, these unusual times have left New Lilinar in precarious turmoil. We cannot have a civil war, yet towns are being razed to the ground and treachery abounds. I fear drastic measures will be needed to keep the people in line."

Steigan wished he knew what to say, that he had some sharp retort for Adonid, but he had nothing.

Then Ithanes' boots slid along the floor. "Then, my dear gentleman, I suggest you follow my lead if you wish to save your ill-managed countries."

Adonid's face burst with red at Ithanes' comment. "Who is this man?" Adonid raged.

Steigan wondered who would speak first and answer Adonid's question. Instead, he noticed Aeribela lean closer to Lord Irragon and whisper, "Father, you cannot trust this man. He was about to hang me in New Lilinar."

"Pa-shaw! You must have mistaken his actions. Surely, I would've heard if such a thing had taken place and now it is irrelevant as we have made peace with New Lilinar. They are now our allies." Irragon straightened in his chair. "Holy Sapere Adonid, it is quite a long story about Lord Ithanes. I suggest we hear about it over dinner as I'm certain my new guests are weary from their travels. Let me set in motion the events to get everyone settled and this evening Lord Ithanes can regale us with the tale of how he has come to be here and what his plans are."

"Dominus Arlyn, your counsel has always been most appreciated. I am wondering we might have a moment to speak in private regarding our new affairs state." Adonid rushed forward toward them and raised his hand as he approached. It settled on Arlyn's shoulder as Adonid looked to Irragon. "Lord Irragon, if I may request use of your council chambers for a few moments, please."

Irragon gone waved his hand dismissively. "My castle is at your service."

Steigan felt Ithanes bristle beside him, but the prior Lord of Dubinshire said nothing. Probably for the best, Steigan thought.

"Thank you." Adonid said to Irragon as he motioned for Arlyn to follow.

Arlyn moved after Adonid, but as he passed Steigan, he touched Steigan's shoulder and tapped two fingers against his nose. Steigan gave a brief nod before Arlyn moved off with Adonid into another room.

Watching the door close behind Arlyn, Steigan felt cut off as if he should be in the room answering whatever Adonid wanted to know from Arlyn. Part of him wanted to barge in. But he hadn't had the courage to follow a moment ago and now his chance was lost.

Irragon pulled rope. "I shall summon someone to find you quarters and bring warm water for bathing," he told them.

With that, Aeribela turned back to her father and began speaking excitedly again.

"You have more friends here with you?" Steigan heard Irragon ask.

"Why yes, Father. I can't wait until you meet them all."

Irragon drew his daughter close in a tight embrace, briefly kissing the top of her head. Yet something about the move felt forced and insincere to Steigan. Had Ithanes' warnings left stains of mistrust on Steigan's own thoughts?

The door behind them opened and a few servants in simple black and gold tunics entered. A woman in a matching dress also followed.

"I understand how hard that must be," Irragon added before acknowledging those coming into the hall. "My staff shall see to your accommodations. We shall visit again at our dinner tonight."

Aeribela came bursting by them and rushed to hug the woman who had come in. They chatted with rapid excitement as the woman brushed tangled blonde curls away from Aeribela's face.

Then they were all ushered out of the main hall.

The castle had changed little in the thousand cycles even though the musky smell of humans, dust, and dampness had intensified. Tables with bouquets of the season's last flowers filled the hallways, their lives cut, fading, and the fragrance not quite pleasing any longer.

Aeribela bobbed happily along beside the woman in the black dress who now held her hands folded before her, head bowed, and seemed to listen intently to Aeribela. Steigan suddenly wondered what her life had been like growing up here in the castle, running through these very halls. It might have been very similar to Keteria's life with King Cirello.

He picked up his pace. "Princess Aeribela?"

She whirled around with a pirouette as her face lit even brighter. "Oh, Steigan, come forward. You mustn't be all the way back there. Up front with us."

"N-no." At once, he saw the look of disappointment draining the excited flush from her face. He hemmed, "I'm sorry. I was w-wondering where the others have gotten to." Steigan flinched, wondering where this studder had come from. It felt strange to have guarded words like this.

"They are being cared for," she answered, her voice now politely calm as if she were hostess for the castle. "Ellis is bathing and cleaning up from our long journey. More water needed to be heated, so it caused a delay. Keteria and Rivic are being cleaned up, as well as being attended to by the physician and High Maege. I believe Laurient is still with them. They are in the best possible hands."

Ithanes, meanwhile, seemed to be perusing the castle, taking long, slow steps as they went through intersections so that he could look both ways as if reacquainting himself with the hallways. Was he noticing anything different or any big changes?

Then he started to shake his head.

"Ithanes?" Steigan moved closer so if Ithanes wanted to speak with a bit more privacy, he could.

"I don't see anything." After a brief pause, Ithanes continued, "Future-sight allows me to see images of people moving through the halls and interacting. I always knew what was coming. Now there is nothing. I am blind."

"Lord Ithanes, you will be quartered here," one of the servants said as he indicated a door. "I will stay to assist you as needed."

Ithanes nodded, but he glanced back toward Steigan and muttered under his breath, *"Rest well, Dominari. Even without future-sight, we need to be in Gohaldinest soon, whether 'tis approved or not."*

They led Steigan into another hallway. Passing one open door, Steigan looked inside to see Laurient standing nearby Keteria while someone leaned over her. Laurient acknowledged him but turned back to watching. Steigan knew he should probably go relieve Laurient soon. He wondered if Arlyn was still meeting with Adonid and what had come of that.

So many things to be done and figured out. Steigan wasn't certain he'd be able to rest yet. He certainly wouldn't be allowed to relax.

Just like the old days in Dubinshire.

CHAPTER 5

"It's true," Arlyn began as he took a chair at the table beside Steigan. He'd poured himself some water, but it sat before him with his fingers lingering on the glass. "Adonid negotiated a peace treaty between New Lilinar and Dubinshire. If nothing else, it should make it easier for us to move about."

Steigan couldn't believe Arlyn took this news so easily. "But why? What does he want?"

"It doesn't matter. I told him that his family is waiting outside of Dubinshire. He is sending someone out to get them."

"Did you tell him that his brother and nephew have magic?"

"What purpose would that serve?"

"You know what he's really doing here, don't you?" Steigan asked, his hands flat on the table.

Arlyn guzzled the water and settled the glass back down before him. "You've seen conspiracies around you for so long that you expect them from everyone now."

"Because everyone has their own agenda. What's your motive for keeping Adonid's plans a secret?"

"I really can't talk about this." He dragged his arm across his forehead and got up to fetch more water. "It's awfully hot in here."

Steigan thought the air in the castle felt rather cool, a clear indication that the snow season was approaching. Even more, for someone who was used to working a forge, it took a lot to acknowledge the heat. "Maybe you're getting sick, old man."

"Days on the road," Arlyn chuckled as he refilled his glass yet again after chugging down the second. "I'm not as young as I used to be."

Arlyn returned to his chair. "Look, Adonid has always been curious. I admit that I shared Onim stories with him that I probably shouldn't have. That's the benefit of being young and stupid. For now, it's important that he thinks we are still obedient to him. He'll be more willing to share his plans with me if he thinks that I'm siding with him and that I still have influence over you."

Steigan wanted to inform Arlyn that he'd never been very good about playing nicely with Holy Saperes and he didn't feel like starting now, but he knew that Arlyn wouldn't understand. Adonid and Arlyn were friends. Much like Steigan found it hard to betray Martias, though the opposite were not true, it would be the same case for Arlyn. Why did Holy Saperes have to be such pricks?

The sound of hooves on stone came to Steigan and, at first, he thought a unicorn galloped through the castle. How would one have gotten in? And why?

But as Steigan turned toward the door, he felt a wave of magic hit him and Ithanes appeared beside him. Ithanes chuckled at Laurient as the centaur entered. Seeing Ithanes, Laurient scowled. "That was not fair!"

46

Ithanes shrugged, then faced Steigan. "Keteria is waking up."

"We thought you'd like to know," Laurient said, gesturing between Ithanes and himself.

Steigan felt hot and cold at the same time. He'd known this moment would come. Now, he was not ready for it. He felt as if he should be better prepared.

Ithanes stepped up to Steigan and put a hand on his shoulder. "Allow me."

"Root rot, Ithanes!" Steigan heard Laurient curse as Ithanes whisked them a way in a flash spell.

Expecting to land inside Keteria's room, Steigan was surprised when they appeared in a hallway a short distance away. There was no way that Ithanes' enchantment was off in that short of a distance.

"I sense you have some trepidation about this," Ithanes said as he started to walk. So, he had intended for them appear outside of the room.

"I wasn't faithful to her, Ithanes. How am I going to explain?"

"She might not live through waking up. That's pretty powerful magic she possessed. Which is going to be harder, explaining to her that life continued, or losing her?"

Neither idea appealed to Steigan, but the question had been put forth and demanded an answer. "Explaining. I think my feelings for her have changed."

"You've had a long time without her, and she left you out of her plans when she cast the spell, so it's not surprising that you feel differently about her now."

"But how do I make her understand. Just like when I came back here and no time had passed for Aeribela, it's going to be the same for Keteria. It's hard to make them realize that I'm the one that changed."

"Yes, you had to live on. How about you take this one step at a time, Dominari?"

They had reached the room where both Rivic and Keteria had been placed. The room was a bustle of activity as people rushed around for various items. Steigan heard someone call for a moist cloth. Steigan didn't want to go through the archway of the door into the chaos beyond, but Ithanes nudged him forward.

"Good, you're here," Valic said, rising from his spot beside Keteria. "She's been calling for you."

Steigan moved stiffly, yet trying to hold an air of confidence like Ithanes always did. He wanted to pretend that he knew exactly what to do right now, not show that he was scared half to death himself. He sat down in Valic's spot and took ahold of Keteria's hand. "I'm here."

A woman pressed a cloth against Keteria's brow. "You must be Steigan then?" she asked as she continued her dabbing.

Steigan nodded. "I can do that if there are other things you need to be attending." He reached to take the damp material from her.

"You focus on seeing her back to the land of the living."

He had zero clue as to how to do that? Was there something he needed to say or do? Could his magic act as a tether?

"You should talk to her," the woman suggested. "She'll follow the sound of your voice."

That sounded like magic if he'd ever heard it. Still, he leaned forward, drawing her hand up to his chest and holding it tightly against him. "Keteria, can you hear me? It's time to wake up now." He suddenly realized how she wouldn't be able to understand him, how strange his words would sound to her, and he switched into ancient. "*Keteria, 'tis time to wake up. Come on home.*"

Chills crawled across his skin as a sudden memory went

through him. He recalled her talking to him in the catacombs, telling him that it wasn't time for her to wake up. Yet, she had spoken to him in the ancient and he hadn't even noticed the difference. Her words had been simple, but he'd understood.

A young manservant pushed his way into the room and tapped on Steigan's shoulder. "Dominari Steigan? Forgive me. Laurient requests your return to the room where you left him promptly. It is urgent."

Steigan glanced back at Keteria. He had just arrived here and now he didn't want to leave. What could Laurient want so urgently? This had better not be a petty game between Laurient and Ithanes.

Ithanes moved up behind Steigan. "I'll sit with her. You go." There was a strange sadness newly arrived in Ithanes' eyes.

Steigan rose, looking down at the boy. "Did he say what is wrong?"

The boy shook his head. "It's urgent. He says you should flash back."

Steigan took a step forward. "Talcor dun."

He entered the room where he'd left Laurient and Arlyn. At first, he didn't see them, but then he noticed that Arlyn had fallen from his chair on the far side of the table. Laurient had transformed back to human and sat holding Arlyn in his arms. A sickly blue-green webbing covered Arlyn.

"Goddess!" Steigan practically shoved the table and chairs out of the way as he dove for Arlyn.

"It's all right. Let me help," Steigan said. He reached to Arlyn's forehead and tried to pull a strand away.

The magic tugged away from his fingers and snapped back in place.

Undeterred, Steigan tried again, but added some magic of his own. "Nalorium breticham." He felt the threads of magic hook around his fingers, but when he pulled, they dissolved away.

"I tried already," Laurient choked.

"Nalorium breticham!" He tried to pull a handful of the webbing away from Arlyn's chest but with the same reaction.

"Birthmark," Arlyn muttered. "What color?" Arlyn's eyes were open and completely black. "Birthmark!"

Steigan glanced down at his palm and answered angrily, "Silver. Come on, Arlyn. Fight through this." He tore more of the webbing away from Arlyn's neck and chest.

The magic snapped, retaliating against Steigan. The force of it pushed Steigan backwards so hard he rolled in an awkward somersault on his right shoulder and ended up face down on the floor.

"No," Steigan bellowed, pushing himself up off the floor. "No, no! Come on, Arlyn."

Arlyn opened his mouth as if to speak. No sound came out.

Steigan's nose tingled as tears gathered in his eyes and he fought them back. He couldn't lose Arlyn now. Please, Goddess, don't be this cruel.

Tears streaked down Laurient's face as Arlyn gasped for breath in Laurient's arms.

Arlyn's black eyes rolled around in their sockets as he fought to focus on Steigan. "Whi... wh... Winctonicht." As he sputtered the word, he flung his hand up onto Steigan's gripping him fiercely. The webbing retracted as if retreating from Steigan's presence. "Winctonicht."

Steigan shook his head. "Don't talk. Save your strength. We're going to get some help." He looked at Laurient. "Why didn't you ask for Ithanes?"

More tears poured down Laurient's cheeks. "It's too late, Steigan."

"No. No!" He reached down to slide his arms beneath

Arlyn. Steigan would carry Arlyn to someone, Ithanes, the High Maege, someone.

A ragged breath left Arlyn's lips and his body sagged.

"Arlyn?" Steigan reached up to feel for breath.

The sickly green webbing dissolved away.

"Arlyn?"

"He's dead, Steigan," Laurient whispered. "Arlyn is gone."

Steigan fell forward over Arlyn's body, an anguished wail rising up from his feet and pouring out of his mouth before he could stop it. For several moments, he shook in grief he couldn't control or stop. Then it subsided enough for him to sit back on his heels. He ran his hand over his face and wiped away the tears. "Why did you call me? Why didn't you call someone who could do something?"

Laurient surfaced from his emotions, swallowing hard. "It was too late. I saw him fall. Then there was the webbing. I called out for you, but you and Ithanes were gone. All I could do was get a servant. I tried to help him, Steigan, but…"

Steigan barely heard the words Laurient was saying as he got his feet beneath him. The floor was no place for Arlyn. Steigan picked up Arlyn and carried the body from the room. Grief returned like a wave, spilling over him and nearly knocking his knees from beneath him. Staggering, Steigan kept going, plunging back into the wake of numbness.

Somehow, and maybe it had to do with Laurient's guidance, Steigan found his way back to the infirmary.

"Arlyn?" Steigan heard Ellis gasp. The rest of the room seemed to turn, noticing them entering now.

"Oh, Arlyn…" Aeribela whimpered as Steigan lay the body down on an empty bed. She reached out to Steigan, gripping his arm. "Magic sickness?"

Steigan could barely nod. His body felt thick and stiff, barely allowing room for his breaking heart.

"Steigan," another woman called out weakly. He moved

toward it as if it were a command and saw Keteria's eyes open and as black as Arlyn's had been. She reached her hand out for him.

Aeribela fell away from him as he stretched for Keteria. Ithanes left her bedside, vacating it for Steigan who dropped down beside her.

"What has happened?" she asked. "You're upset."

Steigan's chest tightened. He sucked in ragged, stifled breaths. He clasped her hand rigidly in his. He could scarcely speak, but he knew he had to. It was to release Keteria. "I'm sorry. I can't do this."

Standing, he resisted the growing ball in his chest fighting to make his world black. He touched Ithanes' shoulder before grief cracked through once more. Hand to his face, he plunged through the crowd and out of the room.

How could his world continue now that he'd lost the man who'd been like a father to him? Until now, Steigan had never felt like an orphan.

CHAPTER 6

*S*teigan stood as Honor Guard as he had done for the son who was not his and for too many friends. But out of all of them, this was the hardest. He watched the flames dance like feathers in the wind over Arlyn's body, a numbness in the pit of his stomach acting as the only thing that kept from bringing him to tears. He hoped the others didn't notice as he wobbled on his feet. Never before had he felt so weak and powerless.

"Goddess, accept this warrior into your welcoming arms," Adonid said, turning away from the small audience who had gathered for Arlyn's funeral toward the edge of Dubinshire Park. He raised his arms as if in triumph end to all the droning he'd been speaking before. Steigan hadn't been listening, hadn't cared what Adonid said about Arlyn.

Steigan felt chilled despite being so close to the fire.

Goddess, this was too hard. All Steigan wanted to do was drop to his knees and cry over all he'd lost. Instead, he locked his knees and remained standing beside Arlyn's burning corpse.

Adonid pivoted once more and started a solemn walk

toward the platform where Lord Irragon stood. Once they were together, they both sat down on the chairs placed there. Greytas stood nearby, guarding Adonid. Steigan silently thanked Adonid for not telling Greytas to be one of Arlyn's Honor Guard. Maybe Adonid knew how much of a slap that would be to the memory of Arlyn since the two had long stopped being friends. If Ellis realized how closely he stood to his real father right now, the boy didn't show it. Making a mental note, Steigan added telling Tethys about Arlyn's death to his long list of things to do once they defeated the Destroyer.

A lick of wind curled through the park and sent smoke and cinders twirling into the air. From the corner of his eye, Steigan watched them float out toward the ocean a very long way down beneath them. There was no way to see the water beneath them. On a clear night, one might see some of the glow from lights in Montikovert reflecting, but even that glimpse was rare. Yet, looking out, one could see far off toward the low horizon where water met sky.

"Are you all right?" Aeribela asked, coming up beside him and laying a hand on his arm.

He wanted to tell her desperately that he was fine, but he felt the unicorns' magic working through him, forcing him to tell the truth. "I knew we would have losses, but I didn't expect this. All the time that I was in the past, I thought about Arlyn and I knew that everything would be all right because he was there and alive. I don't know why I assumed he got out of those ruins of Lilinar, but in my mind I knew you all had made it out safely. Now everything feels wrong. I don't know how any of this can have a joyful ending. And I can't help but to blame Martias for his part in this. How my going to tell Martias what happened to Arlyn?"

Aeribela leaned herself against him and rested her head against his chest for just a moment. The silence of her hug communicated so many things, yet he felt too insecure to accept any of the emotions teetering on the edge of his awareness.

The fire burned in earnest now, stretching flames high into the air. Steigan watched cinders float up and disappear, taking little pieces of Arlyn to the goddess' arms. Yet the goddess was Alityka, and she was just a woman who awaited them in the form of the statue. For magic to have returned, had her spell already broken? Or was that just Keteria's spell? Had it been Keteria's own cracking layer that had caused this? Steigan knew he wanted someone to blame, a solid substance that he could punch and drive all his anger into. But that was not Alityka or Keteria, or for that matter even Martias. For as much is Arlyn had always prepared Steigan, Arlyn had always known that magic would return. Why had Arlyn not prepared himself? If there was anyone that Steigan should be mad at, it was Arlyn for his inattentiveness.

But it didn't feel right to damn the dead.

"Dominari Steigan?" a small voice called to him. Steigan opened his eyes to see Ellis standing before him. Dragzel sat nestled in the boy's arms, his blue-green eyes downcast. "We're very sorry about Dominus Arlyn."

Steigan nodded, hardly noticing that the cahaster seemed genuinely mournful rather than full of his biting sarcasm. Ellis moved on, heading back toward where Laurient stood.

"You should ease up on Sapcrc Lauricnt," Valic suggested from where he stood as Arlyn's second Honor Guard.

"I haven't spoken to him since I left the room with Arlyn," Steigan countered.

"That's what I mean. Laurient called you because he knew Arlyn was dying. He knew you'd want to be there. Imagine if you hadn't gotten to say good-bye."

But Steigan hadn't said good-bye. He watched another cinder take flight toward the sky. "Good-bye," he whispered.

Ithanes had been sitting off to the side beside another chair set out for Keteria. He rose now and approached Steigan. "I'm sorry for your loss," Ithanes said. Then, Ithanes put his arms around Steigan and hugged him. The embrace caught Steigan unaware. When Ithanes stepped back, he grinned. "Keteria said I should come give you a hug. She thought you needed it."

Steigan realized that he probably did, but he wasn't going to admit it and he was glad that Ithanes hadn't asked him if he did.

Ithanes remained by Steigan's side for quite some time, silence easy between them.

The heat of the flames slacked, allowing for more of the day's chill to surround Steigan.

"I've done this for my son," Steigan told Ithanes suddenly.

"You had a son?"

"He was actually Centhya's, hers with another man. What Centhya didn't realize is that I came to love the boy. He wasn't with us for very long. He just fell asleep one night and died. But I remember shortly after he was born, the dark hours when I couldn't sleep, when strange thoughts and worries kept me up, and I'd hear him wake up. He'd smile and laugh when he'd first see me come into his room. Centhya would still be sound asleep, and I would warm milk for him. He would pat his little hand against my cheek as I fed him. When Centhya accused me of killing him, something inside of me just cracked. I just wasn't the same person after that."

"I remember watching Leloran die in every vision I had of her when I decided if we should be bound in marriage. I never forgot any of those visions, even while she stood by me and alive. If it hadn't been for my visions, then I might also know what it is like to lose someone who you have come to love. I am sorry about the loss of your mentor, and I wish I

56

could give you more time to mourn, but the ripples in this world will not allow for the passage of time for your recovery. We must resume our mission in the morrow."

Knowing Ithanes was right, Steigan glanced turned toward Dubinshire castle in the distance. He must finish his mourning and resume his life. "Before Arlyn passed, he whispered something to me about a Winctonicht. I think he wanted to tell me more."

"The mythological Sacred Knight."

"Mythological? So it was some near-death confusion between an old tale and the title I held while being champion for Martias?"

"Most likely," Ithanes answered. "I'm sorry."

As much as Steigan wanted it to be some clue that the Onim had found in the thousand years between his time as St. Steigan and now, maybe it had been too much to hope that someone else would solve their current problems.

"Unless you want to become a horrible monster and then seek redemption from the people," Ithanes continued. "But I say we leave that to someone else. I've seen enough dark days in you and they're not very pretty."

As another silence came between them, Steigan wondered why Ithanes would remain by his side for so long.

Steigan found Ithanes staring at Keteria.

"I worry. Her eyes are still all black. She had not found her way free of the magic sickness and she still holds the cold magic," Ithanes said. "I do not understand this. She should be dead. I find myself thanking this Goddess of yours that you've been numb and pre-occupied by the death of your mentor so you haven't tried to remove the cold magic from her. Or perhaps your feelings for her really have changed significantly."

Feeling like a traitor to his own emotions, Steigan kept quiet.

Then Ithanes blurted out a disturbing thought, "She could be the Winctonicht. Some would certainly consider her a monster now."

Looking at the woman sitting docile with her hands in her lap, Steigan didn't see how Keteria could be a monster. Yet, she had cast the spell to shut down magic for the last thousand cycles. Many had rightfully blamed her.

"She's Cirvel's daughter," Steigan said finally.

"What?"

"The twins I took back into the past, Matoline's children, they were Cirvel's. Matoline is Lihn Harvestendale."

"That explains why she handles the cold magic with such ease."

Steigan nodded.

"She cannot go down into Gohaldinest with us," Ithanes announced.

"Do you say this because of the cold magic she carries, or because she is Cirvel's daughter? Her true lineage has never been revealed to her."

"Both. Those two pieces of information should scare you as well." Ithanes took a step, paused, then walked back to sit beside Keteria. Soon, they returned to the castle.

Slowly, so did everyone else, leaving one by one or in pairs, until only Steigan and Valic remained beside the pyre's last glowing embers still bright in the darkness.

CHAPTER 7

*I*n the dream, Steigan ran.

The forest trees stretched long branches toward him, tendrils which sought to pull at his hair and tunic. The tie on his ponytail had come loose and he'd lost it in his flight. He didn't have time to care. His pursuer drew closer.

He felt it behind him.

Or was it in front of him?

He couldn't tell any longer.

A thin, unseen branch scratched across his face and he barely closed his eye in time. The branch snapped, clutching onto his sleeve rather than falling.

He swiped his hand to pull it loose and dropped it, cursing that it caused a mark on the trail. What else was he supposed to do? Arlyn would never let a carelessness like that happen.

A line of strickleberry shrubs blocked his path ahead. This would hurt if he hit it.

He had no chose; he had to keep running.

Chills crawled along his back and neck. He felt the presence closing in on him.

He couldn't weaken now.

Hurdling the strickleberry bushes, he twisted to fully get his hips up over the branches. Heavy armor dragged him down too fast. Throwing up his arms, he protected his head as he stumbled, his knee twisting beneath him, and he went rolling over the ground.

Opening his eyes even as his body told him how the impact had affected him – nothing broken, he pulled in a sharp breath and realized that he was still alive and needed to stay on the go. Now.

Steigan flipped over onto his stomach and started crawling.

Hooves pounded, shaking the ground.

He had to move!

In crawling, he'd discovered that a couple of his muscles were sore, probably pulled, but he was so far unbroken. It wouldn't stay that way if he didn't get back to running.

Shoving to his feet, he reminded himself of all the training he'd done. His mind may hold a multitude of memories of aging, but his body knew none of the stresses and injuries that had once been his.

A flashing movement told him he was still too slow.

He wasn't going to make it.

They had him surrounded.

Steigan turned, changing directions.

Several white horns spiraled with gold were lowered toward his chest.

Steigan threw his hands in the air and made to turn around. Maybe he still had time if he took another direction. Maybe they hadn't surrounded him and he could slip between them, letting them all continue the chase.

Too late.

They had already closed in behind him.

He was trapped.

The unicorns moved in on him, pressing him backwards with his arms still in the air. He couldn't even pull his sword.

With a small thud, a unicorn horn tapped against his armor and he couldn't retreat any further.

"Please don't," he begged, lowering his right hand toward a unicorn moving in from the side. Tyana's brown eyes stared back at him.

She stepped closer.

"Please?"

Her horn pierced his outstretched hand. He felt the pain and the energy of her body surging forward into his rib cage where the armor didn't quite protect.

Why did Tyana have to be the one to kill him?

Steigan jerked awake. He kicked the blankets off him with fervor, breathing hard and seeking to be free of the last confines of the dream. He rose, crossed the room in his bare feet, and looked out the window over the quiet streets of Dubinshire. He couldn't see the forest from here and he didn't know if that should bring agony or relief.

Still tired from his long night by Arlyn's funeral pyre, Steigan sank down into a chair and rested his head against his palm. How long would he be numb? How long would everyone leave him alone? Soon, he was sure, they would demand his attention return to the fight at hand. Cirvel and Martias were out there somewhere. Ithanes had already reminded Steigan that he had no time to mourn.

He closed his eyes.

He still wasn't ready to live without Arlyn.

"Steigan? Are you Steigan Taburath?"

The question came to him in the ancient tongue. He couldn't believe he'd fallen asleep again so quickly and already into another strange dream. He hoped he wouldn't die in this one too. "*Nay, I am just Steigan. I have no surname to claim.*" While the answer came naturally to him, he couldn't help the scoff that escaped his throat. "Xian Dominari Steigan."

"*Dominari? I didn't realize you were a Dominari as well?*"

A Dominari as well? What a strange thing to say. Steigan raised his head to see the woman in white, Alityka, standing a short distance away from him. This was no dream that held him. He lifted his head from his hand. "*Goddess! Forgive me!*" He wished for the energy to rise and bow to her, but he couldn't find any reserves within himself.

"*I don't understand. For what would I possibly have to forgive you?*" she said, taking half a step forward.

"*Nay, 'tis me. I'm sorry. I should give you the proper respect. 'Tis been a long day and I don't have the fortitude to stand any longer.*"

"Have you defeated Cirvel then?"

Steigan raked his hand over his face. "*Defeated Cirvel?*" The question came with a scoff. "*I wish I knew how to do that, along with how to free my friend from his clutches.*"

Alityka stepped forward, glancing all around her. "*If you have not defeated Cirvel, where are we? This place is not familiar to me.*"

"*Dubinshire castle.*"

Her head twitched. "*Dubinshire? 'Tis not a name I've ever heard. Where is this Dubinshire?*"

He realized that she might not know. "*Gohaldinest was destroyed and Dubinshire built from the ruins.*"

She walked to the wall and stretched her fingers tentatively toward the gray rock. Studying it, but not touching it, she flinched her fingers away before she got too close. Her eyes widened and color entered her cheeks as she stayed at the wall looking at it. Then she placed her hand flat against the stone.

Steigan felt a wave of power come off it.

With a gasp, she spun around toward him. *"'Tis the stone. The magical enchantments have been renewed, but 'tis the same underlying spells. So, Gohaldinest is destroyed and a new city born from the rubble?"*

"Aye."

"Then there is hope."

He wished her enthusiasm rubbed away the sour stain he felt on his soul. Hope seemed impossible if it meant losing those he loved. Since he'd started this journey long ago, he'd surrendered so much of his life and faced enough losses for his two lifetimes. Did any of it seem worth it now?

Was that why she was here now? The Goddess had always come to him with courage-filled words to push him to endure. She seemed different now. Where was her conviction?

"How long ago did this happen?"

"About two thousand cycles."

"Was that when Cirvel ruled Gohaldinest?"

He supposed that was about the same time that the Destroyer of Civilizations lived, so Steigan nodded.

"Where is Cirvel now?" she asked

Steigan shrugged. *"I don't know. I feel as if I've waited days for him to appear."*

"Was he trapped before?"

"Aye. In a painting." Steigan looked back down at the floor. He hoped that she didn't ask how Cirvel got free and forced Steigan to admit his part in it. Although he would in a moment if it would help bring Arlyn back.

The door burst open and Laurient, wearing his sapere robes, rushed in while hollering, "Steigan, come quickly!" As soon as he saw that Steigan had company, he stopped, his gaze going back and forth between Steigan and the woman in white. "I was going to tell you that something was happening, but maybe you have bigger things to attend." He tried to back out, but Ithanes stood behind him, looking over Laurient's shoulder.

Steigan couldn't speak. He had known, somehow, that Alityka's spell had broken the moment she touched the stone. Now she was awaking from the stone statue where she'd been sleeping. The last thing they needed was more magic in the world, for Cirvel to regain his powers.

Too late.

"*Why are you here?*" Steigan faintly managed to ask Alityka.

She glanced to Laurient, who remained frozen in his spot, then to Steigan. "*I had hoped that you could tell me how we defeat Cirvel.*"

"*And how is it that you are here?*"

The look of an internal struggled move over her face, one Steigan recognized as a person not wanting to answer the question asked by a Dominari. Why could she not throw it off herself? He had no time to even reflect on the possibilities before she decided to respond. "*I came via a time travel spell.*"

"*Time travel?*" Ithanes stepped forward around Laurient and toward Steigan but spoke to Alityka as he drew up beside Steigan. "*If that be the case, why not go to the very end and find out for yourself?*"

"*I do not understand. 'Tis what I tried to do. I am at a loss as to why this 'tis happening.*"

"I suggest we take her with us, show her," Ithanes suggested to Steigan. "Perhaps she needs to see this as part of her quest. She may need to see what happens in order to empower her actions."

"See what?" Steigan asked, still at a loss.

"Trust that she is here for a reason. Bring her." Ithanes spun away, ending any further questions or debate, and leaving Steigan to wonder what had happened while he'd been asleep.

Steigan stepped forward, slowly raising a hand toward Alityka. *"Come with me... us, please? I do not know what answer you are searching for, but my friends claim this might help."*

She looked uncertain, but then started forward. She didn't take his hand, but she didn't need to. Moving along with them was enough.

A small crowd gathered outside of a room just down the hall. Ithanes waited as if holding Valic and Keteria back. Ellis sat down on the floor by the wall holding Dragzel. The cahaster looked shocked to see Alityka.

Ithanes waved his fingers, urging Steigan and Alityka forward. He halted Alityka right before she entered. *"Be strong, my lady,"* he advised. *"'Twill be a bit of a shock, but 'tis all right, I assure you."*

Laurient stepped up to Steigan, right as he entered the room and caught sight of the statue of the Goddess. "We figured the Temple was pretty much abandoned, so Ithanes, Valic, and I went to go get the statue while you were... preparing Arlyn... you know. We figured we'd tell you about it in a few days, but then this happened."

As Laurient moved aside to let Steigan through, Alityka had already approached the statue and had begun to study it. *"I am stone."*

Steigan realized why they'd called him, thinking that something was going on with the statue. The grayness of the stone he'd become so accustomed to was now changed and magic radiated from it. Flesh seemed softer and more the appropriate color for skin. The white of her dress seemed closer the one which she wore now beneath her armor. Edges which had once seemed melded together now parted.

"How did this happen?" Alityka asked.

"You fought Azote and cast a powerful spell," Laurient said.

"*A spell to stop Azote?*" She turned toward Ithanes. "*But there were ramifications too?*"

"*Aye, while it turned Azote to stone, the same happened to you.*"

"*I must say then that 'tis a scary possibility. I would have to be standing very near him for the spell to have the exact effect on both of us.*"

The chatter beside Steigan seemed to fall away as he watched the statue growing more and more to life with every moment. He felt his heart beginning to pound. A foretold prophecy occurring right before his eyes. Steigan looked down at the torch shape on his palm. It remained silver. He pressed the thumb of his other hand against the sign proving his lineage to Rivic.

A small sound escaped the mouth of the woman once a statue as her lips separated. She breathed in and her eyelids once closed in concentration fluttered as if trying to open. Then her knees gave way.

Steigan caught her, swooping her up in his arms. Red hair tickled as it swayed against his arm.

He turned to see Alityka staring agape at him as he held the once statue form of her. Steigan couldn't meet Alityka's gaze and too many people stood between him and the door.

"Let's take her to the infirmary." Pivoting sideways, Steigan managed to maneuver with the woman out of the room. Steigan heard them behind him as he moved down the hallway. He took the first infirmary room he came too, but it was Ithanes who magically opened the door before him.

Settling her down on the bed where Keteria had been before recovering, he kept a hold of Alityka's hand, feeling it growing warmer as her heart pumped flowing blood through her once more.

"*Rivic is here as well? He slumbers?*" the other Alityka asked, moving to Rivic's bedside and touching his cheek.

"*We are told that someone bearing a golden torch marking on*

66

their palm will appear when it is time for Rivic to awaken," Laurient said.

"A torch marking?"

"Aye. You are said to have put a mark on Rivic's palm that would come down through his true lineage until the time of your return and Rivic's reincarnation."

"Ali, Ellis bears the mark!" Dragzel shouted. *"I saw it on his palm while he slept."*

Though Ellis had no idea what Dragzel had said, the boy's eyes fearfully widened as several gazes turned to him.

"Do you have a golden mark on your hand?" Steigan asked.

Ellis hesitated, then slowly raised his arm to show the golden torch mark on his palm.

"He's the reincarnation," Laurient said.

Clasping his hands together, Ellis held them against his chest. "Rivic's reincarnation? What does it mean that I'm his reincarnation? What will happen to me?"

Steigan shook his head. "Nothing."

"We don't know what it means," Ithanes cut across him.

"I won't let any harm come to you," Steigan went on, sending a glare to Ithanes. "I made you that promise and I intend on keeping it."

"We have made it across the span of two thousand cycles," Alityka whispered behind Steigan. *"Gohaldinest has fallen. We are nearly won."*

"And yet there is much of the battle to go, my lady," Ithanes added.

Whether it was the emotions of the day or Ithanes' reminder that their foes remained out there in the world, Steigan suddenly felt sick and dizzy. Fighting the vertigo, he rushed to the window and flung it open. He leaned over the sill, purging the yellow contents of his empty stomach until nothing more remained and yet his body continued to heave.

When the convulsions calmed, he wiped his mouth and tried to not think about how he'd vomited in front of the woman who was once his goddess. He didn't want to turn to face her.

Yet he felt her at his side, a gentle hand coming to his arm.

"Are you all right? I fear your long day incites you to feel eternity. All the bad must have some payment of good in it for balance."

"Your return brings hope and that 'tis... a balance of good... I hope." He tried to make his tone sound light and positive, but all he could think about was that there was no pleasantness which could balance out the awfulness of Arlyn's death. The return of one life at the taking of another didn't settle the scales.

"While I have found much encouragement in coming here today, I have not found the answers I seek. Perhaps we are to discover them together to give us both emboldened solace of our victory."

He wasn't quite sure what she meant, but felt the magic surge around them with the casting of a hasty spell, as if she wished to get it out before either he or one of the others in the room stopped her.

When the world calmed around him, he found himself standing in complete blackness. Alityka's hand sought him out and gripped him tightly. *"Where are we?"* she whispered.

The eternal darkness of death came to mind, but he refused to say it aloud. *"I don't know."*

A ghost rose like a white wisp from the depth and swayed before Steigan. *"One-time travel spell inside of another is a dangerous thing. I have rerouted you here for your safety."*

"Galault?" Alityka said.

"You are in the shadow room. I'm merely an apparition."

"You seek the ending for answers to a quest you have not

walked," the ghost named Galault told them sternly. *"I must insist you stay on that path. I am sorry that you each grieve."*

Alityka broke, *"My father, my sister, everyone I've ever known. I'm about to lose them all. What will I have left?"*

Galault smiled. *"The greatest love you could ever find."*

Steigan wished he could see Alityka in the oppressive darkness, but all he felt were her warm fingers within his to reassure him that she was still there.

"Galault, please," she continued, *"I have to know that we win, that we save this world. Why can we not go speak to our future selves to find out how we are victorious?"*

The ghost swayed before them. *"Struggles do not end just because resolve one set of conflicts with another. You will save the world and for a time all will seem right with the world. But life continues and new quarrels will emerge. Believe me when I tell you that what you gain from this adventure is stronger than the fears and doubts you have now. More trying times will come, but if you do not fill yourselves with the fortitude you gain here and now, your hunger will devour you in the darkness of other things to come."*

"But how are we to defeat a genie?"

"Wait, a genie?" Steigan stammered, not sure what that was but not wanting it to be greater than a gargax or even a gaxlor and fearing it would be.

"Your headstrong persistence continues as always. I have little time left to explain but let me say that some adventures turn out differently than we planned them."

"Galault, please, you know what happens. You have the answer I need. Tell me, or when I return, I will continue trying to find the answer on my own."

"What are the answers she seeks?" Steigan put forth.

Alityka and the apparition ignored Steigan. *"Again and again, I will cast the spell until I get to the end and find out the* answer for myself. Would it not be simpler to tell me rather than to continue to block me?"

"Believe me when I say that you would not understand the answer you find there. 'Tis too early for you to comprehend what needs to be done," Galault said as if he were instructing a child.

Steigan noticed how Galault seemed to be able to throw off Alityka's Dominari magic as easily as Steigan's own.

The apparition turned to Steigan. "As for you, you cannot save everyone. I know that hearing such a thing makes a heaviness in your heart that is difficult to bear. You always believe there is a way."

"I couldn't stop Arlyn from dying," Steigan admitted, feeling the weight of his words as if they were boulders being laid upon his chest.

"'Tis right. You cannot be in all places at once. Even you are not that powerful." Galault paused for a moment and the apparition seemed as if it were debating its next words. "Nor is everyone given to you in your charge. Some things would be best if you didn't accept their responsibility. You don't have to take care of everything assigned into your keeping. That might be a lesson your life depends upon you learning."

"I don't understand."

"Time is up. Return now to where you need to be and continue moving forward on the paths of your missions."

The black room dissolved.

At some point which Steigan couldn't identify, he no longer felt Alityka's fingers in his. Yet the sensation of her being there remained warm on his hands. When he reappeared in the room where Alityka recovered from being a statue, the other Alityka was not with him.

CHAPTER 8

*S*teigan and Ithanes reached the square alcove in the hallway where the tapestry hung representing the doorway to Gohaldinest. Steigan hadn't paid much attention to the tapestry before. Standing back and looking at it now, he saw a celestial pattern in the black and silver weaving.

The steady click of feet on the stone floor pulled his attention away. At least five people marched down the corridor, four of them in step with each other and one person off.

"I want to go into Gohaldinest with you," Adonid said as he and the domini with him came to a halt. He tipped his head back, raising his chin, and giving himself a more authoritative look. Greytas stood by Adonid's side appearing as fiercely stern as he could.

Ithanes seized Steigan and dragged him away, then huddled close. "We cannot have them going down into Gohaldinest with us."

Steigan glanced back at Adonid. As much as he disliked the position he'd been put in, he didn't see how he could keep Adonid out either.

Ithanes tugged on him once more to get his attention.

"Those men are no longer your superiors. You have no allegiance to them. When are you going to quit letting them rule over you? It would be best if you just put them to sleep and let those of us that need to go into Gohaldinest make the journey. Don't let them be sightseers just because they once held command over you."

Steigan knew Ithanes was right, but that didn't make the actions any easier. "I'll do what I must." He stepped back over to Adonid and Greytas. "Very well you may accompany us to Gohaldinest. But there are some things you should know about before we venture down there. Let's step aside so that I can tell you about them while Ithanes prepares. The ritual to open the door to Gohaldinest is quite intensive and Ithanes will need several moments of private concentration."

They moved back against the wall opposite the tapestry while Ithanes began his rituals.

"Now this is very important," Steigan stated as he raised his hand. "Gohaldinest feels like a city, yet the effects of being underground make it far stranger. It is dark when you expect sunlight. The devastation that has been caused can be strange and horrifying at the same time."

Steigan watch the fascination and horror grow in Adonid's eyes. He had Adonid clinging to his words. Greytas appeared a little more skeptical. He'd put up with several cycles of Steigan's and Martias' antics, so the mistrust was probably justified.

"There are creatures down there…" Steigan held both his hands in the air. "Mezzipalor."

As Greytas and Adonid both fell into a deep sleep, Steigan lightly pushed them back against the wall so that they would easily slump to the floor.

"Very well done," Dragzel said as his long slivery body slipped from the shadows. "Your deceptions know no end, do they?"

"Leave, cahaster. You will not be slipping into Gohaldinest either."

Dragzel sat back on his haunches and folded his arms over his chest. "I believe you will change your mind just as soon as you hear what I have to tell you. I have good reason to go into Gohaldinest with you and I suspect you will decide to take me *and Ellis* along."

Steigan scoff. "And what reason would that be?"

"Ellis is the reincarnation. I need the Guardian's help in order to restore Rivic."

"You had best not be lying to me."

"You would know if I were, wouldn't you now, Dominari? Am I lying to you?"

Steigan felt only truth from the cahaster. "Fine, go get him."

Dragzel dashed off.

Enough magic swirled on the air that Steigan could taste it as he turned to face Ithanes now in his silver and black robes. "We should have left in the middle of the night. At this rate, we shall be taking the whole castle with us soon," Ithanes complained. "I'm not certain we should be taking anyone beyond you, me, and Aeribela."

"Why?"

It wasn't a question Steigan had to ask, for Ithanes looked ready to answer anyway. "Ellis is far too curious, and we still don't know what it means for him to be the reincarnation of Rivic. Taking him down could be dangerous especially with the cahaster there. The Guardian is under my control, but her children have no such binding to my power. This could very well be a ploy to bring back Rivic as a Necroatheling. We know so little."

A strange silence came over Ithanes and he began to pace. "I wonder if Rivic is the Winctonicht? I suppose it is possible."

"You said the Winctonicht is a redeemed champion. How can that make him a Winctonicht? He's a Necroatheling."

"That's awfully harsh toward your relative. Perhaps you don't get chosen to be a champion. Perhaps it is a matter of title only."

"I don't understand what you're getting at."

"You'll notice that both Necroatheling and Necronosti have the root word of 'black.'"

"Yes."

"When you turn from that path to walk in the light, you actually gain the title of Winctonicht. Which means?"

"Sacred knight," answered Steigan, feeling a dirty taste in his mouth at the thought of a Necroatheling being a Sacred Knight as well. "Was Rivic trying to become a Winctonicht?"

"I think so. But he has had a dark taint to his soul. As a toddler he destroyed two villages and killed everyone in his family except for his twin sister. 'Twas not something he could have controlled because he was so young, but it left a befoulment on his mind. I'm afraid he never felt pure enough to be a Winctonicht. But that doesn't mean it's not going to happen when he's reincarnated. That may be the redemption he needs to clean his soul."

Steigan felt the embers of a jealous rage beginning to flare in his chest. He didn't want Arlyn's last words to have been about a Necroatheling. He put his gaze to the floor.

"Lord Ithanes," Irragon shouted, as he stormed down the hall toward them. "What is this craziness my daughter spouts about going into Gohaldinest to accept the powers of the cursed city?"

Ithanes sighed, shook hit off, and rolled back his shoulders. "My dear Lord Irragon, I have surrendered my city to you. Gohaldinest is still mine. I must do whatever it takes to safeguard my city from the Destroyer."

Irragon spotted Adonid and the domini on the floor and

stepped warily around them. "Including this? Whatever. I understand you already didn't want them attending you into Gohaldinest. But my daughter? She is my heir."

"And she shall become like every ruler of Dubinshire has been up until I put a stop to it. It is time for the rulers of Dubinshire to wield the powers of Gohaldinest once more."

"Why not me then? I won't have you put her in the path of the Destroyer."

Ithanes stepped forward toward the Lord of Dubinshire, keeping a level gaze with him. "Your perception of my intentions is inadequately false. I would prefer it if you would start thinking more like a lord of this city than as a father. Once we have returned from Gohaldinest, I fully intend on sending you to Hallon with the rest of Dubinshire's people where you meet all be safe. Your daughter will be going with you. These precautionary measures are being taken so that the Destroyer cannot merely take back his city should I fall."

"And if the Destroyer were to defeat you, that would send him after her. I will not have her put in such danger."

"You presume that he would know who he is looking for. From Hallon, you should send her on the fastest ship to the north continent. The further away from all this but she is, the better. However, I do not plan on being defeated here. Fate has brought many of us across time to gather us all here to stand against the Destroyer. I trust that the magical essence of all things knows what it was doing in making such an assembly. I have no doubt that Dubinshire will bear new scars from the coming battle, but as before, it shall be rebuilt better than its predecessor by its people."

Irragon appeared hesitant and ashamed for having admitted his fears, but they had only been the ones on the surface. Now, he forced out the thing he was most afraid of. "Will she be changed? I hear that sometimes those who take on the power of Gohaldinest are different afterwards."

"One cannot gain an understanding of the arcane secrets without having it touch upon their own darkness. I cannot say how this will affect your daughter for I have not known her long, but from what I've seen of her, she is a smart, bright girl. I suspect her lightness will be more than a beacon holding the shadows at bay, but will cast them out entirely."

This seemed to appease Irragon somewhat.

Ithanes redirected his attention at the sound of additional footsteps coming down the hall. "It sure is busy here today. So much for my quiet contemplation."

Laurient walked beside Aeribela. She smiled at the sight of her father. "Have you come to see me off then?"

With a careful glance to Ithanes, Irragon nodded and placed a stiff arm around his daughter. "You look ready for the occasion," he said as he indicated her black dress. "I sent someone by your chambers earlier and they told me that you weren't there. Other than getting ready, what have you been up to today?"

"Practicing, Father. Laurient has been helping me work on my magic."

Laurient gave a nod as he slid over toward Steigan, pointed at Adonid, and whispered, "What happened to our Holy Sapere?"

"Prior Holy Sapere."

"You do love correcting people, don't you?"

Steigan shrugged. "I don't know what happened to them. They got tired."

Laurient gave a slow, disbelieving nod of his head. "Right. Hope the same thing doesn't happen to me when I say that I want to escort Aeribela into Gohaldinest."

Ithanes leaned in and muttered, "No. Steigan, I told you we should have gone in the middle of the night."

"I'm here," Ellis announced coming around the corner with Dragzel by his side. "We ready to go?"

Laurient jerked his thumb toward Ellis. "The kid gets to go, but I don't?"

Ithanes rubbed his head.

"Whoa!" Ellis said as he inspected Ithanes in the black robes with silver sigils and the thick jewelry, particularly the hoop and cuff hanging from Ithanes' ear.

Steigan walked over to Laurient and put his hand out in a gentle manner. Adonid's presence must be affecting him as the action felt just like the way Holy Sapere Adonid would hush the audience during a speech. "Gohaldinest isn't just village you go wandering into to see who you can trade with. It's not a pleasant place and it can be dangerous."

"Even more reason for me to go," Laurient protested.

Ellis had stopped examining Ithanes and moved on to look at the tapestry on the wall.

"Fine," Ithanes shouted, "but everyone needs to have a reason for going. Your reason shall be to keep an eye on the boy and the cahaster while we are down there. Now, if you please, I need some quiet in order to focus and gather the magic for the spell. Anyone who is not going with us should leave." He gave a pointed look to Irragon.

Irragon hugged Aeribela once more. "I'll have someone fetch these men back to their rooms after you are gone," he said to Ithanes.

"That would be appreciated." With a hand on Ellis' shoulder, Ithanes guided him back to the others. More specifically toward Laurient, showing he was serious about Laurient taking charge of the boy. Then Ithanes faced the tapestry and raised his arms about his head. "Wha'ssa shalor."

The hallways off to the sides of them fell into darkness, closing them off to this small space. Steigan looked up, noticing probably for the first time that the ceiling arched above them.

"I'm pretty sure it wasn't like that a moment ago," Laurient whispered out of the side of his mouth.

"Satatie recor'malem hari sacodion vanache chekom ra tanasae," Ithanes chanted as all the magic around them seemed to syphon toward him. "I'tae lanic gnik eepd su amanadae."

The tapestry hanging on the wall rippled as if shaking off long years of collected dust. The air filled with a musty scent. The tapestry seeped back into the stone, leaving a door of iron and wood before Ithanes.

Ithanes twisted back toward them and reached a hand toward Aeribela. "Are you prepared?"

Aeribela looked nervous, but she moistened her lips and stepped forward to join Ithanes. "P-plon myk rad—"

"Stronger. You cannot be timid in this!"

Aeribela straightened, her shoulders rolling back as she stared at the gateway and took in a deep breath. "Plon myk radenish fa vencor tora vin grith allion warch'do nee iths groben da tali'ack suda tae."

Nothing happened.

"Again," Ithanes commanded.

"Plon myk radenish fa vencor tora vin grith allion warch'do nee iths groben da tali'ack suda tae."

The portal swung open, a gossamer veil of silver shimmering over the entryway.

Then came the release of long arcane magicks that Steigan had forgotten about. It nearly swept Aeribela off her feet, but Laurient was there, catching her.

"I did it," she said, smiling up at Laurient as he brought her back to her feet.

"You did," he affirmed proudly.

Steigan felt a sting go through his chest and, in the space of a heartbeat, his mind replayed the events of the last few days. Aeribela and Laurient had gotten to know each other as they come up the hill. She had said that Laurient had been teaching her magic, time that would've let them grow closer together. And now, he insisted on going into Gohaldinest to protect her. In that span of time, they had fallen in love. She now looked at Laurient the way she had once looked at Steigan. Now he had to accept that he had lost her to Laurient. Steigan didn't want to admit even to themselves how much that hurt even while it brought with it a certain relief.

Ithanes moved toward Steigan. "I hope it wasn't too cruel. I could do everything but open the door."

"Lady of Dubinshire," Steigan acknowledged.

Ithanes nodded, but there was something in his eyes that told Steigan that he regretted turning rulership of Dubinshire over to Irragon so early. It was always hard for Ithanes to admit his mistakes.

Ithanes approached the doorway. As he reached it, his trailing foot slowed in his stride and then he stopped altogether. He stood there, seeming to stare into the darkness for a long moment. Then when he turned to face the group, his eyes locked on Steigan who saw sudden immense depths of fear within Ithanes' eyes.

"I want to warn you all as we enter Gohaldinest: always keep a watch out of your surroundings. Things in Gohaldinest have a mind of their own and they rarely have good intentions. After a thousand cycles of being locked away, they will be particularly vengeful."

Dragzel slithered from around Ellis' legs and approached Ithanes with caution. "Do you know if my mother has been sleeping through this time, or has she been starving?"

Ithanes knelt down beside the cahaster. "I don't know. I would hope she has been hibernating, but let's send her a little something just in case. Miex'calidori pratady. Cha'chrispin." A light blue aura surrounded Ithanes, and he wiped some of it away from his arm and placed it inside the magic bubble he'd created. "Do you wish to add something, or a message that you are coming?"

The cahaster pressed his face against the bubble until his muzzle pressed inside it. He spoke something, but the words could not be heard outside the bubble. Then he pulled his head out.

With the bubble held in one hand, Ithanes motioned Steigan forward with the other. "What was your message?" Ithanes asked the cahaster.

Dragzel looked back over his shoulder and bared his teeth at Steigan. Then he leveled an equal glower at Ithanes. "I said I was coming with the reincarnation of Rivic. That's all."

"I shall be kind and respect you, creature, but I will never trust anything that has its origins in Gohaldinest," Ithanes explained as he released the magic ball and it zoomed into Gohaldinest.

Dragzel cowered backwards, his head low even while he stared up at Ithanes with his blue-green eyes. "I suppose that's quite understandable, considering your mother and all." As if expecting retaliation for his words, Dragzel looked around and zipped back toward Ellis.

If Ithanes had any irritation over the cahaster's words, he didn't show it. Rather, he turned once more to look at the group. "Remember my warning and take heed. From here on out, we stay in groups. No one is safe on their own." At that, Ithanes moved first through the veil and into the blackness.

CHAPTER 9

The staircase which Ithanes had once led Steigan down into Gohaldinest was now taken over by thick, white spider webs. Steigan drew his sword to cast them away, but Ithanes raised his hand.

"Burn them," Ithanes chided.

Steigan released his sword to let it fall back into the scabbard and raised his hand. "Cazidor." The webbings burned quickly away.

"See? You always make this too hard," Ithanes said as he continued on into the streets of Gohaldinest.

Even with five magical balls of light floating around them, the bright ring did little to expel the darkness from around them. If anything, the sepia color of the city had intensified. It brought back memories of the tone that the sky had turned when a forest fire once raged outside of Whalston. The sunrises and sunsets had taken on this brownish-orange color which was both beautiful and eerie at the same time. Even in the middle of the day, the sunlight on the ground had an unnatural orange hue. Dust motes floated around him now like ash had then.

They walked along, two by two, with Steigan and Ithanes in the front, Dragzel and Ellis next, and Laurient and Aeribela last. Steigan heard the cahaster shudder behind him.

"Not like you remember, beast?" Steigan asked.

"I disliked Cirvel long before it became fashionable with all you people," Dragzel said. "Being down here brings back few good memories for me. No one likes cahasters."

"I should wonder why."

Ithanes warned, "Be nice, Dominari. The walls fell down around him. The powerful injustices done to him may still linger in these stones as they do his mind. Let us not make the two connect."

"You make it sound as if the city has life and breath of its own," Aeribela said.

"It does. Make no mistake about that. Gohaldinest stood as a city of magic long before Cirvel took over here. What he did only enhanced its strength."

A shiver of being watched ran through Steigan. He swung his gaze around, but he saw nothing. Wanting to mention it to Ithanes, he went to speak and saw Ithanes' eyes narrow on him. Then Ithanes let his gaze drift over to the left.

There, standing in the shadows, Steigan saw a woman standing. "Is that…?" But then, as he took another step, he saw that the woman had merely been an old wooden beam held up at an angle by stone.

"Guard your mind, Dominari. You must hold your focus elsewhere."

"I saw her too, Steigan," Laurient admitted. "Ithanes can claim it was our imaginations all he wants, but I know what I saw."

Ellis' steps began to slow as he paused to look. Laurient grabbed Ellis' tunic's collar and urged him onward.

"Do you even know your way around here?" Dragzel asked. "You're not taking a very direct route."

"There happens to be a broken catapult and the stones from a rather large fallen section of wall blocking the immediate path to the castle. We have no choice but to go around," Ithanes replied.

"But we're going to see the Guardian, right?"

"For which our easiest way is to go through the castle and into the tunnels."

"There is another way," Dragzel informed them.

"You told me *no adventures*," Ellis said to the cahaster. "We're going to follow Lord Ithanes."

Dragzel spit a series of sparks but slumped along after Ithanes anyway.

They turned down another cobweb filled street, which Steigan blazed clean in a moment. One building leaned into another, stone littering their path so they had to climb, crawl, and duck through the clearings. Ithanes and Steigan waited for the others to finish the trek through the debris.

"Tell me something, son of Rivic, do you think that means nothing?" Ithanes asked.

"I don't understand," Steigan said.

"Rivic learned at the feet of the Destroyer. He took his oath as a Necroatheling. Then he turned on the Destroyer and helped Alityka overthrow the Lord of Gohaldinest. Do you think he gained nothing from that experience? Maybe 'tis possible that he fashioned Lilinar to be his own Gohaldinest?"

A new fear stirred in Steigan's stomach. "He was a dominus. He wouldn't do that."

Ithanes began to walk, once again leading the way. "Aye, you're right; he was a dominus. But you don't understand the origins."

"Enlighten me," Steigan said bitterly.

"Cirvel trained maeges. First, an acolyte began their magical training and he weeded out the weak. Those who passed became a dominus. 'Tis a fancy word for lord or lady, coming from the word 'dominate.' Once you are ready to move up, you become a Black Prince, or Necroatheling as you know them."

"You carry the title of Lord. Does this mean you are a dominus too?"

"Lords and kings of the land are outside the system as well. Those designations came about after the fall of Gohaldinest and new rulership was being established throughout the land," Ithanes explained. "But my father bound my blood to the Destroyer to give me the gifts due to a Lord of Gohaldinest. I am closer to a Necroatheling. I easily could be if I chose to let my soul be housed within a cahaster for safekeeping and performed the blood-killing."

"Blood-killing? That's why Cirvel meant when he told Martias to kill me."

Ithanes paused as if letting that sink into Steigan's head for a moment. Then he tipped his head. "We must go this way." He turned toward another wall of fallen stone.

For a moment, Steigan thought Ithanes meant to climb the stone, but he kept walking toward the pile.

"Come," Ithanes called back, motioning with his hand, but not looking back.

Steigan began to follow. Ithanes disappeared into the stone. *A mirage*, Steigan thought.

An explosion shook the whole of Gohaldinest, blasting Steigan backwards off his feet. He tumbled and somersaulted backwards over the stone street until his head slammed against the wall of a ruined building. His ears filled with a high ringing tone. A cloud of dust discharged from the illusionary pile of stone and real stone had fallen and rolled out into the road.

"Tell him my next bobble is a doozy."

The memory of Ithanes' mother telling him that when

he'd taken the twins back to King Cirello skipped though his mind. She had somehow known that Steigan would be meeting up with Ithanes again in his newer timeline.

"Ithanes?" Fighting back the blackness creeping in at the edges of his vision, Steigan rose and dashed across the street. He coughed as grit filled his lungs and his eyes. "Ithanes!"

Laurient was there by Steigan's side, arm over his face to protect his eyes as he too fought through the dust. Steigan sent his magical orb of light forward, hoping to glimpse how much rock they would have to clear to reach Ithanes. "Stay back," he told the others. Then, softer, he whispered to Laurient, "There could be more traps like that."

"Look," Laurient said, pointing.

Steigan saw a form walking through the dust and realized that it was Ithanes. He wiped his robes, no longer quite as black as they had been.

"You will have to do better than that, Mother!" Ithanes called out from the dark, hazy depths. "I am a true Lord of Gohaldinest. You cannot kill me down here now."

Steigan and Laurient helped Ithanes over the debris back to where they stood. Ithanes turned and surveyed the site of the explosion, then he looked to everyone else.

"I'm glad to see no one injured. That certainly put me on my toes," Ithanes said as he stepped further out into the streets. "Come along, Dominari. Don't look so shocked. I've had much practice at avoiding my mother's attempts at murdering me. Even after a thousand cycles I know to be wary and prepared for her treachery."

"She knew, Ithanes," Steigan muttered. "When I went back with Matoline, I saw her. She knew I was out of my normal time and that I'd be seeing you again. She warned me."

"I remember her warning to you, and I recall you helping Cirello battle your aunt while your mother gave birth. Now

85

leave the dead be." He gave a quick look around. "I guess we shall have to go this way now."

"You remember seeing me when you were a child?" Steigan asked as he glanced back to see Laurient returning to Aeribela.

"Aye, from the moment when I first saw you again in Lilinar when Keteria called us all together to fight the gargaxes. There you were, sitting in your seat so jealously watching me and Keteria talking. I knew you were Cirello's rightful heir and I kept waiting for you to stand up and announce it. You never did. I just didn't quite remember Keteria and Tanold being left in your stead, but I was young and just starting to learn about my own powers back then, so it made it all very confusing. Don't look shocked. Why do you think I always wanted you by my side?"

"Maybe he does know his way to the castle," Dragzel muttered behind them. "We're here, at last."

At a place where a staircase had crumbled away, Ithanes grabbed onto what looked like it had once been a fancy metal railing.

"Dominari Steigan and I will go upstairs. There is something I must get while I am here. Please wait in this area for us to return shortly," Ithanes said. Then he nodded to Steigan and began to climb the deteriorating stairs.

Steigan followed the short distance to the top. Coming out on what had once been an upper floor, he couldn't help his thoughts going to the ruins of Lilinar and the jagged outcroppings of stone that had been roofs and floors there at one time. Was Ithanes right? Had Lilinar been Rivic's personal Gohaldinest? Was the fact that both civilizations now lay crumbled in ruins with prosperous cities rising from them a testament that time needed to bury the past for good? The parallels seemed too strong to be coincidence.

"What are we after?" Steigan asked.

"Some very old relics."

A staircase which circled a decent sized square room opened into a hallway where wrought iron made diamond patterns in what used to be latticework windows. Broken glass sprayed all over the black and white tile floor. Steigan felt as if he'd seen this hallway before and a shiver came to him.

The door ahead to the left hung by one hinge, letting it sit at an odd diagonal angle. Ithanes pushed it open and ducked under it, holding it for Steigan to follow.

A long table which had once been in the center of the room now lay cracked and shattered. Boulders had been pushed off, evident by the long scratch marks left in the wood and the offending stone just over the edge. The table had been set back up as close to normal as possible, though it was disturbingly offset from the breaking. A thin, once white and now gray runner tried to hide the enormous break along with a teapot and two upside-down cups on a silver platter. Chairs had been set around the table where there weren't boulders in the way. A couple of them leaned sideways, legs cracked beneath them. Someone had worked at replicating how it might have once been. Steigan admitted that the sight made him a little nauseous and he had to look away.

Each of the room's four walls had a doorway.

"This way," Ithanes said as he went to the doorway off to the left.

"How do you know your way around here so well?" Steigan asked.

Ithanes hand fell on the silver handle. "My father insisted that I spend time with my mother down here while I was younger."

"Your mother lived down here while you were growing up? I guess I always figured that she had been with you until your father passed away."

"Everyone in your world has the perfect family life, don't they?" Ithanes didn't bother to bury any of the sarcasm of his tone.

"I know from experience that they don't."

Ithanes scoffed, then opened the door. "That was Lord Cirvel's antechamber where he actually met with people he didn't want to entertain in his larger quarters. It's said he did quite a bit of reading in here too, as well as practiced magicks. This is where he kept some of his most powerful items."

At first, Steigan couldn't see anything within the dark room. He cautiously approached the door, and as he did so, various items inside began to glow. He felt the magic calling to him. Orange light pulsed to life.

"Cold magic," he said, feeling himself responding to its essence.

Several candles in sconces on the walls sprang to life with flames, lighting the whole area.

"There's more."

Ithanes crossed into the room, going too far back right corner where he opened a door. He motioned for Steigan to enter before him.

All sort of stones and boxes on the counters and shelves began to pulse blue and yellow. Several books on shelves across the room creaked as if begging for Steigan to pick them up. A wand rolled back and forth in its long box. Everything seemed to have a life of its own.

Ithanes moved up behind him. "My mother use to bring me in here. We'd have tea in the antechamber, then she'd bring me in here. She liked to taunt me with all the magical items. She'd make me stand in front of this cabinet and shout that I was the Lord of Gohaldinest and the doors would shake, but they never opened. She'd laugh at me and scream that I wasn't the rightful lord of anything."

"I'm sorry," Steigan found himself muttering, realizing how much pain Ithanes must have gone through as a child to make him into the poised ruler he had been. Steigan had only seen Ithanes truly happy once: at the Springsday Festival. Ithanes found peace when Leloran was around him. "I think I now understand why you never wanted to give the Destroyer a hold over Freygorio."

"This room is why I put Frey in the timelock. He needed a childhood away from Dubinshire and the deep roots of Gohaldinest." Ithanes reached out and swung the doors to the cabinet open.

Inside a long staff of twisted wood floated in midair. Around the room were various tools for magical practices and several books on shelves that only stretched partway across to make room for the hardwood shaft. Ithanes reached for it. His fingers went through the wood he tried to grab.

"No!" Ithanes screamed. "I am the rightful Lord of Gohaldinest." He tried a second time to take a hold of staff. Again, his fingers fumbled only on air. He turned to Steigan. "What am I missing?"

Steigan shook his head. He reached inside and his fingers also closed around empty air. He tried for something else, but he couldn't actually touch anything within the cabinet. "Is it all an illusion?"

"No," Ithanes venomously denied. "The items are there, but we don't have the ability to get it. I thought I would now that I am the sole lord, but there must be something more."

"But Cirvel is no longer trapped," Steigan said with hesitation about angering Ithanes again. "He is the rightful Lord of Gohaldinest."

With a disappointed look on his face, Ithanes slammed the cabinet door closed and lay his hand flat against the wood. "I need the staff or this whole trip into Gohaldinest is for nothing."

Steigan thought of Galault helping him out with the key in the catacombs of New Lilinar. Was if possible Galault watched them now? Did Galault know what they were after?

"We can't let Cirvel get this. Do you think if I burn the cabinet, the mirage of items will disappear too?"

Steigan nudged Ithanes aside. "I might be able to help. Vochey cabinet." Then he gave the cabinet a little push. "Galault, I need the real staff back. Can you send it?"

The cabinet disappeared.

"What did you do to it?"

"I sent it to the same place that holds my weapons and armor when I'm not wearing them."

Ithanes nodded. "I hope the dimension is safe."

"There's a man who watches over it, a watcher of worlds. I trust him completely. If he finds his space in danger, he will send it somewhere safe and let me know me immediately."

"That is a lot of faith. I'm not certain I can place that much confidence in your friend, especially with tools like this."

At a clatter behind Ithanes, both men jumped at the sound and discovered the staff rocking on the workbench.

Ithanes slowly reached out toward the wood, quickly pulling his fingers away after the briefest touch. His fingertips rested a moment longer the second time. Then he settled his hand against the staff when he realized it wasn't going to vanish and he picked it up. Gripping it in both hands, Ithanes moved slowly around in front of them as if he couldn't believe he really held onto it.

A smile grew across his lips. "I may have to have you deliver an apology to your friend." As the smirk reached his eyes, he looked to Steigan and asked, "So, prince of Lilinar, are you ready to go meet a most magnificent creature?"

Steigan wished Ithanes wouldn't call him that. Lilinar had fallen and he was largely responsible. But Ithanes didn't really care for his response, as he was already halfway out the door. Ithanes had the old relic that he'd come to acquire and while Steigan didn't understand how a long shaft of wood could help, he knew enough to trust Ithanes. Steigan followed.

They went back down the stairs to where everyone waited below. Steigan had to admit his own surprise for he half expected Ellis and Dragzel to have disappeared.

"Let's continue," Ithanes ordered.

Once again, everyone took their positions and let Ithanes begin the second journey of their expedition.

"We are definitely being watched," Dragzel said.

"Stop, Dragzel. I told you. You're scaring me," Ellis scolded the cahaster. Though he tried to keep his voice low, Steigan heard it and he figured that Ithanes had too.

"It's true," Dragzel protested. "Something else is alive and down here in Gohaldinest with us."

"Nothing can survive on its own. No food, no light. You saw what it took for us to get in here. I tell you, there's nothing else down here."

"The cahaster is not wrong; we are indeed being watched, though I do not understand how that is possible. Dragzel, you care to take point for us and lead the way down to your mother?" Ithanes asked as he brought the group to a halt. "We need to rearrange. Steigan, you will follow Dragzel. Ellis, you're behind that. Aeribela and I will take the center, and Laurient will follow behind. Everyone needs to stay sharp. There is definitely someone here who dislikes my plans."

Steigan gave Ithanes a questioning look, hoping that it would be enough for Ithanes to give him an answer. He wanted to know what they were up against.

"It's unbelievable, unimaginable even," Ithanes said. "My mother still lives."

CHAPTER 10

*I*t hadn't been just Steigan's imagination playing tricks then. He must really have seen her, Ithanes' mother, in the fragments of light scattered along in Gohaldinest.

"How is that even possible?" Laurient asked.

Ithanes shook his head as if he didn't know, but Steigan wondered if Ithanes still had suspicions and a vague idea of how his mother still walked among the living after all this time. Ithanes always had some sort of clue or theory, but he obviously didn't want to share it.

They took the new positions that Ithanes had assigned them and began to proceed once more. Steigan could hear Ithanes and Aeribela talking quietly behind him, but he couldn't tell what they were discussing. Meanwhile, ahead of him, the cahaster weaved along down the path. Keeping his body low, Dragzel swung his head back and forth as if he checked the shadows of the corridors and streets around them.

Dragzel stopped, his head jerking up right as his ears

pivoted toward a sound. Steigan heard it, a click and a clatter as if something rolled over the cobblestone.

Then he saw the little ball heading toward the cahaster.

Something rolling out of the shadows in Gohaldinest couldn't have good intent.

Steigan jumped forward, seizing the little animal, and shouting, "Talcor dun." It felt like only a short distance, since Steigan had only moved them from the path of the tumbling object. Before everything came back into focus, he added, "Miex'balish," to put up a magical shield.

He heard both Ithanes and Laurient cry out, "Miex'balish palikiem a't." They had decided on much stronger protective spells than Steigan had.

Ellis creeped to the edge of Ithanes' shield spell, looking down at the little metallic object that had stopped just beyond.

"Ellis, get back!" Dragzel shouted, trying to wiggle from Steigan's arms.

The area filled with the sound of clanking as the little objects rolled from every direction toward them.

Ithanes reached out, seizing Ellis's tunic, and throwing the boy backwards. "There's too many –"

The first object exploded. Debris slammed into Ithanes' shield.

Laurient tried to catch Ellis, failed as the boy smacked into the cobblestone. Ellis' head slammed hard against the rock floor.

"Miex'calidori," Steigan said as he dashed back for the others.

Several of the other metal balls exploded as Steigan's magical bubble went up. A couple had made it inside due to miscalculating the edges of the spell in his haste. Shrapnel flew in all directions. Some crackled and hissed, evaporating as it hit the shield spells. Another piece hit Laurient, making him cry out in pain and fall to the floor beside Ellis.

Several more of the objects rolled out of the darkness and lined themselves up around Steigan's bubble spell. As the dust and grit settled outside, Steigan saw someone walking toward them. At first, she was silhouetted by the light from the magical orbs floating high above them. Then she stepped into the light and Steigan saw that it was Ithanes' mother as if she had never aged a day over the last two thousand cycles.

Aeribela and Dragzel knelt down beside Laurient and Ellis. The scent of blood in the air told Steigan that the injuries were bad. He didn't dare look though, instead keeping his eyes on Ithanes' mother for whatever action she had next.

She stepped to the edge of the spell which currently encased and protected everyone and felt along it with a hand. She gave Steigan a delightful smile, like an adult mocking the child's attempts at a sophisticated project. He knew she could take down his spell without a word, but she would indulge his attempt anyway.

Ithanes moved over toward her, the end of his staff tapping against the stone with each step.

"'Tis good to see you again, my son," she said. *"Why not take down this barrier between us so that we may share a loving embrace?"*

Steigan wondered if her intentions were to have Ithanes remove the spell himself.

"I'd rather throw myself into a strickleberry bush. Stand aside, Mother."

"You may possess the Guardian's staff, but you are still not a Lord of Gohaldinest." She tilted her head to the side. *"Oh my. It seems you have injuries among your party. You really should have them seen to. We can take them to my place."*

It was getting harder to breathe within the bubble, the

coppery scent of blood thick on the remaining air. Steigan felt he should cast the spell, but he wondered how long Ithanes' mother would continue to toy with them. He didn't want to use the energy if it were needed for escape in just a few moments.

Then a sickening thought came to Steigan: sound didn't travel through a magic bubble. She had already dispelled it, but somehow held on to the essence of it remaining there.

Ithanes turned the staff, gripping it in both hands and shoving it out toward his mother. She retreated several steps back.

Steigan knew he had to move. He didn't know how he would get everybody out of there, and he'd have to trust that Ithanes could hold his own, but he knew he had to act now. He dropped down on the cobblestone beside Ellis, who had a large pool of blood growing around his head, and Laurient. He spread his knees to touch both of their bodies on the floor, glad that they were kind of close together, and reached out for Dragzel and Aeribela. "Talcor dun."

It was a sloppy way to take a lot of people, but with two of them immobilized, he had no other choice. They didn't get far, but Steigan had given them some safe distance.

"Can you use a flash spell?" Steigan asked Aeribela.

She shook her head. "We haven't gotten there yet."

Steigan heard the bombs rolling along the street like dogs chasing after them. He had no choice but to keep going. "Talcor dun."

When they appeared this time, it was in complete darkness. Only the damp, musty, earthy scent of Gohaldinest surrounded them. Steigan couldn't see where he was going to go next, nor did he know the ruins well enough to make an attempt.

Aeribela created another floating orb of light high above them. "It's the least I can do."

Laurient moaned and sat up. Aeribela knelt beside him and tried to keep him from moving. He grabbed onto her hand while muttering reassurances that he was all right. His other hand though, which lay on the stone, told a different story. He was bleeding, but not badly.

Ellis still had not moved.

"That woman is an oracle." Laurient pressed to his feet with Aeribela there to aid him.

"She's Ithanes' mother. He got his future sight from her," Steigan told them.

"You don't understand. Her powers as an oracle are stronger than that of Ithanes' future sight. We can't hope to defeat her."

Steigan looked down at Dragzel, who now pressed his forehead against Ellis' arm attempting to get the boy to respond. The cahaster caught sight of Steigan looking at him and whined, "He won't wake up."

"Can you keep going with them while I go back to help Ithanes?" Steigan asked Laurient.

"But Ellis seems far too injured to move," Laurient said, kneeling down beside the cahaster.

"Safety first, then we can treat the injuries. But you have to be strong enough to do this."

Laurient didn't look happy. Blood continued to pool from Ellis' head and covered the sparkling gold flecks in the streets of Gohaldinest.

"We need to get them to my mother. She can heal him. I know she can," Dragzel said, but confidence barely covered the fear in his voice.

Steigan felt so at odds about what he needed to do even while he knew that they had stayed in their current location for far too long. He looked back down the road, but there was only sepia walls fading into blackness. He reached out trying to sense for Ithanes' magic but felt nothing. Had Ithanes already fallen under his mother's attacks? Steigan knew his shielding bubble would have disappeared the moment he flashed away. Had he done it before Ithanes could prepare his own defenses?

An explosion rocked through the streets, showering pebbles and grit down upon them. Somewhere, in the not too far distance, rocks clattered in a landslide.

Then Ithanes, dirt smeared across his face, appeared at Steigan's side. "Everyone, get as close together as you can."

They all huddled around Ellis. Ithanes raised his staff and muttered the spell to cancel Aeribela's orb of light. Once again, they were shrouded in darkness. Steigan felt that it didn't matter though; as an oracle, Ithanes' mother could still see them.

Steigan felt Ithanes beside him start to rotate the staff in the air. "Ny'sek shaytal kadvian ol'la mybaepul."

Another blast erupted through the streets, making them all bump against one another in the blackness. As the noise subsided, Steigan swore he could hear the familiar clatter of the metal bombs rolling toward them.

"Sena'la toka!" Ithanes roared.

A bright white light so intense that Steigan could feel its warmth surrounded them. Then he felt movement similar to a flash spell but with much more force to its movement. The light lowered until there was nothing visible.

At first, the darkness around Steigan was so thick that he wasn't certain he'd come out of the spell except that he could feel himself blinking.

"Everyone call out your name. If you hear someone next to you, reach out and take ahold of them," Ithanes said.

"Laurient. I have Ellis."

"Aeribela."

"Steigan."

Steigan felt a hand knock against him and realized it was Aeribela.

After a short moment of silence, the cahaster added, "Dragzel."

"I believe you are on my cloak," Ithanes said. "You can take it in your mouth."

Dragzel snorted. "Unlike you humans and sub-humans, I can see perfectly well in the dark."

"Was that a jab at me?" Laurient asked.

"No, I'd forgotten about you being a centaur. I was calling Steigan the sub-human. He can't see me in the dark to kick me!"

Ithanes ignored Dragzel. "Is there anyone who does not have a hold on someone else? We're going to have to move toward the door together. Dragzel, can you guide us?"

"You put us here. Don't you know? Is that why you wanted me to bite your cloak? I'm just a guide now, am I?" A pause in the dark. "Yes, of course I will, if this will help get us to my mother faster. Can we be moving now? Go to your left."

"Who's left? Who is in the lead?" Laurient asked.

"My left," Ithanes growled as if it should have been obvious.

Little bright flashes of light glittered around him in the air. He raised his hand. Magic, little essences of magic.

"Don't let them bedazzle you," Aeribela said from beside him.

Steigan tried to follow the sound of her voice, but the sparks kept drawing his attention. He seemed like he could almost hear music playing. A woman's voice sang inaudible lyrics of a lilting tune.

"Steigan, are you coming?" Aeribela's voice seemed to come in from all directions and swept away the song.

"I am," he called back. His own voice sounded distant.

The little flecks of white danced in the murkiness around him. They looked so pretty. His eyes wanted to drift closed. The melody came back to him, wandering to him like a lullaby once again.

"Steigan, come on."

"Dominari," Ithanes called out.

"Over hill and way, come home, come home," the voice began to sing. Steigan saw an image fading in through the darkness to his right. A part of him would have thought it was a Shant'olin except for the fact that the ghostly shape had a distinctly human appearance. A pregnant woman in a white gown sat in a rocking chair. She rubbed her hands over her belly as she moved back and forth.

Steigan took a step toward her. Even though he'd only seen her once, he knew who she was. "Ma?"

"He let go of my hand," Aeribela shouted.

"Steigan," came Laurient's voice.

"He's going back," Dragzel informed them. "Someone will have to go get him."

Steigan stepped through the darkness, drawing closer to the white outline of the form he saw before him. He wanted to swipe away the white flashes that kept flaring before his eyes, but he felt that if he interrupted his vision through movement or blinking, the apparition would disappear. "Ma?" he whispered again, seeing Corina with her long braid hanging down over her shoulder.

She seemed to take on full color as he got closer. She rocked a little faster in the chair as she circled her hands over her belly. Corina gave a little press at one spot, her face lighting up with a smile.

"*He has the soul of the champion, doesn't he?*" King Cirello asked as he entered the ghostly vision.

Another tall and lanky man wearing robes of black and gold swirled up behind the rocking chair where Corina sat.

Though he was balding on top, he had long black hair that hung down his back. He looked quite similar to Ithanes and Steigan knew this had to be Ithanes' father. The man leaned forward and spoke to Corina for a moment, then faded. Corina looked to Cirello and answered him, *"Nay, not any longer,"* Corina answered. Her eyes filled with pain as she looked up Cirello. *"I could not do it. I had Lord Epious cut his magic from the bloodwave and replace it with mine. I'd rather give up my magic than surrender him."*

"I understand," Cirello said, kneeling down beside her rocking chair. More of the castle room fabricated around the images Steigan was seeing and he felt like he could move to the window and look out to see the city of Lilinar beyond.

Ithanes' mother approached. *"I am sorry, but you will still have to relinquish your child."*

Cirello jumped to his feet. *"Still? Lord Epious told us that if we did this our son would be safe."*

"You know you should have consulted with me first. He will be safe," she answered, *"until the moment he discovers the book and takes back the missing thread of his life. I never said he would remain with you."*

Corina wrapped her arms around herself as if she could hold her belly closer to her. *"I don't want to lose him."*

Ithanes' mother faded while Epious stepped forward, his gaze firmly on Cirello. *"Your child will be taken, and those you are given you must raise as your own. Your kingdom depends on it. You know what I say is true."*

Lord Epious was talking about Keteria and Tanold; King Cirello was being told about the exchange.

"Steigan!" Aeribela's voice cut through the ghosts, shattering them to curling wisps which spun away back into the blackness. "Hurry!"

Steigan waited, willing his parents to return. Had that been a memory? Had that event really happened? Why was he being shown that moment, unless to let him know about part of him missing, cut out and stolen away to be put into a book? When nothing happened, he started to walk through the room again.

"Steigan," a boy's voice whispered to him.

Steigan turned and saw Ellis. "Ellis? You're all right?" As he reached out to grab the boy, his hand went right through Ellis. Another ruse.

"It's messing with your mind, Steigan. Come on. You've got to get out of there," Aeribela's warning came from behind him.

"I had to hide, Steigan," Ellis said. "Keteria can find me. She knows how."

"Dimensional magic," Steigan whispered and the boy nodded in response. It explained why he hadn't been able to find the boy; he'd been looking in all the wrong spots. Ellis wouldn't even be found in Gohaldinest.

"They are looking for Dragzel," Ellis said as he bent down and scooped up the cahaster. "He can't stay here long, but Galault will send him to you when he can't stay here anymore."

Of course, Steigan thought. Galault had taken the boy, protected him. "What about you?" Steigan asked. "Dragzel shouldn't come back without you."

"I need Keteria. Only she can pull me out."

Something didn't feel right. "Come on back now, Ellis, you and Dragzel both.

A gray mist moved over Ellis, darkening his image for a moment. Ellis lifted a hand. "Steigan, help us. Come and get us."

Steigan stepped back, knowing that this sight was false. The real Ellis was no longer there.

"Steigan, we've got to go." Aeribela's voice seemed further away than ever.

He turned, seeing nothing but the tiny sparkling flickers on the curtain of black. "Aeribela?"

No answer came.

"Aeribela?" he shouted again. Still nothing.

Putting his hand out before him, he began to walk in what he hoped was a straight line. Even if it slightly askew and wobbly, he would eventually run into something, right?

Like a trap, his mind replied, thinking about going through the dark tunnels under the city of Lilinar with Tanold. He felt his old panic at small, confining spaces coming back to him. His chest tightened. The flashes moved in closer to him. Why couldn't he see with so many of them going off around him?

"*Steigan*," a female voice whispered as a woman in a rocking chair illuminated what seemed like across the room.

"Steigan," Ellis muttered, making Steigan whirl around half expecting to find the boy behind him. The spectral wisp curled out of sight.

"*Steigan*," King Cirello sobbed. The king's white outline rushed toward Steigan. Cirello's ghostly white face shouted, "*What have you done with my son?*"

"Steigan." Ithanes surfaced before Steigan, drifting right by his face between him and Cirello.

A hand grabbed Steigan's arm and Steigan jerked away, half expecting to see another apparition rising before him. Instead, he saw Aeribela.

"Come on," she said. "Quit watching these ghosts."

"Are you real?" He reached out to touch her face. She didn't melt away, but she did give his hand a good shove away from her.

"I'm real. Let's go."

"I saw Ellis," Steigan said as he followed her once again. "He's in an alternate dimension."

"Laurient is carrying him. You can't trust anything you see in the shadow room."

"The shadow room?"

"It's what we just walked through." As Aeribela said these words, Steigan realized that they were back in a tunnel, albeit dark but no longer completely black with the spectral flashes. The little, magical ball of light illuminated the walls and floor once more. He saw that Dragzel walked just slightly ahead of her, the bottom edge of her cloak in his teeth.

"Aeribela," he said, grabbing onto her arm and trying to slow her pace. "I saw my parents."

She didn't reply, but kept a determined step with Dragzel at her side.

As they walked along and Steigan's eyes adjusted to this darkness, the walls seemed to take on a green shade. Algae clung to the rocks and showed up as just a slightly lighter green. Steigan found himself looking all around now.

They came around a corner and saw the others waiting for them there. Ellis was still being carried by Laurient.

Steigan took one last look back the way they had come. The corridor seemed to end in darkness. "What exactly is shadow room? What does it do?"

"It shows you illusions," Ithanes said flatly. "There is no truth to them."

"I've been there before though with Alityka." He tried to make sense between what they were telling him and speaking interdimensionally with Galault.

Ithanes added, "You saw nothing real in that room. Just exaggerations from your own mind. It takes your fears and pushes them to the extreme, makes them seem real for you."

Steigan couldn't get it all to reconcile in his head. How could all that be so false when it felt so true? Maybe his Dominari magic affected the room and made it unable to lie to him as it did the others. He walked over to Laurient and inspected Ellis. Other than him still being unconscious, the boy seemed all right. Someone had performed a light healing spell to stop Ellis' head from bleeding. Everything seemed all right, but something in Steigan's gut still nagged at him.

"We should be moving along now," Ithanes said. "It's best not to stay in one place for too long."

Steigan reluctantly agreed. He hung back, letting Ithanes take the lead, so that he could be alone with his thoughts for a moment. If Ithanes didn't want to hear about his vision in the shadow room, then Steigan would have to conform his own thoughts with other truths he knew.

The off-colored walls gave way once again to the regular gray stone which most of Dubinshire was built from. As the underground hallway brightened as much as it could, Steigan found himself starting to feel better as if the shadows were falling away from him into the footsteps he was leaving behind him.

As he found his emotions steadying, he began to wonder if Ithanes was right about the shadow room playing with his head. How often had Ithanes told him to mind his thoughts while in Gohaldinest? No, Ithanes' father, Lord Epious, had told Cirello that his son would be taken and replaced. That had indeed happened, meaning some of what the shadow room showed someone had to be true.

CHAPTER 11

"*L*isten," Aeribela whispered as they continued winding through Gohaldinest.

Steigan felt himself involuntarily looking around as he shifted his concentration to his hearing. His gaze searched the walls as if scanning them, but also looking through them as he tried to find the sounds she wanted him to listen for.

Scratching, like long nails gripping onto stone as an animal scurried back to its den, sounded within the shadows of branching hallways.

"Probably cahasters," Ithanes said from in front of them.

Steigan nodded to Aeribela. "He's probably right. We saw several of them when we were down here before."

Aeribela gave a little scoff as she smiled. "That's better than the rats I was thinking about in my mind."

He gave her smile, knowing that he was trying to lighten up the mood. "Don't discount that yet. I haven't actually seen what's making the noise."

She shivered and turned away, but not before Steigan saw

the scared look on her face. "Wait," he said catching her arm. "Are you all right?"

Her lips trembled as tears she'd been restraining began to stream down her cheeks. "Do you hate me?"

"What?" Steigan stepped backwards, stunned by her question. "Why would I hate you?"

"Because if it weren't for me, you wouldn't have been looking for the books and you wouldn't have gone back to the past. You would have never become Saint Steigan."

"I became Dominari Steigan."

"I'm not sure there's a difference. You're still the Bloody Saint," she spoke, her voice trembling fairly close to a sob. "It's all my fault you had to go through that."

"What makes you think that?"

"The shadow room."

"You saw me being angry with you in the shadow room?" He didn't even wait for her to answer him. No wonder she had been so abrupt with him. Yet, even for all her words saying that his visions in the shadow room weren't real, she believed hers. Was that one of the mind games of the shadow room? "If I hadn't gone back in time, I wouldn't have written myself clues that took me across to the Temple in time to rescue you from hanging in the courtyard. All of those events were set in motion long before you were born. We were never meant to avoid them."

"But have we accomplished anything? Are we any closer to figuring out how to stop the Destroyer? We failed at stopping the return of magic and the Destroyer is free. What if we've already lost?"

He wondered how many fears the shadow room had awoken in her. "We're still alive. As long as I have breath in me, I will keep fighting. With Cirvel free, I'm glad magic has returned. I need all of my abilities, and not just the magical ones, if I'm going to take him out. If I hadn't gone back, I wouldn't have even learned my magic. Do you realize how vital that is to our quest?"

Aeribela inhaled, then released a shaking breath while nodding her head. Afterwards, she rolled her shoulders and stood just a little taller, and then she smiled. "Let's do this."

"We're here," Ithanes announced.

Steigan looked up and felt all of his breath leave his chest. Larger than the double gates of Lilinar, this entrance seemed to stand another half a length taller and nearly double the width. It arched at the top. The whole thing was a conglomeration of wood, metal, stone, and magic. While it filled Steigan with a sense of awe, it also brought trepidation. The magnitude of what this gate held behind it had to be worthy of its construction.

Steigan felt the goose bumps rise on his arms in wave after wave. He had a hard time finding his tongue to speak.

"How do we go about opening that?" Laurient asked.

"We don't. To do so would break the enchantments holding the Guardian inside. That's not something we want," Ithanes answered.

"No, probably not," Steigan said.

"Rokhesta." The long staff in Ithanes' hands began emanating magic that could never be contained in a mere fallen branch modified into a walking stick. On the end, a long, dark, sharp arrow-like needle grew from the top.

Looking at it made Steigan want to recoil. "Send it away," he ordered in a gruff tone.

Ithanes shook his head. "Our having it might be the only thing that keeps us alive. Everyone take a hold of my cloak." He waited in the center while everyone reached out to grab onto the material. "Talcor say'ta Guardian venchae."

Steigan felt the teleportation spell pull at him, but it seemed to him like he drifted within darkness for longer than an ordinary flash spell. Yet as he knew that complete feeling had returned to his body, he also grew aware that he was in a space with barely any light. He glanced around, taking in the large gate behind them, stone walls, and a large black mass curled tightly around itself in front of them. Steigan could scarcely make out wings tucked around the beast's body and a tail that came to a sharp point.

"Welcome," a deep voice growled at them.

As the monster spoke, hot steam floated into the room and little flashes of fire emanated from the beast's mouth and backlit the long lengths of its teeth.

"Good day, Guardian," Ithanes said as he stepped from the center of the group and bowed.

Steigan wondered if he should do the same and awkwardly followed suit.

Ithanes tapped the staff against the hardened dirt floor as if to draw the dragon's attention to it.

"I hope you have not come here to interfere with my plans," the Guardian said.

"I have not," Ithanes answered.

"Then why does a Lord of Gohaldinest come before me after I've been alone all these years? Why bring the staff unless you mean to torment me?"

"How have you learned our current language if you've not had anyone to converse with?" Steigan asked.

The beast turned its head in Steigan's direction so that it could look at Steigan with one of its dark eyes. "I am gifted with the knowledge of all languages." It swung back toward Ithanes. "Now, why have you come?"

Ithanes took in a deep breath and rolled back his shoulders. "The Destroyer is free. I must know if he has a weakness."

The Guardian opened up its large mouth and began to laugh. "You think you are the one to defeat him? More powerful people than the lot of you have tried."

Dragzel ran out before the group. "Please, mother, help them. They are working with Rivic and Alityka. They have made it across two thousand cycles, and I have brought the reincarnation to you."

The Guardian seemed pleased to see Dragzel. For a moment, the creature closed its eyes, but when the large scaly lids opened again a sad calm had come over her. "I am not sure I have the strength to do what needs to be done now. I thought I could overcome, but..." Her words trailed off as her head came to rest on the floor.

Dragzel lowered himself to the ground and scooted forward. "Please, Mother, you have to try." He rubbed his miniature muzzle against her much larger face.

Ithanes stepped forward. "If you are weak, then my request becomes of the utmost importance. I require you to provide succession of Gohaldinest to Lady Aeribela of Dubinshire."

The Guardian scoffed from deep in her throat. "You think that has any bearing on any of the larger plans going on around you? You are a fool if you do not understand that Cirvel created the myth that I am the bestower of his powers as a means of controlling those who thought to box him in."

"Explain yourself." Ithanes leveled the long-pointed end toward the Guardian and stepped forward.

"I warned you, Lord Ithanes, if you strike me with that, I will eat you all right now. It's been a long time since I've had anything but the company of rats and while I do not require food, something more tasty than the flesh of rodents does have an appeal."

For a long moment, Ithanes and the Guardian stared off. In the end, Ithanes lowered the staff and retreated.

The Guardian raised her head. "I am not the one who gave Cirvel the powers of Gohaldinest. I do not have the ability to do that even if I wanted to. Those powers came from the imagination dragon who created this world. In order to transfer the powers as you wish you will have to talk to Cirvel or this other dragon."

"And where might we find this dragon?" Laurient asked.

Ithanes glanced back over his shoulder to scowl at Laurient while the dragon answered, "Considering this world still exists and we are all still alive, I'd say that Leschemal is still asleep."

"Leschemal?"

"How very little you know, Lord Ithanes. In all your arrogance, you have no clue about the things going on around you. If you had any sense at all, you would keep yourself and your friends out of the plans I devised over twenty centuries ago."

"You sound like my mother, yet neither her loyalty to the Destroyer nor yours will allow him to win."

The Guardian began to laugh. "There shows your arrogance again. How do you know whose side I'm on? Now bring the reincarnation forward. That is true work I must do."

Dragzel motioned Laurient to come forward with Ellis, but Steigan held out his arms to bar Laurient's route. "What do you intend on doing to the boy?" Steigan asked. Without Arlyn, Tethys' son would no longer be looked after unless Steigan did it himself.

"Restoring an essential piece of Rivic's soul to him. The Onesong is stitched like a fine fabric. You cannot remove one strand without others giving way. If you ever want to put things back together, one must catch what falls away. The cahaster houses Rivic's soul, but to fully return it properly to Rivic's body, we had to capture what was lost when he became a Necroatheling. In doing so, Rivic's own magic will pull his soul back to him naturally. Otherwise, we are left to doing so magically, which can cause complications. As I said, these plans I have put in place were done long ago. I will not allow the likes of you mortals to interfere."

"Steigan," Laurient whispered, "don't upset the nice dragon who could eat us in one bite. Let me through."

Steigan dropped his arm and allowed Laurient to proceed.

"The boy is injured," the Guardian commented as Laurient placed Ellis on the ground.

No one seemed to want to respond to the dragon. Steigan thought the story too complicated to tell. How much did the Guardian know about what went on in Gohaldinest outside of this lair?

"It happened in Gohaldinest," Aeribela said finally. "We haven't been able to go back for medical attention."

The Guardian gave a slow blink of her dark eyes before looking the group over again. She seemed to shake her head as if disbelieving the people before her. Steigan felt it weird that he should pick up on such thoughts, accentuated further when the dragon's gaze landed on him.

"Open his hand. I must have his palm," the Guardian ordered.

Laurient knelt and worked at unclenching Ellis' fingers. Once he had them open, the Guardian placed a dark talon on the boy's palm and whispered magic in a language Steigan didn't understand.

Steigan felt a searing pain go through his palm.

"Ah, another thread," the Guardian muttered, once again focusing on Steigan. "Someone better catch him. He's going to pass out as I pull this."

As much as Steigan wanted to insist that he was all right, when the dragon resumed speaking in the odd language, he wobbled on his feet. Aeribela tried to hold him, but it only worked for an instant before Steigan crumpled to his knees.

He bowed forward, catching himself on his hands and letting his swooning head hang.

"There it is," the Guardian said as pain burned through Steigan's hand and subsided just as quickly.

Steigan raised his itching palm and when he went to scratch it, he realized that the mark was gone. He pressed his thumb into the spot where it had once been, missing it and feeling like something had been torn from him all at once. For a long moment, he remained kneeling on the cold stone floor and rubbed the spot where his birthmark had been.

"I am sorry, Dominari, for pulling that from you and what will soon be taken. I do hope one day you realize that your powers were fading long before now." The Guardian turned to Dragzel, passing on a black thread which dangled from its talon to the cahaster. "Take this to Rivic, return it along with his soul."

Dragzel took the thread in his mouth and dashed off.

Steigan wanted to demand what the Guardian had meant, but he still felt too woozy.

The Guardian whispered another spell over Ellis. "He will sleep until you are out of Gohaldinest. He will wake shortly after that and be as new. Then, if you are smart, you will all sail to the northern continent and live your remaining days happily until this world ends."

"I have not come all this way to leave without you giving me what I need," Ithanes raged. "How do we defeat Cirvel?"

Steigan rose to his feet, still a little weak, but knowing that he had to buffer Ithanes' temper once more. He had to find the energy for that.

"Do you even realize what you have coming toward you?" the Guardian asked. "He has a whole armada of black ships waiting to return to the seas and invade this country. He has an arena of Necroathelings who have done nothing but tear themselves to pieces over and over as they prepare for the time of their lord's return. Do you believe your little ragtag team could stand against all that? I sense nothing from any of you that would suggest even the slightest possibility of success in overcoming all that."

Only Ithanes didn't seem somehow disheartened by the dragon's words. Everyone else lowered their heads or shuffled nervously about. The loss of hope Steigan felt weighing on his chest seemed like something that would never disappear again.

The Guardian continued, "Truly, your only hope is getting help from the dragon who created this world, and since he despises everything about his creation, that hope is slim. As the only one who possibly has any control over the dragon, Ithanes, it would seem that you are the only one whose life holds any value. As for the centaur that I smell among you but I do not see, you are the greatest peril in the group."

"Why is that?" Ithanes spoke before Laurient could raise the question and give himself away.

"If you don't know why, then I suggest you find out. Now learning the truth might be your greatest downfall. This will be a delightful game to watch. Now be on your way and leave me be." The Guardian rose up on her stout legs and began to turn in a circle.

Aeribela stepped forward and shouted, "Guardian, as a Lady of Dubinshire I require your aid." With short, quick steps, she positioned herself closer to the Guardian then knelt to the ground and bowed her head. "Please, Guardian, tell us about the centaurs and guide us to bringing the dragon who created this world to our side."

The Guardian finished her turn and lowered her head close to Aeribela. She sniffed the princess, and it took a lot of strength for Steigan to hold himself still. But as Laurient didn't move to protect her, now that Steigan was aware of

Laurient's feelings for her, Steigan knew he had to trust Aeribela as well.

"Finally, someone with the sense to ask for information rather than rudely demanding it. Maybe some of you will learn after all." The Guardian sank back down on the floor and crossed her forelegs over each other. "The centaurs were not always such as they are today. They used to walk upright on two legs, but they betrayed the imagination dragon and angered him into cursing them."

Aeribela raised her head. "What did they do?"

The Guardian shook her head. "Cirvel could not speak of it, ever. If you ask me, I suspect an egg was destroyed. That is the only thing which could enrage a dragon for such a curse as well as anger a novihomidrak into silence."

"That would be horrible indeed," Aeribela asked. "Why would anyone want to hurt an unborn dragon?"

"There are many reasons, my child. None of them end well, but rarely does humanity care for something beyond the span of their lifetime when it can increase comfort now. Look at how I have been abandoned in these caverns, or how the unicorns are driven to smaller and smaller areas of forest so that more towns can be built from the wood and land, or how the wastile are no longer wild but hatched in pens to die. These tragedies have ramifications, but not that you will see in your lifetime or even those of your grandchildren. To your eyes, it does not exist. Nature tries to adapt and push back as best as it can, but when those warnings are not heeded, terrible are the consequences."

"Then what is needed? We have come so far and we can't give up on trying to save our world and its people now. What must be done?"

The Guardian stared at Aeribela for a long moment, as if sizing up another to see if they were friend or foe. "Stand up, my child. There is something that must be done if you have the courage for it."

"Aeribela?" Ithanes warned from behind as she got to her feet.

"I do," she affirmed, never taking her gaze from the dragon.

"Are you certain? This is not to be undertaken lightly."

"Aeribela, step back," Ithanes said, even as Steigan hurried forward shouting, "I will do it." The sound of the two men practically drowned out her enthusiastic agreement.

The dragon stretched out her foreleg, cutting Aeribela off from the others. "She is the only one who holds promise, the only one I deem as worthy. I would just as soon snack on the rest of you. But she will need you after I am done."

The Guardian breathed out quickly. Steigan threw his arm over his face as grit and heat blew in his direction. He felt Ithanes stumble blindly backwards, nearly falling over. Steigan caught him. Nearby, Laurient yelled out Aeribela's name.

The great roaring sound came to a stop suddenly, as did the heat. Steigan felt like he'd stepped from a forge house on a cool spring morning. As he made certain that Ithanes had his balance, Steigan glanced for Aeribela and found her lying on the stone floor. He broke away from Ithanes and ran for her. "Aeribela."

"She will be fine," the Guardian stated, drawing back her leg to allow both Steigan and Laurient around to Aeribela. "She will be sick for a couple of days, but when she wakes she'll be fine. Let her rest. That is the best thing for her."

"What have you done to her?" Laurient shouted at the Guardian as he tenderly brushed ringlets away from Aeribela's reddened face.

"I have done the best for you all that I can at this point.

Rivic will need a sapere, as will Cirvel if you can get him to turn from his diabolical path."

"It's only diabolical when you don't understand the full scope of his vision," a female voice came from the darkness.

Steigan knew who had spoken. He drew his sword as he stood and turned. The tip of his blade came right up to the collarbone of Ithanes' mother. Another step and he could put it through her throat. But would that kill her?

"Frankly, Dominari, of everyone here, your scope of vision is the narrowest. I, however, have a bit more clarity. I understand how the pieces come together." Using the spine of a book she carried, she pushed Steigan's sword aside and walked around him toward Ithanes.

Ithanes accepted the book that she offered him though Steigan wasn't certain that was the best choice for him to have made.

"You have done well, my son, and you have made your mother very proud. I reward you with this book which she will need when she wakes in order to understand her duties."

Ithanes inspected the outside of the book, then opened it randomly toward somewhere in the center. "Dragon language?"

"She has been blessed with dragon magic and she will now be able to read it."

"Blessed? You call this blessed?" Laurient called out angrily. "I call it burned alive."

Ithanes' mother leaned over to look, her face wrinkling slightly in distaste. "I've never seen a sapere created, but I assure you she will be fine."

Laurient slid his arms beneath Aeribela, clenching every time she moaned with pain, and picked her up. "I want to return to Dubinshire now."

Ithanes never glanced away from his mother. "Why would you bring this book to us? What's in it for you or your

Lord of Gohaldinest which would make you want to help us?"

"Maybe it is time we call a truce between us."

"I don't even know why you think that would be possible considering all you have done."

"I have taught you to see multiple sides to a situation and how to best protect yourself. Has your scope of vision become as myopic as the Dominari's?"

The Guardian turned her great head toward Ithanes' mother. "Enough. They do not see how all the pieces come together yet. Hopefully, they will at least realize that Ithanes' and Aeribela's lives are of the utmost importance, that they are as vital to this mission as Rivic and Alityka."

Steigan hated hearing that he wasn't important. He had been hoping that the Guardian would validate what he had seen in the shadow room and tell him that he needed to find his missing piece. Instead, he felt like he'd been relegated to Ithanes' bodyguard and nothing more. A dominus whose only worth was laying down his life in battle.

After sliding his sword away, Steigan picked up Ellis and went to stand by Laurient. He also was ready to be back in Dubinshire. No, he was ready to be back home in Whalston. He wondered about Arlyn's house and the forge. Arlyn had said it was destroyed, but perhaps some could be salvaged. Whalston would still need a blacksmith. Steigan wasn't certain he wanted to return to that demanding vocation and life, but what else was he supposed to do? Return to a fallen kingdom and sit on the throne of ruin? Now more than ever, he felt uncertain of his future and of who he was.

That wasn't true either. He was a Dominari, a champion for the unicorns. They had chosen him and that was what made him special. He didn't need a dragon to validate that.

Yet the dragon had just told him who he was supposed to

protect. What other initiative did he need? None. Protecting the four who were essential to this quest was his duty.

Steigan caught the dragon looking at him.

Ithanes ended the angry conversation with his mother, breaking away to return to the group. "Return us to Dubinshire, Guardian."

The dragon spoke a word and a moment later Steigan found himself along with the others back in Dubinshire.

CHAPTER 12

*T*he only thing worse than listening to Ithanes tell Irragon to head to Hallon without his daughter because plans had changed, and Irragon's subsequent learning of Aeribela's tragedy, was discovering Alityka, Rivic, Keteria, and Dragzel all together in the library. They all looked up at Steigan as he entered, but Keteria's eyes were filled with questions.

The few books they had on the table were closed, pushed away from them. They'd been talking rather than research-ing. He supposed it was only natural since each of them, save for the obnoxious cahaster, had been recovering from their long sleeps.

Steigan tried to ignore their silence and walk by the table, but Alityka was the one to speak up, "How was your trip into Gohaldinest?"

"I am restored and have my soul back. Thank you," Rivic noted to Steigan.

Steigan nodded and strode forward toward the books again. He reminded himself that these were the important people with the grand quest, not him. He could be absorbed in figuring out the Winctonicht puzzle and leave them to saving the world. Yet even in the isolation of his mind, he realized that Rivic might now hold the key to freeing Martias. He stopped and looked at Rivic. "You have your soul back?"

"*Aye*. Flesh and soul have been reunited."

Alityka gave a soft smile. "Rivic had to become a Necroatheling in order to get close to Cirvel, but we knew he couldn't stay that way."

"I'm not certain I understand. Are you saying that when you become a Necroatheling, you have to surrender your soul?"

"*Aye.*"

"Rivic, for the hundredth time, you are supposed to say 'yes' now when answering in the affirmative. Please forgive him," Alityka said, "he's having problems adjusting to some of the new language."

"I like saying 'aye!'"

"*'Tis fine. I understand. Sometimes the ancient is easier for me as well,*" Steigan said.

"See, Ali? He gets it."

"Will you sit and join us?" Alityka asked. "We were discussing our next plans."

"I'm sure Steigan has other important matters to be about," Keteria spoke up, her dark stormy eyes challenging him to counter her words.

It made him want to drop down into a chair, but he resisted the urge. "I do have research to be done. My friend is going to be changed into a Necroatheling, if he hasn't been already, and I'd like to find a way to save him."

Alityka gestured to Rivic. "We know something about that. Come, join us."

Steigan considered, then pulled out a chair and took his place. Maybe they could explain about what the Guardian had said about capturing a something a little extra so that Rivic would truly be whole again. If he was to restore Martias to his former self, that might be important.

Dragzel curled up next to Keteria. "So, where did Cirvel get the cahaster to store your friend's soul? We saw no signs of cahasters when we were in Gohaldinest and I haven't seen another of my kind for ages." The challenge shining in Keteria's eyes now sounded in the cahaster's voice.

"I don't have an answer to that," Steigan admitted.

"Then how do you know your friend is a Necroatheling. Maybe you are being deceived, again."

"Dragzel, what has gotten into you?" Alityka asked. She faced Steigan. "He does have a point though. Dragzel, did you see any cahasters when you were in Gohaldinest? Did the Guardian have any with her?"

"None." Dragzel glared at Steigan and gave no more information.

Rivic leaned forward over the table. "I'm not surprised. Cirvel knew the supply was getting slim when I was made into a Necroatheling. Of course, the Guardian was busy incubating me and my sister as novihomidraks for a span, so none were being born then."

"How do creatures like that," Steigan pointed at Dragzel, "get created?"

Dragzel gave an indignant snarl in return.

"Dragons have cycles," Rivic said. "They often alternate between creating novihomidraks, for which they need a human child to incubate, or they can with the help of a mate create a dragon egg. If a dragon doesn't have a mate, she can choose to spawn several live cahasters. These litters usually range from five to twelve, commonly around eight, little dragonette creatures." Rivic smiled at Dragzel. "Being smaller, they are generally free to go out and help the mother dragon with things, like bringing her treats and taking care of her."

"So without cahasters, is the Guardian starving herself?"

Rivic chuckled. "No. Dragons have no need to eat. They are primordial creatures of the universe. That is their supply. It is also what makes them a great contradiction. They understand the infinite abundance of the universe, but they are natural hoarders. They reproduce and they horde. That's what they do."

"That was a pretty sparse cave," Steigan said, thinking back to the meeting with the Guardian. "What does she horde?"

"Pride." The one word was spoken quickly and surely. "Many dragons don't horde physical items. They can be. But Salvarae hordes pride. She wants to be very proud of her novihomidraks and her cahasters. That is why she stopped producing them for Cirvel."

"And she's proud of this one?" Again, Steigan pointed at Dragzel.

While Dragzel held himself on his best behavior and merely curled into a tighter ball to put more of his back to Steigan, Rivic smiled and answered, "Yes, she is. He's the first to actually learn to speak, and he's adapted from the ancient tongue to the modern. I'd say Dragzel makes her very proud. He might be the only reason she's still alive. Dragons have telepathic links with their cahasters. Many times the dragon doesn't like the meaningless thoughts of cahasters and will tune them out or sever them, but Salvarae remains in near constant communication with Dragzel."

"Why does Dragzel not like you?" Alityka asked.

Steigan pointed a finger between himself and the cahaster. "We've never gotten along, since he tried to turn me over to the gargaxes."

"He was making my life miserable long before that,"

Dragzel snapped. "But I'm trying to leave all that behind us now that milady Lihn asked me to stay behind so she could save the babies."

"Babies?" Rivic asked. He exchanged a glance with Alityka.

"Milady Lihn had twins," Dragzel reported. "Beautiful babies. But Steigan took them into the past to hide them, made Lihn call herself Matoline."

Alityka and Rivic both looked at Steigan as if waiting for more of the story. Steigan couldn't help his quick look at Keteria, who stared wide-eyed at the cahaster. She happened to raise her gaze at that moment, catching Steigan's. "Ma-Mat?" she asked. "Her name was Matoline."

Steigan froze, trying to hold himself so still that he'd give away neither confirmation nor denial.

Keteria continued putting the dots together, her voice sounding flat and struggling as if she were trying to wade through a swamp. "She didn't have children. But twins? Me and Tanold..." She covered her mouth with her hands and sagged a bit in her chair. "I discovered we weren't really Cirello's children. We were her twins. That's why she looked at us like she did, she was our mother but couldn't tell us. Why?"

Once again, all eyes seemed to turn to Steigan as if they expected him to give them all answers.

Instead, it was Alityka who broke the silence. "Keteria is Lihn's child?"

Dragzel looked quite pleased that he'd gotten them to this realization without him having to actually spell it out for all of them. His smug look said it all as he set his head down on his from paws and let out a sigh.

"But it was said there were twins," Rivic added. "What happened to your magicless twin?"

"He died," Steigan answered quickly. "A long time ago."

Keteria looked a little shattered by the news, even though she had to realize that it had been a thousand cycles ago and there was no way someone without magic was still alive through that many ages. "At least he is with Ma-Mat, together now in the afterlife." She spoke the words, but they didn't sound right. Even Alityka seemed to notice the false tone to them.

"So we have an even bigger problem now." Rivic's face grew dark. "Keteria is Cirvel's daughter and if he learns that…"

"Right," Alityka answered.

The silent exchange that crossed between Alityka and Rivic didn't go unnoticed. "What?" Steigan asked. "What will happen?"

Keteria's eyes widened and she seemed to hold her breath.

"He will use her to locate her markers on the bloodwave, then he will be able to separate out all humans of this planet, essentially removing humanity from the bloodwave and killing everyone," Rivic said.

Keteria looked horrified at the prospect. Steigan leaned forward over the table to offer new information, "She has no markers on the bloodwave."

"What? How is that possible?"

"No, Rivic, think about it." Alityka reached out and put her hand over Rivic's arm. "Lihn was a unicorn; she'd have no markers there. Cirvel was half genie and half human from another world which is why he can't track himself on the bloodwave."

"But Keteria was still born on this world. She'd have markers."

"She might not. Keteria is the combination of two power-ful, non-human beings. When I capped the spell and she was removed from our time before her birth, it might have been enough to essentially make her disappear."

"With your spell putting everything to sleep…"

"Exactly! It was like her magical markers were put to sleep as well."

While Rivic and Alityka marveled over how the magic had escaped, Keteria grew pale and turned a fraction green. Distress lengthened her face. "I knew Cirello wasn't my father. But to learn it's the Destroyer…. I'm sorry. I need a moment." She rose from the table, barely skirting around it and bumping Rivic's chair with her hip as she fled.

Steigan slapped his hand down on the table in front of Dragzel. "Way to go, cahaster." He started to follow her.

"She needed to know," Dragzel shouted after him.

Even though Steigan hurried into the hallway, he didn't see her, yet the scent of magic lingered in the air like perfume. He reached out, touching the remnants, and getting the invisible tendrils to gather around his hand. "Talcor dun," he said and felt himself whisked away after her.

He appeared out on the streets of Dubinshire. A cold wind sent dry leaves skittering over the cobblestone. Steigan realized that he was in the business district not far from the park. It didn't look too different than when he'd lived here.

Keteria stood near one of the buildings, her hands shrouding her face as she stared inside. She didn't turn to look at him as he approached, but she did speak. "Remember the baker's shop. It was right here, wasn't it?"

"It was. And I do. That was a very long time ago."

She dropped her hands to her sides and turned toward him. "Better times."

He didn't know how to respond, so he didn't say anything, but he stepped forward and put his arms around her.

"It's true, though, isn't it?" she asked, gripping him in her own tight embrace. "I'm Cirvel's daughter."

"We are not our parents or their actions. And I have to believe that even Cirvel has the goal for you which most parents have for their children: to be better than them."

She sobbed against him and when she quieted, she tilted her head back a little to look up at him. "You are Rivic's lineage and a cousin to Searn. That must mean you are the true prince of Lilinar as I've heard people saying. You are Cirello's son."

"Lilinar is in ruins. It doesn't exist anymore."

"That's kind of how I feel about my life right now; it's in ruins and probably shouldn't exist. What's he going to want from me?"

"Nothing." He tightened his grip upon her. "I promised Matoline a long time ago that nothing would happen to you. I mean it. Cirvel will never know that you are his daughter."

"I know that you would never say anything, but there are others who know and might say something, like Dragzel or Ellis."

"Even though I don't think that the cahaster should have said anything to you, he felt that you deserved to know the truth before you discovered it in another way. Now it's out in the open with everyone. I know we will all circle around you to protect you from whatever Cirvel thinks he can do. At least we know his plans to use his child to find the blood-wave markers will never work for him." He released her and stepped back. "Are you going to be all right now?"

"I don't know. I suppose this will take some time to process. I am glad you followed me though." She glanced back to the shop. "It does remind me of that day we were going to Dubinshire Park and it felt like it was just the two of us."

"It wasn't. Your guards were with us."

"But now we're alone."

Keteria leaned in to kiss him and Steigan felt fear drench all the way from his stomach to his feet. He put a hand on her shoulder and held her back. "I can't do this. I'm sorry."

"You don't love me anymore, do you?"

"I loved you so much back then, but now, I'm not in love with you anymore. You, having cast that spell, left me. You took the whole thing upon yourself. And it didn't even help things. It made them so much worse." He glanced away from the sorrow growing in her eyes. He wished he could soften his words, but she deserved to know that his feelings for her were gone. That didn't mean that it wasn't hard. "I was brokenhearted for a long time until I finally realized that I needed to get over you. I had to give myself permission to release you and to love again and that was one of the hardest things I have ever had to do. I can't put myself through that again, not now that I am healed from the whole thing."

Keteria bit down on the inside curve of her lip. "So that is it? You won't even allow me to have a second chance?"

"It never works out between us." Steigan shook his head. "I do love you, but I am just not in love with you. That is a vast distinction and an emotion which allows me to want the best for you. I loved Centhya when she was in love with Searn and if I could have, I would have given him back to her in a heartbeat. As it was, I had to do the next best thing for her which was to take care of her. But it was mediocre at best, a sense of camaraderie and companionship, but not the passion she deserved. When I find the right person for me, I want to feel the swell of energy and passion that we both deserve. I want to be in love with someone and I want them to be in love with me."

"I am in love with you. I took the cold magic from me to save your life because I loved you. Do you think I would've done that if I didn't feel this way for you?"

"I'm sorry, Keteria. It just isn't the same anymore."

"Because I'm Cirvel's daughter. You probably started hating me the moment you discovered that." Her shouts nearly covered up the footsteps of someone approaching.

Steigan raised up a hand and paused to listen. It was probably just someone coming to check up on them.

Then, the chilling voice spoke, "Well, isn't that interesting information? I think that makes me love you even more."

Before Steigan turned, the cobblestone opened up beneath his feet and he fell into a pit up to his waist. Earth closed in around him, sealing him in the hole. He barely had time to realize what had happened when the ends of a dark purple cloak swept over the ground near him, stopped, and the Necroatheling knelt beside him. "Tell me," the Necroatheling ordered, "is this before you made the leap back to the past, or after? Have we already met a thousand cycles ago yet?"

Steigan didn't want to answer, but the unicorn magic worked over him. "It's after."

"Good. I do have to admit that the question was a bit of a cheat though. I felt the cold magic I'd given you here. I never imagined it would be inside of Cirvel's daughter. No wonder she holds it so well, like the true princess she is." With a crass little smile, Martias-na looked Keteria over. Then he turned back to Steigan. "Your leaping through time does seem to be good for your youthful appearance. You were older then. Now you're back to looking like a boy, the one I had weak and nearly dead on my cottage floor before the Destroyer. This means that you and I are very close to our epic battle. Alas, since I am here, you can guess the results."

Steigan glanced around for Keteria and found she was gone. Had she flashed out of here? Would she be getting reinforcements?

"Tell me," the Necroatheling continued, "how many of

you are there within the castle? How many powerful maeges will I be going up against when I walk in there?"

"Enough to kill you," Steigan ground out.

"Oh, you wound me, Steigan." Martias-na stood up. "Don't worry. I won't be going into the castle right now. See, we didn't attack Dubinshire until the first snowfall, which I suspect is coming any day now with all the trees having lost their leaves. Too bad someone wasn't here to clean the streets beforehand. Between the slush and the blood, it got awfully slick. It was then that I took Keteria. But this time, I thought I might even give you an interesting advantage."

Martias-na paced around Steigan, the cloak swaying against his human legs. It helped Steigan remember that his friend was a centaur and this enemy took human form; the two were not the same.

"Right now, out there in a very special cave close to the spot in the forest where you found Tyana, Lord Cirvel and I are in a timelock and he is training me." The Necroatheling touched his face. "But he did a better job of our timelock than yours, for I came back merely having aged two days. Already I am starting to recall awaking with Keteria nearby. I didn't know why her eyes held such fear when I first saw them. She refused to speak for several days. Cirvel, though intrigued at the sudden appearance of her capture, was not kind. Perhaps I should tell her that it would be best if revealed who she was to keep Cirvel from some of his inter-rogations. Funny now, having these two sets of memories." Martias-na's gaze drifted skyward.

"You took Keteria?"

"I did."

Steigan struggled to free himself. "Talcor dun," he said, going nowhere and hearing Martias-na chuckle at him.

"There is a single absorption stone beneath your right foot. Someone's going to have to come dig you out. Though I do have to admit that slitting your throat before that happens does have a certain appeal. But why should I get into a rush when I know that inevitability is coming?"

Steigan tried to push himself up and free either an arm or a hand, but the earth around him held him in place.

"I did hold you while you died," Martias-na continued. "Your blood flowed warm over me until that moment when the life left you, then I felt the chill set in."

Steigan tried to ignore him, knowing he really needed to get out of this hole. Cold moved through his body and he knew it was more than the damp, unsettled earth packed against him. He'd long ago accepted the fact that he might one day might die while protecting Sapere Martias, might die in his friend's arms. But now that they were enemies, hearing these words made Steigan nauseated. His hands were shaking from it.

Martias-na dropped down onto his hands and knees. He leaned forward, putting his face close to Steigan's. "You know that I cannot lie in your presence. I kill you. How does that make you feel?"

"You might be better off to slit my throat now. You've already proven that events can be changed."

"How very right you are!" The Necroatheling straightened. "So why don't you gather your friends and come to rescue Keteria before I wake up from the timelock? I think you should see what you're fighting for, or rather against. Come see how inevitable your defeat is."

Martias-na disappeared, leaving Steigan to struggle in the hole until maddening tears took over. Steigan screamed in rage so long his throat began to hurt and exhaustion took over. It seemed like forever before Valic found him and nightfall before the dominus pulled Steigan from the hole.

The Necroatheling had quite a head start on him.

CHAPTER 13

*V*alic and Ithanes were the only ones who knew the full extent of the conversation Steigan had had with Martias-na when they all went riding out with Laurient and Alityka. Rivic, knowing Cirvel would sense his novihomidrak magic, had stayed behind to take care of Aeribela and Ellis, and Ithanes had tried to convince Steigan to stay behind as well.

"He needs to come," Alityka said finally. "Galault always told me that I made several time jumps, but as of now I've only a few. Steigan needs to fill me in on the other jumps where he's encountered me, and traveling will give us that time."

Ithanes had suggested they all carry an absorption stone so that Cirvel and Martias-na wouldn't feel all of them coming. At most, the unicorn magic might be sensed, but could be presumed as a herd moving through the forest. All this meant traveling by horseback or walking.

Since horses were scarce, most having been taken when the citizens of Dubinshire fled to Hallon, they opted to have the horse they did find to pull a wagon. It bounced over the rutted road, jostling Steigan as he felt the absorption stone in his pocket and thought about Martias. Rivic had been a Necroatheling and come back. Alityka remained friends with him. Was it possible Martias could also be restored, reincarnated with soul retaking flesh again? After their last encounter, did Steigan even want that?

A cold wind stirred against Steigan's face. He glanced back in Dubinshire's direction even though he could no longer see the city. He worried about Rivic as a solitary defense of the castle, even though Alityka assured them all that he was capable of handling it; the taunt of Martias-na attacking at first snowfall chased the anxiety of leaving Rivic alone. The growing chill around Steigan felt like a dreadful omen.

He glanced up to see Alityka watching him. But all Alityka did was look; she never said what was on her mind. Steigan never asked.

Two days of wagon travel like this had left Steigan cramped and wanting space. Steigan longed to stretch out his legs. "I've been able to call my unicorns to me," he said to Alityka finally when he was unable to take the confines any longer. "Are you able to do the same? I'm just thinking that if two of us got out of here, there'd be more room."

"I tried while we were in Dubinshire, but I got no answer," she said.

"I know. Me too. But we are further away now. Maybe they didn't want to get stuck in the snow. It should be more temperate here."

She thought it over for a moment, then began to nod. "I like that idea. We should give it a try."

Steigan reached up for Valic to signal him to stop for a break. Aching, he climbed down from the wagon and helped Alityka out. She seemed just as stiff. Ithanes groaned as he moved. Laurient was the only one who didn't seem afflicted by the stagnation of the journey. He took the reins from Valic and held the horse steady while Valic climbed down.

Laurient looked around. "Maybe Chief Jepssa and his tribe will be in the same location and we can get a hot meal soon." He rubbed his hands together as if in anticipation.

Alityka walked toward the forest. Steigan followed behind her slightly and gave a whistle. Alityka whipped around. "Do you want to bring the gargaxes to our location?"

Steigan physically stepped back at her verbal assault. "I'm calling the unicorns."

"That's how you do it? By making three shrill sounds? It's amazing you're still alive."

"How do you call them?" Steigan asked, refusing to look around at the others who he knew would be watching him.

"I reach out for them with my mind."

"And how is it that they know your location or that you really want them to come? You might just be thinking about them and they would appear. That could be dangerous for them."

"Like you would endanger us by practically shouting for them."

"Ali, Steigan," Laurient interceded, "let's keep the tone down. If there are gargaxes nearby, we certainly don't need your screaming at each other to draw them either."

Steigan felt something snap inside him and he put hand to his head. He closed his eyes, momentarily feeling dizzy and ill.

A unicorn strolled from the forest, but it took a moment for Steigan to focus on it and realize what it was and what it was doing. The white animal stretched one leg forward, bending the other, as it bowed before Alityka.

She returned the courtesy with her own flourish. "Thank you, Tigma. I am honored."

Steigan thought he might retch. With his hand still to his

head, he stumbled away from the others toward the edge of the road. His feet didn't want to walk quite right beneath him.

"Dominari?" Ithanes asked.

"Yes?" Alityka responded.

Steigan lost control and vomited into the leaves and dead weeds. He heard Ithanes come up beside him, a doubly odd sensation since he didn't have the impression of magic along with the movement.

"Are you all right?" Ithanes asked.

"Probably just sitting still for too long and having this stone suppress my magic."

Ithanes motioned for Valic to bring the waterskin anyway and Steigan flushed his mouth out.

"Maybe you should go back to Dubinshire. If you left the stone with us, you could flash there," Valic offered, but Steigan suspected that Ithanes was also about to voice the same suggestion.

"I'm fine. I swear." He returned the skin to Valic and started back toward the wagon. He caught sight of Alityka standing with the unicorn. Only one had come out of the woods.

Alityka came over, the unicorn, Tigma, following her. "You should ride. I'm sure the wagon is very uncomfortable for you. I'm smaller. I'll be fine."

The image of the unicorn bowing before her recoiled through his stomach. He let it fuel a heated anger. "Great, let's do that. Come on everyone, let's get moving again." He waved his arms flippantly as he moved toward Tigma.

Ithanes and Valic shook their heads as they climbed back in the wagon. Ithanes' lip gave a little snarl as he settled into place.

The unicorn stepped away from Steigan and glanced at Alityka.

"Let him ride," Alityka said as she planted her foot on the wagon and started to lift herself into the back.

For a moment, Steigan wanted to slap the unicorn's flank. But Tigma blinked her dark brown eyes and jutted out her head just a little toward Steigan. He reached out taking her large head in his hands, feeling the unicorn's soft warmth against his palms. His heart ached for Tyana. Why hadn't she come?

He placed his forehead against the flat of Tigma's long nose. "I'm sorry. I don't mean to be angry with you. What happened to me?" He saw that he couldn't ride her. If only Tyana had come.

"Get out of here," he said to Tigma. "It's too dangerous."

Steigan turned back to see the questioning looks they were giving him from the wagon. "They will sense the additional unicorn magic and we can't take that chance. We must keep going like this." He climbed up in the wagon and retook his position.

They travelled until nightfall and started early the next morning. Laurient took to his centaur form, knowing they risked exposure in the quick flash of magic it took for Laurient's transformation, but it did put more room in the wagon.

The land began to flatten and soon they came to the road leading south toward Plenelia.

They weren't far along traveling the path eastward when a man stepped out waving his hands over his head. "Hail!" he called out as he got their attention. "I don't suppose you have a healer among you."

Steigan quickly glanced the man over from his messy brown hair to worn wheat colored tunic and brown leggings. No visible weapons, and a girth that spoke of plenty to eat. His eyes were weary as if his hardship had come recently.

"Please, we've been looking for a healer."

Steigan signaled for Valic to stop.

"Be careful. It could be a trap," Ithanes said.

"They would have to do better because in requesting a healer, we could have just shouted we didn't have one and kept going. Still, I will remain vigilant." As the wagon slowed, Steigan jumped down and walked up to the man. "We have no healer with us, but many of us have seen combat and have basic wound repair skills. If someone is hurt, we might be able to help."

The man shook his head and his shoulders slumped forward with defeat. "This is no wound, but it's like no sickness I've seen."

"Show me. I will have a look."

The man led Steigan a ways off the road and into the trees. As they went, the man muttered that his name was Torsep. He spoke quickly of trying to find help and were driven from the city.

Among the trees, Steigan found many people wrapped in blue webbing. Some lay on the ground. Others, in early stages, sat cross-legged. There were a couple clutching onto tree and trying to climb into the branches. Many had eyes that seemed to glow in vivid blue.

"I promise they will not hurt you," Torsep said. "They are scared and many have lost loved ones along the way."

"Where did you come from and where were you going?" Steigan asked.

"We came from Hallon. We could not go back up the direct road to Gohaldinest because Lord Irragon's soldiers held us back. We were trying to get to Dubinshire. We'd heard there were still people there, people with magic, and we hoped the skills to tell us what was happening to us. Last night, we were scattered by a horde of winged demons."

"Gargaxes."

"Yes, the legendary beasts are real. Those of us who fled and managed to regroup are here."

Steigan pulled the absorption stone from his pocket and set it on a rock. "I can help, Torsep. Your people are magic sick. Soon, they will have control of their magic. And after this, you must head back to Hallon. No one is safe out here with the gargaxes." He walked in among the camp and started pulling magic away from the people.

"What is it that you do?" Torsep looked around at the first one who were already starting to pull from their stupor and shake the webbings off of them.

"I am pulling some of their magic from them temporarily. As the magic enters them and doesn't find an outlet, it builds up into this webbing. If I can take just enough off of them, then they can find their own way to balance their magic. This will only happen once and afterward, they will under-stand naturally how to channel their power."

"Why is it happening now? Is this because of the gargaxes?"

"No. This world has forgotten magic." Steigan noticed that Ithanes and Alityka had entered the camp and were now going around pulling magic from people. "This is a sickness, but we've forgotten how to deal with it. Those that are here will be able to return to Hallon and help others. I would imagine there are people all over, in every city, that need this."

"I was among the first and I survived. Others haven't. Why?"

Steigan thought of Arlyn. He felt his eyes filling with the tears from his own loss as he saw it reflected in Torsep's gaze. "Some come through the magic on their own. Most people will have this when they are young, about five to six cycles. For others, the magic is too much and, with the old ways lost, the strategies to help them are gone. We weren't prepared for this. If it eases your mind, I was like these people and I had to be shown how to get through my magic. I have lost people to this magic sickness too. Right now, there are no easy answers but we must stick together to look after one another."

As they finished going around to all the people in the camp, Steigan wondered how many others were out there in the forest, alone, scared, and sick. Rather that reaching out to find them, he fetched his stone and slid it back in his pocket. They still had to remain hidden and now that this pocket of heightened magic would soon settle, Steigan couldn't take the chance of his group being found. He hoped that Torsep and the others would find any additional survivors out there.

"Thank you," Torsep said, coming up to shake Steigan's hand.

Steigan shook the man's hand, then put his fist over his heart in salute.

Torsep's eyes widened. "You're a dominus from New Lilinar. A dominus with magic?"

"The magic has no preference; it goes to the people capable of handling it."

Ithanes came up alongside Steigan. "The world will see chaos and prejudice. It will take a lot to come together as a people united on this planet."

"For now, you have seen me pull the people from their magic sickness. Please, go help others in need."

Torsep nodded.

"We need to go," Ithanes said to Steigan.

Soon, they were back in the cart and traveling again. The disuse of this road, if it could even be called that, quickly grew to a mere tread worn path where only Laurient traversed without issue. By afternoon, the trail seemed to be fading out before them, leaving nothing for them to be following.

Valic urged the horse to pull the wagon a little further

and stopped in a light covering of a few aspen trees. "We walk from here," he announced.

Steigan stretched once his feet had landed on the ground among the yellowing weeds, which brushed against his calves as he went to help gather the supplies and pack them on the horse.

"Root rot," Laurient said after coming back from a short jaunt out. "It looks like Jepssa has moved the tribe further into the valley for winter. No hot meal for us. I did find a spring and got the waterskins refilled though."

Ithanes nudged Steigan's arm as Steigan carried over more supplies to be packed. "Aren't you supposed to be talking to her about her time jumps?" He directed his gaze toward Alityka.

"She hasn't said anything to me or asked me," Steigan said.

"Maybe she's waiting for you to start the conversation. Maybe she's shy."

"Alityka, shy?" Steigan had never known the woman in white to not speak her mind and be forthright with the conversation.

"Well, you've been awfully standoffish since she awoke, not like when you traipsed in and demanded that she watch her own awakening. The girl has been turned to stone for two thousand cycles and faced a gaxlor, not to mention being trained by Cirvel when he was out destroying villages to restrain magic. Excuse her if she's not all happy and ready to charge back into the mission. You've done your share of brooding. How many times have I had to go and talk to you?"

"All right, already. I'll go chat."

"Good boy." Ithanes walked off to check that everything was out of the wagon.

Steigan didn't have a chance to speak with Alityka until they were underway once more and following the trail through the flatlands. Foothills were off to their left, and while this route left them a little exposed and out in the open, it was easier to travel. If Martias was where he said that he and Cirvel were, Steigan figured they had two days of travel before getting into the northern section of the Palin Mountains.

He noticed Alityka looking off toward the foothills with the mountains rising further behind them. "Do you see something?" he asked.

Alityka startled. "No." She lowered her eyes as if embarrassed. Her lower lip trembled and she struggled with finding what she wanted to say for a moment. "Can you sense them out there?"

"The Necroatheling?" he asked, assuming she meant Martias-na.

"No, the unicorns. They are gathering. Something's strange. Maybe they are feeling the presence of Cirvel and his new Necroatheling nearby." She tried to shake off the feeling.

"I don't –" Steigan broke off, afraid that if he voiced it, his words would become utter truth. Yet, he felt urged to answer. "I don't feel anything."

"Nothing?" she asked, shaking her head.

"No." He met a fear now entering her eyes and knew that he needed to change the conversation. "We should talk about your time jumps while we have the opportunity."

"Right."

Maybe she was shy, Steigan thought as he watched her cast her gaze to the ground once more. "I'll start." He exhaled deeply, wondering just where he should begin. "I first met you in the forest outside of Whalston. You were dancing around a fire."

"Haven't done that," she muttered.

"You seemed to know my quite well, so it's not surprising," he offered as if to give her some comfort. "Then there was the catacombs of Saint Steigan's tomb. You told me to face my demons."

"Haven't done that either."

"The enclosed space of Lilinar castle when I found the statue? You recognized Rivic's cloak."

She shook her head. "Is this leading us anywhere?" Alityka snapped.

"Sorry. Maybe you should tell me of your time jumps."

"No, I'm sorry." She waved her hand around. "This is just bringing back memories of trying to lead Azote as far away from Gohaldinest as I could. The unicorns out there..." She placed her palm to her forehead and let her fingers cap her shaking head.

He hadn't thought that she might be suffering through her own memories. As someone who had lived in two different timelines himself, he certainly understood dealing with those forlorn emotions. "What happened? Do you want to talk about that?"

"I was trying to get Azote far into the mountains. We had many of us trying to distract the gaxlor, get him away from Gohaldinest and where my father had his camp waiting to attack the city. There were groups along the way, but I was making the solo run for a cave where we were going to perform the spell."

She paused, looking once more toward the mountains. "I lost so many unicorns. They would run as far as they could and another would be waiting. While I was on the road, it was fine. I'd make the change to a fresh unicorn and we'd continue on. But once I was in the mountains, the rocky terrain was too much for many of them. I had spells on myself to keep from hitting the ground if I was thrown. They had initiated it and, after the first couple of times, I got the hint of what they were doing and used my own magic rather than theirs. They were sacrificing enough for me." She forced both her hands down to her sides and marched forward while taking steading breaths until she could speak again. "So many fell. I tried leaving them behind at first, running, knowing I had to continue on. But then I would hear their screams as Azote came upon them." She started wiping her hands over her mouth as she tried to keep from going to tears.

"I'm sorry."

She glanced up and nodded her head, acknowledging that he understood her pain. "I had to kill them. If they fell, I had to kill them." She melted into sobs.

Steigan grabbed onto her, embracing her and holding her up while she choked on the emotions. Ahead, the rest of the party turned at the sound and Steigan motioned them to continue. They seemed rather reluctant as they turned and continued.

"Sorry," she said when she finally reached a point where she could compose herself. "That memory is just so fresh."

He put his hand to her head, his fingers tangling in the depths of her reddish-blonde hair, and he held her against him until he felt her breaths steady and regular.

After a length, she glanced up at him, her eyes reddened but dry. "Thank you. I probably needed to get that out."

"Probably," he said with a small, sad smile. "It couldn't have been easy. But better death come swiftly by your hand than tortured at the gaxlor's claws."

"That's what I told myself each time." She stepped away from him, indicating that she was ready to carry on their conversation. "Very well. Back to our time jumps. What was the next time we met?"

CHAPTER 14

Since the time when Steigan had been in the mountains with Martias, following the trail of the domini fighting in the Palin Wars, Steigan hadn't been this way, yet the brisk cool felt familiar. He knew snow would be falling soon and he felt an urgent need to get out of these mountains and fast.

"Which way, Steigan?" Ithanes asked as he surveyed the ranges before him from the peak of a hill they'd climbed.

"Martias-na wasn't specific. He just said it was a cave near where I found Tyana, my unicorn."

"They all look the same and without being able to sense magic, we could be right on top of them and never know it." Ithanes fastened Steigan with a hard look. "Or we could be completely in the wrong set of mountains."

"I know."

"Let us not forget that there might be Plenelians out here too. Many of them hunt and forage this deep in. They have to," Valic noted, "unless they want to trade with outsiders, which is not something they're fond of."

Suddenly, Alityka brightened. "We can't sense their

magic, but the unicorns can. That's why they've been gathering and following us. I can feel their magic. They can lead the way for us."

Steigan paused, glad that no one looked to him for confirmation of Alityka's ability to do what she'd said. He felt nothing, as if there were no unicorns around.

"Brilliant, Dominari," Ithanes said. "Send them out."

She nodded, then moved away from the group.

Steigan glanced up and found Laurient's questioning eyes staring at him. Laurient turned away quickly, thankfully leaving Steigan alone.

Alityka stood on the rise, her reddish gold hair teasing in the breeze. She lifted her face, eyes closed, as if to feel the wind better against her skin.

Sensations seemed to rise through the ground, heating Steigan with well-placed anger. He wanted to storm over to her, demand if she realized that Azote was out there, waiting alongside his master, and yearning for the blood of more unicorns. Did she want more to die? He started to move toward Alityka. Then he flinched and the emotions rolled off him, leaving him alone and empty. He once more thought he might purge the light contents of his breakfast into the weeds.

She glanced in his direction, and once Steigan noticed, he turned away. Had she sensed his emotions? Huffing, he walked off and started down the hill.

She'd said that she reached out the unicorns with her mind. Steigan tried that now. *Tyana, if you're out there now, please...*

Please what?

Please come rescue him from his hopeful imaginings, tell him that he wasn't losing his Dominari powers? Steigan reached down and picked up a rock from the ground. As if he could channel all his anger for needing validation of who he was, he chucked the rock as far as he could.

He found himself wanting to do the same with the absorption stone. His fingers quickly found it in his pouch and –

Laurient caught his arm. "Mate, what are you doing? Let's not be rash."

"Something's wrong with me," he admitted to Laurient, though he noted he was speaking the words because he wanted to.

"We're heading off to kill your best friend and his petty master. The stone is messing with your mind, making you feel weak. You know what we're going up against. Of course you feel like something is wrong with you. But tossing the stone away now isn't the way to solve it. Wait until you can throw it beneath Martias."

Laurient was right. Steigan lowered his arm and dropped the stone back into the pouch.

"Any more intervention needed?" Laurient asked.

"No, I'm good," Steigan lied.

Alityka chose that moment to call out, "This way, we need to turn some. They say the terrain will be easier for us to follow."

With the unicorns guiding their way, it did seem to go much quicker and the animal paths through the hills hid their own tracks well, but sleeping at night seemed more confined. Alityka did find spots where other animals had bedded down before them, usually leaving a musky scent behind that Steigan found distracting for some time each night until his nose got used to it. Laurient seemed comfortable with it, and the others took no notice.

The trees seemed taller than Steigan remembered, and some of the landscape appeared familiar as if it had never left his dreams. Of course, much of these hillsides he'd travelled twice; once to get the unicorn down and then again to assist Martias who had injured his ankle. He remembered finding Greytas and Brynne, who had not been happy at seeing him. Not that they ever were glad to see him, but this time had been particularly bad. Greytas had flogged Steigan's behind with a willow branch. Fortunately, Martias had come and snuck him out of the domini camp and they fled all the way back to New Lilinar. Two days later, a dominus came in and gave Holy Sapere Adonid the news of where his missing sapere and Steigan had been. Steigan would have taken another beating from Greytas rather than the dressing down he'd gotten from Adonid and the Council of Elders. One cycle he'd been held back after that as his punishment.

"Steigan," Valic called out, breaking Steigan from his thoughts.

Steigan moved toward Valic, searching in the direction he was pointing.

Morning light warmed their backs and made everything ahead of them seem bright. The trees, naked of their leaves, creaked in the breeze while the evergreen pines whispered to each other.

"I think there's a cave," Valic whispered.

Between the branches of the shrubs and bared trees, Steigan saw a faint luminescence coming from within a darkness against the mountain. The glow certainly behaved like candlelight. Steigan turned, motioning for the others following behind to remain silent and watchful as they progressed toward it.

For this whole trip, Steigan had kept his mind off the one thing he should have been planning all along. Laurient had even tried to usher his thoughts onto that path, but Steigan had decided to sit it out. Now, standing in front of the cave, that one thought tromped through his mind: what was he going to do with Martias? Once they went into that cave, something would happen. Battle most likely. He doubted Cirvel and Martias would just laugh at them finally having appeared and beckon the new arrivals to join them for brunch. Why did his head feel so scrambled?

"Remember," Ithanes said as he huddled close, "we are here to get Keteria. I know you all would like to take on Cirvel and the Necroatheling, but we don't have the ability to take Cirvel down and if Cirvel found some way to store the Necroatheling's soul, we can't defeat him either."

Steigan was glad that Ithanes had given this reminder, but Steigan also recalled Martias-na saying that a Necroatheling's weapon never missed. Martias had also foretold of Steigan's coming death.

Ithanes continued, "We can't defeat them right now. It's just not possible. Everyone got that? We have to get Keteria because she is the key for Cirvel to complete his plans. Understand?" He finished by looking right at Steigan.

Everyone around him murmured their agreement. Steigan remained silent, but nodded.

"All right. Steigan, Alityka, and I will go in. Valic, you hold the entrance. Laurient, with the bow in the trees. If it gets passed Valic, it's your job to take down," Ithanes ordered.

Ithanes and Alityka both moved toward the edges of the cave entrance. Ithanes flagged Steigan to walk one way or the other, but Steigan, absorption stone in his fingers, walked right toward the center of the cave's mouth. Once the darkness started to press in around him, he tossed the stone as far into the black depths as he could. He heard it ping against something unlike rock.

Inside the cave, a beast grumbled.

"Steigan," Alityka shouted. She rushed over to him, seized his armor and tunic, and tried to pull him back.

In a thunder of footsteps, something huge rushed from the cave. As Steigan fell from Alityka's throw enhanced by a push spell from Ithanes, a dark beast slammed into Alityka, knocking her backwards to the ground.

"Ancient oaks," Laurient shouted.

Steigan rolled as he heard wings flap above him. A cushion of air pressed him to the ground, making this head give a painful thrum, as Steigan caught sight of a large beast with a long, flexible tail launch into the air. It wasn't as large as the Guardian, but it certainly looked like the dragon under Dubinshire, except this one sparkled in the sunlight. It kept rising, flying to the east. With its wings fully extended and floating on the air, the beast seemed to give a shake and the black of its scales fell away to become as white as freshly fallen snow.

"Goddess," Valic whispered as watched the creature's flight while he staggered toward Steigan to help him up.

Ithanes kept his eyes on the dragon too as he helped Alityka to her feet. She had a bloodied lip and a smear of dirt across her face, but otherwise looked uninjured.

Laurient's bow let loose an arrow. It shot right by Ithanes and Alityka. Steigan whipped around to see what Laurient had fired at.

Martias-na leaned against the mouth of the cave. He had his left hand out, the arrow stopped mid-air before him. Meanwhile, his right hand pointed toward the dragon. "That would be what you're fighting against," he announced. "In the cycles while under Keteria's spell, he has actually grown and thrived, but he is still small compared to what he can grow to become. Now don't worry; he's just gone out to stretch his wings. He'll be back soon. We might want to be through here though because he's not big on having visitors." With that, Martias-na braced his stance and gathered magic in his hands. The arrow Laurient had fired clattered to the ground.

With one sweeping gesture, Martias-na brushed aside Valic's rushing attack as the Necroatheling stormed toward

Steigan. "Are you ready to die, Steigan? Have you come to terms with your demise?"

Laurient let another arrow fly, but it veered and clattered into the rocks around the cave.

Steigan worked at pushing himself off the ground, trying to push the shock and pain from his body. He noticed that Alityka was already on her feet and heading toward Ithanes to regroup.

Martias-na charged forward toward Steigan. "Answer me! Are you ready to give up and plunge yourself on my dagger? You do realize this might be the only way you save your friends. As you become a martyr, they gain their chance to get away. Shall I give you that one last request?"

Steigan rose to full height and drew his sword. Then he focused on the Necroatheling. "I've had a lifetime to think about how to kill you. Are you done with your questions so I can begin?"

Martias-na drew back in shock, his face elongating with alarm. "What's this? I don't feel your bizarre magic twisting its way through my being. You are no longer tethered to the unicorns. They have turned away from you."

"Steigan, withdraw," Alityka shouted.

Steigan found Valic circling around. Two domini who had trained together going up against a former sapere were odds that Steigan liked. However, even trusting Valic to have his back, Steigan felt something missing.

"Arlyn is dead," Steigan said, knowing that Martias should know that at the very least. Maybe Martias could make his peace with that in death.

The news did seem to take Martias-na a little off balance. "How?"

Valic saw his opportunity to move while Steigan distracted him.

"Magic sickness. When Keteria's spell broke," Steigan answered.

"You can lie to me now. How do I know this is true?"

"You don't."

Valic rushed for the Necroatheling. Martias-na brushed him aside with a flare of magic. Inside the shadow of the cave, there was a crunch and Valic screamed in pain.

Steigan ducked, coming in close on the Necroatheling, but Martias-na had a sword in his hand which Steigan had never seen him draw. It hadn't been in the Necroatheling's hand before, but it was in that critical moment when Steigan attacked and blocked Steigan's effort.

Their swords clanged as Martias-na drove Steigan back toward the forest. With a well-placed thrust, Martias-na knocked Steigan to the ground and sent his sword scattering away though Steigan didn't remember actually losing his grip on it.

"Without your unicorn magic, you are weak," Martias-na raged as Steigan tried to pick himself up.

Alityka jumped between them.

"Oh, now she's got power. The one true Dominari." Martias-na cast a spell which Alityka easily deflected before firing back her own. Tigma dashed in from the side, smashing into the Necroatheling and trampling him under hoof.

Alityka raced over to Steigan and helped him up. "You've got to withdraw, now," she shouted, glancing back.

Martias-na laughed as he started to rise and dust himself off. "Now that's a fighting partner. Whew! I'm going to have some bruises after that trouncing."

Alityka tugged Steigan, dragging him along while Tigma stood between them.

"Come here, unicorn," Martias-na said.

The unicorn skittered.

"We've got to help her," Steigan told Alityka as he tried to go back for the unicorn.

Before he broke away, Ithanes shouted the words to a spell more powerful than Steigan thought he'd ever heard Ithanes say before, superseding even the enchantment used to open the portal to Gohaldinest. At the same time, Alityka flashed to the other side of Tigma and returned with a sister chant to Ithanes' magic. The both aimed their spells at Martias-na. The Necroatheling hollered as he vanished.

Alityka and Ithanes collapsed near simultaneously to the ground, Ithanes to his knees and Alityka stretching out as if she were sleeping. Tigma nudged Alityka's spent form with her nose. After replacing his sword in his scabbard, Steigan tried to see if Alityka was all right, but Tigma turned to guard the Dominari.

"I'm here to help. Friend," Steigan said, holding his hands out to his side. Had the unicorns really turned their back on him as Martias-na had said? No, he wouldn't believe it. They wouldn't. Or, if they did break the bond with him, he wouldn't have given in so easily to defeat against the Necroatheling. He'd be a heartless fighting monster.

Tigma backed off reluctantly and allowed Steigan passed.

"Alityka, are you all right?" he asked, picking her up.

"I'm fine," she muttered, trying to sit on her own.

Steigan saw Laurient helping Ithanes, but Valic hadn't emerged from the cave yet. What had happened to him? He looked around for the Necroatheling once more just in case they weren't as safe as they hoped. "What did you do to Martias-na?"

Alityka fluttered her hand at him as she set about gaining her feet beneath her. "Ask Ithanes. It was his idea. Root rot, I have one heck of a headache."

Laurient head into the cave ahead of the others. Ithanes merely seemed tired, grumbling that his future-sight would be off for the next fortnight. With his normal complaints in place, Steigan knew Ithanes would be fine.

When Steigan glanced around, Tigma had slipped back to the forest.

Alityka rubbed her head, groaning, as she stumbled toward the cave.

"He called you 'the one true Dominari,'" Steigan muttered more to himself than to Alityka.

"You don't get it, do you, Steigan? I am the Dominari. I was a Dominari long before you were even born," she snapped. "The power can't be divided between us. You were a placeholder. Now I'm back and the magic must return to me. I am the rightful titleholder."

"But why would they do that, choose me only to release me? They could have broken the bond and it would be more effective in their mission."

"Because I am here. I am the first, the primary. You were someone merely dabbling with my powers. Do not act childish about the loss you have endured. You are still a fighter and a strong one, if you would act that way and remember your training."

Steigan let her walk ahead, the hurt filling him too deeply. She didn't seem to even notice. He probably could have slipped out to the forest just as the unicorn had and no one would witness his disappearance. How long before they cared?

The Guardian had indeed been right about him: he was nothing special.

CHAPTER 15

*T*he dank, musty cave fell quickly into blackness as if sunlight didn't dare to leave the mountainside to enter. Over many cycles, roots had bored through the rocks and dangled like the remains of a curtain to further hide what the cave held.

A groan issued from deep inside, along with Laurient's soft reassurances that all would be well.

"What if I don't want it to be well," Valic growled back. "Oh, just kill me now."

Steigan moved forward, trying not rush, but not wanting to be slow either. Cirvel and Martias could be somewhere inside, but whether they were still training in a timelock or hiding in the shadows for their moment to attack, Steigan didn't know. His eyes weren't adjusting to the darkness as quickly as he wished. Or was it really that pitch-black in here? He suspected the latter was true.

Alityka and Ithanes knelt down beside Valic as well as Laurient.

Steigan realized something had to be wrong for them all

to be crouching around Valic rather than assisting him to his feet. Curiosity gripping him, Steigan went for a closer look.

Valic's leg rested at an odd angle and a bone protruded through a tear in his leggings. Blood pooled all around the area. Ithanes and Alityka discussed in low tones between them how to handle this while Laurient gripped Valic's hand.

But Valic caught Steigan's eyes with an intense look and Steigan nodded. There was still work to be done. Steigan began searching the rest of the cave, leaving the others behind to help Valic, who already knew how dire his situation was.

Steigan explored into the depths where there seemed to be more room than needed for the beast who had fled. He was pretty certain he was alone this far in. As much as he didn't relish the thought, he knew he'd have to create an orb of light as the blackness encroached around him more. What if something or someone lay hidden, waiting to strike in the moment when Steigan blinded himself with his own magic?

He was confident he was alone, yet that remaining fraction of uncertainty left him unsettled.

Steigan glanced back over his shoulder, tempted to call out to Ithanes to ask what had happened to the Necroatheling, but Ithanes seemed to be working hard to stabilize Valic's leg. Their voices were starting to raise in agitation.

Returning to his search, Steigan dared to create the light he needed to see.

They were not alone.

The gray stone looked like an enlarged gargax with a much shorter muzzle but teeth which misshaped its face. Its head, which had been tucked down, now raised slowly and brought dark eyes to stare at Steigan, who discovered that it wasn't rock at all.

"Fear me, little man," it growled in a low tone.

A wave of energy surged from the monster and Steigan realized that the beast had been suppressing its presence. Fear like he'd never known before nearly knocked him to his knees. No, he had experienced something similar before, when going to the castle in Lilinar with Searn, and Laurient had been using magic to play with Steigan's mind. But this was worse.

"Azote," Alityka screamed out behind Steigan.

"Alityka, stay. You can't move now," Ithanes yelled.

Alityka's curse got lost amid Valic's scream.

"Vochey," Steigan said, calling his sword to hand rather than taking the time to draw if from his scabbard.

The monster raised a thick foot and stomped forward. Steigan retreated two steps. A massive, lumbering hand drew back in a fist level with the gaxlor's shoulder and Steigan saw it would punch toward him in a moment. He didn't even wait for the beast to move toward him, but ducked proactively while raising his sword to attack.

The gaxlor anticipated his moves, bluntly knocking the weapon aside as if it were a stick, and thrust his other stout fist into Steigan's gut. The armor took the blow, but the distribution of the impact carried Steigan sideways. He fell to the floor and skid.

"Not everyone is afraid of you, Azote, especially when they learn you were once beaten by a girl, twice."

Along with the new voice in their presence and the strong sensation of magic, Steigan looked around until he discovered a Necroatheling cloak standing near him. Strangely, he noticed that the hem was torn off.

"Well, if it isn't Rivic-na," Azote said. "Cirvel's favorite little plaything."

"Better a plaything than his lapdog," Rivic countered.

Azote issued a mocking laugh, then attacked.

Rivic evaporated to smoke, reappearing behind Azote. "Cada vetch."

Azote grunted, partially collapsing as if a heavy weight had come down on him.

Steigan rolled to his feet, ready to attack, but Rivic waved him off and pointed toward the others near the mouth of the cave. He took that to meant that Rivic had this handled and Steigan should worry about getting his friends out of here.

Azote, for as hard as he tried to resist the weight dropping down on him, collapsed. "Silkalae shamesh," Rivic said. "Paltradin gargeshga octra'halcarda ramisen."

Steigan had just reached the others when he noticed Rivic following behind. Rivic dropped down beside Valic. "Bit of a mishap, my friend? Let me see what I can do about it."

Behind them, Azote grunted. Rivic looked back. "That's holding him for less time than I thought."

"Rivic, should I?" Alityka asked.

Rivic shook his head. "Stay together. I'll need everyone here, right beside me."

Steigan hated waiting and felt powerless, especially considering the magic coming off Alityka and Rivic, and watching them as if they were of one mind, speaking in half sentences to each other.

Rivic began chanting in low, guttural tones as he held his hand out over Valic's leg. Valic flinched and winched, as did Laurient who still held onto the dominus' hand. After a moment, Rivic said, "Praektor," and the skin healed over where the bone had protruded only moments ago. "You're going to have to be careful on that leg," Rivic added as he urged the others to get Valic up. "The bone is together, but it's weak. Support him while we get back to Dubinshire."

With Valic injured, it was going to be a long trip back to Dubinshire, even if they used their magic and flashed back.

"Swalon sudinada kali Dubinshire binpada," Rivic said.

Steigan barely recognized the cold magic fluttering around him as they appeared back in Dubinshire.

"Yes," Laurient hissed in triumph before adding, "let's get Valic down to his room."

Ithanes and Laurient helped Valic while Alityka remained with Rivic. Steigan wondered what he should do and he decided to follow Ithanes' group. Instead, Rivic stepped in front of him and lowered the deep purple hood. "Now that we have the foolhardy quest out of your system, are you ready to take care of the bigger picture?"

"We still haven't gotten Keteria," Steigan answered with a look at Alityka.

"We don't need to make a move toward them. They will come to us with her. They need to be here more than we need to be out there. That lesson nearly cost you your friend's life. If I hadn't been there, been able to heal him, he'd never be able to fight again unless he did it from a chair. As it stands, we shall pray he manages to live through any ensuing infection so that he can fight at our side again."

"You agreed with me that since she's Cirvel's daughter we needed to go and get her back."

"No, you didn't listen to my protests. You weren't listening to anyone. You wanted to face that Necroatheling."

Steigan thought back over the quick meeting they'd had before heading out. He'd been enraged by Martias-na leaving him in the ground. He feared what might happen to Keteria after the Necroatheling's taunts. Maybe Rivic was right that Steigan hadn't been willing to listen.

"It wasn't all for naught," Alityka said, raising her gaze from the floor as she reached out to touch Steigan's arm. "We still used the time to talk about the time jumps. The spell that Ithanes and I did will keep the Necroatheling from time jumping again for a while. I had to push back against Ithanes' portion of the spell to keep myself out of the lock Ithanes was initiating."

"And the unicorns had full opportunity to return all your powers to you," Steigan said. He now saw that for just what it was.

Alityka didn't bother denying it; that would have been a lie, something a Dominari couldn't do.

"Did you know this was going to be a disastrous trip?" Steigan asked, wondering if Rivic had something akin to Ithanes' future-sight.

"No. I didn't know what was out there in the cave until I felt Leschemal leave and Azote remaining. I had hoped that the amassed power I was feeling was just Cirvel and his new Necroatheling."

"Do you know where they are now?"

"They have moved back to Lilinar."

"New Lilinar," Steigan corrected.

A faint shadow of irritation passed over Rivic's face. After a moment, he continued, "Just remember that they can travel as swiftly to Dubinshire as we did from the cave. Some of the warding Ithanes has finished will keep them out, but do not expect it to hold for long against Cirvel. Gohaldinest has long been his domain and he understands Leschemal's enchantments better than anyone. He can use that knowledge to create a slip hole. The old dragon has never stood against Cirvel, neither in flesh nor in magic. Make no doubt about it; Leschemal wants to destroy this world, but he enjoys watching Cirvel try to save it."

There went Rivic, being a subservient Necroatheling to his master. Could Alityka not see it, not hear his loyalty in his words? Steigan couldn't stand here and listen to lies about how Cirvel wanted to save the world. He turned away. "I will be ready. Will you?"

Steigan realized that he walked away from the challenge

he'd just thrown down, and that action made him feel like an even bigger coward. He heard them talking softly behind him as he left. Rivic the Necroatheling and Alityka the true Dominari. They both had more power than, well, anything he'd had lately now that the unicorns had turned away from him.

Danger was coming and Steigan, for the first time, found himself woefully unprepared.

CHAPTER 16

*S*teigan entered the storage room of the livestock pen and shut the door behind him. The scent of bagged grain itched his nose. If yellow had a smell, this would be it. A few shelves nearby had salt licks and other supplies, but he'd come here for none of that. Only the familiar odors of something akin to a stable. He wanted to be back home, in Whalston, helping Sim and Lucinia.

The closed his eyes, shutting down the unfamiliar sights and merely letting the fragrances surround him. It still was too strange and unknown.

His chest ached so badly like his heart had shattered into a million pieces and the shards now tried to rip from his chest. How much more pain did he have to endure? How much longer until someone told him he could rest? If this quest, if life, kept kicking him down, why didn't the fates just strike him down now and be done with it? Was this what his real parents had done to him by removing the thread? How could his own mother want him to be incomplete?

Steigan bellowed all his rage and slammed his fists into bags filled with grain.

He just didn't know what he was supposed to do anymore. Had this been how Martias felt all along, a stranger in a strange land and with unclear purpose? Steigan could see so many times when he should've been a better friend. If he had been, would Martias be a Necroatheling now?

Steigan collapsed down onto a stack of the bagged grain and put his head into his hands. He felt so tired and unsure.

"Steigan, why are you hiding out in here? Laurient asked.

Steigan hadn't heard the door creak open. "Maybe because I wanted to be alone."

"Valic is sleeping. There's some swelling and redness around the break, but the wound is clean, so everyone thinks that it will heal."

"And by everyone, you mean Rivic?"

"Yes. I just didn't figure you wanted me to say his name." Laurient came over and sat on a nearby stack of bags. "Look, mate, I don't think it's a good idea for you to be by yourself right now. That was a little harsh, what Alityka did to you, her words. She could've been a little softer and not rip the carpet right out from beneath you. But I don't think she's the most gentle person. It might be a trait you Dominari have."

"Well, I hope I'm not like that anymore now that I'm not a Dominari, but right now I really wish to be alone. Excuse me if upset your delicacies here, but would you really please leave?"

"No. I told you that I don't think you should be alone right now. Everybody else may not want to see it, may not care about you, but I do. So I'm going to sit down right here with you and not be gentle with you either if that's the way you want to play."

"Fine. I'll leave." Steigan stood up and made for the door.

Laurient started to follow. Steigan turned and as Laurient approached and Steigan took a swing at him. Laurient must have been expecting it because he parried Steigan's strike and the one that followed. Laurient landed his own against Steigan's jaw, sending Steigan reeling backwards into the grain.

"Now, care to share your thoughts with me now or do we keep trading blows?" Laurient asked.

Steigan scuttled from the bags of grain and stood up. He tried to seem as calm as possible as if he'd cooled down. He even managed to look up at Laurient with a collected smile. "Share my thoughts, huh?" he said, adding a clever chuckle as he stepped closer. Then he swung.

Laurient hadn't fallen for it either and he caught Steigan's blow. Twisting Steigan's arm, he slipped his foot in and knocked Steigan off balance, once again landing him on the grain. "Ancient oaks, you ought to be glad I came in here rather than someone else. How long do you think Ithanes would put up with your nonsense? Or Valic if he could walk? I suspect both would have left before even letting you begin to take out your anger on them. But me? I'll stand here and take your punches as long as you like while trying to knock some sense into you too. Be glad it's me, Steigan."

Steigan came up, tackling Laurient to the dirty wood floor. They rolled into the shelves, knocking salt licks from above. One banged into Steigan's armor, the other slamming into the back of his head. "Saint's blood." He reached up to touch his head.

Laurient used the moment to push Steigan off him. "If there was enough room in here for me to transform to a centaur, I'd land four hooves in you. Knock it off already." Then he noticed blood on Steigan's fingers. "It got you good, didn't it?"

Steigan sat up, still pressing his hand against his head. "Can't believe a little thing like that drew my blood." He picked up one of the offending salt licks and tossed it against

162

the wall. It thudded to the floor, breaking a couple corners off which rolled further away from the main body.

Laurient went to pick it up, including the extra pieces it had shed. "See, Steigan, this is us," he said, holding up the salt lick. "We try to hit the big monster, but it just tosses us away. If we don't hold strong to who we are, we shatter. But it made a dent in your head. If we keep coming..." Laurient threw the block, forcing Steigan to raise his arm and block the hit. It stung as it slammed against the bone of his forearm, sending reverberating pain up to his shoulder. "...we can continue to damage the monster."

Laurient picked up the salt lick again, crumbling it in his hands, "But if we let the monster tear us apart..." He tossed the salt crumbles at Steigan, who didn't even flinch as the grains didn't reach him. "...we lose."

Steigan picked himself up off the floor and returned to the bags to sit.

"I'm not done. If we let one member who has come loose from our group go off half-cocked..." Laurient pitched one of the broken pieces at Steigan. It bounced off and rolled back toward Laurient, who placed a foot on it. "...then the monster's minions can crush that person." Laurient stepped forward with the audible crunch of the salt lick beneath his foot. "Do I make my point?"

Steigan tested his head again to find the bleeding slowing. "Point taken." Though he didn't feel he needed Laurient's dramatic lesson to have learned it.

Laurient returned the remainder of the salt licks that had fallen to the shelves. "I also think Irragon needs to have some new salt licks made. These aren't holding together too well. Or you've got a very hard head. You know, I think that might just be the case. Maybe I should take some of these with me for the next time I need to knock some sense into you." Laurient smacked his hand on one of the shelves before returning to sit down by Steigan. He brushed dirt and spilled grain from the sleeves of his shirt.

"We haven't even gotten Keteria," Steigan said. "Do you think she's all right?"

"Keteria is a very powerful maege on her own. I think she'll give them what they're in for and they've got it coming to them."

Steigan knew Laurient was right. After a long moment of silence, Steigan asked, "Why am I here, Laurient?"

"Well, your mommy and your daddy shared a special embrace and then—"

"I know how I was born, but why am I here, in this battle? Rivic, Alityka, Ithanes, they are all more powerful than me."

"Sapere Laurient, coming right up. Well, my child, the Goddess calls on you to hold the line of what is right in your world."

An old memory struck Steigan. "Alityka did tell me that I needed to learn what I was becoming. I always figure that she meant I was to learn about my Dominari powers, but she said she hasn't been through that time jump where she initially sets me on my journey. She wouldn't have told me that if she knew that my powers were going to be revoked, would she?"

"I don't know. Women, mate, they are unfathomable creatures."

"I'm missing something. Ithanes' father took something from me before I was born, a thread."

"Well, I know that most things in this world that become lost to us can also be returned. Do you know where Lord Epious put this thread?"

"No. He probably disposed of it."

Laurient looked displeased. "Look, Steigan, if you take an important aspect out of child before the kid is even born, do you just toss it out with the trash?"

"I don't know."

"No, Steigan. The answer is no." Laurient rolled his eyes. "You put it away in a very safe spot just in case you discover that the child needs that ability, or if you want to give it to someone else."

That thought brought a chill to Steigan. "Do you think Ithanes has it, that Epious gave it to his son?"

"No, I think that would have irritated King Cirello into war. Not a good plan for keeping peace between countries."

"So what else could Lord Epious have done with it?"

"Well, I can tell you it's not going to be in a feed storage room, but if something is lost, it can be found. Let's go look for it."

Steigan nodded, then followed Laurient out.

They were back inside the castle and heading down a familiar hallway before Steigan realized that Laurient was seeking Ithanes. "You think it's going to be that simple?" Steigan questioned. "We ask Ithanes and he's just going to say that his father stored all his important items in a little jar?" But as soon as the words left his lips, Steigan knew that might not be far from the truth. What if finding his thread was as simple as looking in Ithanes' curio cabinet?

Laurient shrugged. "I don't know. But I know we've got to start somewhere. Ithanes and his father spent quite a bit of time together, so who knows what father told son? I can guess that Ithanes' future-sight has probably revealed this moment to him. Or possibly where we find your thread. Ithanes could very well have the answer."

Steigan wondered if Ithanes did know and had been keeping it from him all this time. He tried to imagine how he would react to learning that Ithanes had been concealing this secret waiting for Steigan's direct inquiry. He didn't like where that thought took him. It made him run a hand over his face and head.

"What's wrong?" Laurient asked.

"Nothing," Steigan lied, hating that he could speak them so easily now and the fact that Laurient didn't realize the untruth. With his recent thoughts and actions, Steigan knew he'd always been unworthy to be a champion of the unicorns.

Ithanes, carrying a thick book, came down the hall toward them, lost in thought until Laurient called his name. While he listened to the beginning of Laurient's request, Ithanes quickly began to roll his eyes and look agitated. His lips tightened. Finally, he took a deep breath and interrupted Laurient, "While I fully empathize with Steigan's plight, I have no time to assist. I am trying, without my future-sight mind you, to keep the Destroyer of Civilizations from getting into Gohaldinest." He shook the book at them. "You might not realize it, but if he succeeds in returning to his seat of power, we are all doomed. I suggest you speak with Aeri-bela. Her future-sight still works and she might speed you along your quest a little faster. Then, maybe, you can come back and assist me with the bigger mission."

Steigan and Laurient watched as Ithanes walked by them.

"Little touchy without his future-sight, isn't he?" Laurient asked.

"Just a bit, I'd say."

"Let's go find Aeribela then." Laurient started off.

"How are things going with the two of you?" Steigan ventured.

"She's healed and feeling much better. But..." Laurient glanced over to see Steigan looking at him. "But she's powerful and... I don't say that she's changed, but she's different, stronger. She might very well challenge Ithanes soon with her new temperament."

"And how do you feel about that?"

"I wish I didn't have to watch as another person in my life

rushes headlong and heedless into the battle. I liked it when she was willing to hang back with me a bit."

Steigan chuckled. "You know, she came to Whalston looking for the books. She wanted to march right into New Lilinar to look for them. I think she's always been on the forefront. She had a lot scare her and maybe it pushed her back a little. But now she's home, defending it. She probably needs your support now more than ever."

Tears gathers at the brim of Laurient's eyes. "Mate, you may not be a Dominari anymore, but that hasn't made you any less wise. Thank you. I think I needed to hear that."

"The Goddess calls on you to hold the line of what is right in your world."

"Look at you throwing my own words back at me." Laurient laughed. "But you know what? That doesn't quite work here."

"You're right, but I had to take the shot anyway."

They continued in silence, leaving Steigan to deeper thoughts. How was one to find the missing thread of one's life if one didn't know where to look? The question plagued Steigan more and more as he tried to fathom where Ithanes' father would have hidden a thread. What would it even look like? Would it be like the magical black thread the Guardian had given to Dragzel to return to Rivic? Could it be used like thread or did it need a special container? Could it just fade away? Would it even survive a thousand cycles?

Steigan noticed they turned a different direction than toward Aeribela's chambers.

"Ithanes wanted his room back with the curio cabinet, said he couldn't trust anyone to look after the bobbles in there, especially after meeting his mother still alive in the ruins and certainly not around the book that Aeribela had received from Ithanes' mother. She took her father's quarters," Laurient explained. "After looking at the book, feeling the book, I'm not sure I blame him."

"What's wrong with it?"

"Nothing. Aeribela says it's very helpful. Apparently it's written in dragon language. She and Rivic have spent quite a bit of time pouring over it. He says that his sister, Nyree, wrote it. But when they are reading it and talking about passages from it, the writing seems to sparkle off the page. They don't notice it." Laurient paused as if the next words he wanted to say scared him. "Then they both start speaking in this strange language. They don't seem to remember that either. I can feel the influence of this book on them."

"That's really why you say that she's different," Steigan commented.

Laurient nodded.

They had arrived at the heavy door to Lord Irragon's chambers and Laurient knocked. Aeribela beamed when she saw Laurient and she flung her arms around him. "I see you were successful," she whispered, letting Steigan know that Laurient had been sent out to stop Steigan's pity party thanks to her future-sight. She released Laurient, then waved to them. "Come in."

Sunlight from large windows on the right wall lit the rectangular room they entered. Across room sat a four-poster bed with thick red curtains that gathered in a peak over the bed, letting the material dangle over the poles. Closer to the door was a square, wooden table surrounded by four chairs padded in red velvet. Several pieces of framed art covered nearly every inch of the walls. A fire blazed in the fireplace, chasing the chill from the room. The scent of burning herbs reminded Steigan of the night he'd met Alityka in the forest. He saw a similar metal canister to the one Alityka had been wearing on her wrist sitting open on the wooden hearth.

"Did you have any luck?" Aeribela asked Laurient as she took a seat at the book-filled table with her back to the wall of artworks.

"No. But I'm going to head back and see if I can talk to him a little more. I think he needs a pep talk right about now too." Laurient leaned in and kissed her cheek before leaving and closing the door behind him.

Steigan guessed he should take a seat as well, but he glanced over the paintings on the wall. Most were brightly lit landscape scenes of valleys, as if the Lord of Dubinshire wanted to be reminded of the land beyond his forest mountains. One painting had a dreary city lost to a gloomy rain. Two more were of people standing in regal poses, but Steigan couldn't guess if they were of any importance beyond that.

"We were hoping that Ithanes would reveal something when Laurient went to ask him about your thread," Aeribela said before Steigan settled into his chair.

"Yeah?" he responded absently. "How about you? Have you seen anything?"

"Future-sight doesn't usually extend too far beyond one's lifetime. I've been looking for a spell that might aid us," Aeribela explained. "Ithanes' father would have no idea that we are searching for it now, but we shouldn't assume he didn't think about someone seeking it. Besides, you saw this in the shadow room. It might not be true at all."

"What if the shadow room couldn't lie to me because I was still a Dominari?" Steigan asked, willing her to be open-minded. "Might that not change things?"

"I'm not sure that's possible. Besides, the Guardian had mentioned your failing powers as a Dominari and that it had been happening for some time. How can we be certain the shadow room couldn't show you falsehoods?"

He wished she hadn't asked such a question. He hated

feeling it, without others echoing the acknowledgement of his waning abilities. "Aeri, what the shadow room showed me wasn't fears. It showed me possibilities. Besides, it wasn't Lord Epious said that I would find the book with the thread; it was Ithanes' mother. She taunts people with her visions, but how often have they not come true?"

"I'm just saying that it would be unusual for Epious to have accurate future-sight over such a time gap. Not impossible, just difficult. He still might have known something. Besides, the shadow room is meant to mess with your head and mislead you. Nothing in there is quite as it seems."

He hated admitting that what he saw wasn't actually the truth, but he hadn't even been born yet, so who was he to say what was real or not? "What if Epious or Ithanes' mother burned the book? Or put it in another dimension?" Steigan asked. "I never met Ithanes' father, so how am I to know what he did? And Ithanes' mother... well, she acts under her own purposes. We might never know if she's lying or not."

"I have what you need," a voice said beside them.

CHAPTER 17

The sunlight coming through the huge windows didn't stop the sudden draft against the back of Steigan's neck. His armor suddenly felt protective on him, like a layer of safety between him and whatever had spoken near them. His senses took in all of the room around him and Aeribela including the herbs burning on the logs in the fireplace, a familiar scent of when Alityka had first set him on this mission as well as a reminder that events might never be what one expected. He'd thought the woman in white to be helping the bandits, but everything had been wrong from what he'd imagined.

He'd thought he'd been a Dominari, but all that now proved to be false.

That didn't mean Steigan didn't know who he was. Even without the title of Dominus, he was still a protector of those around him. Immediately, that meant Aeribela.

Steigan spun around, rising to his feet, to face an old man with a white beard who looked out of a painting at him. The gloomy city had disappeared and, in its place, this man and a sullen library behind him. The scent of burned wood heightened, leaving Steigan tasting the singed air. Everything was not as it seemed. "Galault?" Steigan whispered as he took a step forward.

Galault extended a white-covered book out in front of him as Steigan approached. Galault's hands trembled and he seemed barely able to walk as he shuffled forward. His beard had grown longer and whiter than the last time Steigan had seen him. Galault, so brittle with age, Steigan feared the watcher of worlds might crumble to dust before handing over the book. The book itself didn't look much better. A portion of the blanched cover had darkened and the once gilded edges of the pages were brown and faded to yellow. It smelled of smoke. "It was hidden among the books in the Temple library in Lilinar," Galault said.

Steigan suddenly realized why the incinerated room behind Galault looked so familiar. "Is that why Cirello burned the library? Was he trying to destroy the book?" Steigan asked, the memory of it still sharp in his mind. Though so many other memories had faded, he had always wondered why that one stayed so clear. It had been the most traumatic, he knew.

Galault's eyes looked deeply saddened as he handed the book to Steigan. "It is. He never wanted you to become what you must in order to defeat the evil which has plagued this planet for far too long. But do not blame him; no parent ever wants their child to face dangerous situations. Believe me when I say that King Cirello would have rather dealt with the situation himself than to have the burden rest on your shoulders. Someday, your children will do things that you wish they never had to do." Galault leaned against the frame of the painting, his body very much round compared to the flat look that the Destroyer had in his painting. Strong magic held the portal open even while Galault appeared weakened. "Every parent wants their children to have better lives than they had, and in that same token, parents don't want their children to have to struggle to make their world better, yet it is a double-edged sword. To have a better life, the world must improve and that only happens through the sacrifices people are willing to make."

This watcher of worlds must be the wisest man, but why did Steigan garner such attention. "Why do you do this for me? Why do you keep watch out for me and help me as you have?"

"Because you have created me into the man I am," Galault said with a faint smile that turned the wrinkles in the corner of his eyes upward.

"Why? How?" Steigan shook his head. "That seems like so little in exchange for what you have done for me."

Galault dropped his gaze to the floor outside of the painting. "My previous words tell you all you should ever need to know." His shoulders drooped as he took a step back. It seemed almost like he sunk into himself as all the turmoil he'd ever known cloaked back over him and took him in. "I must take my leave now."

"Wait," Steigan said. "Is there anything I can do for you? I know you said that I made you into the man you are, but it still feels so slight. I have to know if there is something else I can do for you?" He didn't know what. What did a watcher of worlds need?

Galault's head trembled as he fought with age to raise his eyes to look at Steigan. "The one thing I would ask is the one thing that you mustn't do." As Steigan made to speak again, Galault held up his hand. "If it were up to me, I would ask that you strangle your first child before anyone knows he lives.

"You are from my future then?"

Galault gave one more wave of his hand. "When you meet me for the first time, all will be clear. Until then, you know what request I would make of you and know that I forgive you for not fulfilling it. Even though it is my fondest wish, for you to kill your son would irrevocably change all our destinies."

"Why? What happens?"

Galault raised a crooked finger and shakily pointed at him. "You of all people should know that I cannot tell you. I leave it in your hands as to whether to heed my advice or not. That is the only thing you can do. You have been warned."

"That is terribly cruel," Aeribela shouted as she rushed up behind Steigan, her own index finger jabbing right back at Galault. "How dare you come in here and say that to him? Who do you think you are?"

"That, milady," Galault said, with a fist over his heart and giving her a bow which made several bones in his back crack, "is indeed a good question. I am merely a humble watcher of worlds."

"Get out!" She slammed her hand on the table as if she wished to use that energy to punch Galault instead, but knew it was wrong to strike an elderly man, especially one inside a painting.

"Aeribela, not now," Steigan snapped.

Her blue eyes turned fiercely on Steigan, but quickly softened. "He doesn't have any right talking to you like that."

"He just might," Steigan replied gently.

"I don't… I don't think so."

Steigan faced Galault once more. "I thank you for rescuing the book and bringing it to me."

"You might not thank me after you've gotten back that thread of your life," Galault said. He took a step backwards and vanished from view.

"Who would tell someone to murder their first child?"

Aeribela whispered harshly. The thought had made tears come to her eyes. "What a cruel, old man."

"He has saved my life on a number of occasions," Steigan said, watching as the painting of the gloomy city settled back into place. "I'm certain his suggestion was not given lightly." A family… might he be destined to have one after all this? Even after all he had done? Steigan pushed the arising optimistic thoughts and buoyant sensations away from him.

"But you never could, Steigan, especially not without a reason," she continued. "It's not in your heart. Why would he even try to plant the seed?"

Pain twinged in his chest. He knew Aeribela was correct, but he also knew that he was right about Galault. He needed a distraction from that fantasy that might never come true. "At the moment, that is all irrelevant. We need to focus on what is right before us. None of us can afford to live in a future not yet here." Steigan picked up the book Galault had given him and touched the top edge of the pearly leather cover which was untouched by fire. Light umber letters wrote out the title in magical letters. Parts of them had singed in the heat and had a golden shimmer to them. "Piece of the White Snow," he read aloud. "A Letter Against the Shadows." He flipped the cover open, and his heart sank with disappointment when he didn't see a thread lying inside. He riffled through the pages hoping one would just kind of stop indicating the presence of something between the pages. There was nothing. "I don't even know what I'm looking for," he admitted.

Aeribela reached out her hand and waited to see if Steigan would offer her the book. A part of him didn't want to give it up, but he wasn't certain why he'd suddenly become so distrustful of her. He let her take it from him.

She leafed through the book. Then she returned to the

beginning and began reading. "Maybe it'll tell us something more."

"Maybe I'm wasting my time with all of this." Exasperated, he started toward the door, but a couple steps before he got there, he turned back to Aeribela. "I should be out there, tracking down Cirvel and Martias. I can't stay here and wait for them any longer."

"I think you're tired. You should go and try to get some sleep." Aeribela rose and handed the book to him. "You should take this. If a watcher of worlds brought it to you, then it needs to be safeguarded in your keeping."

Steigan accepted the book, but wanted to refuse the responsibility for it. He'd had his fill of books.

"I think I should remove this painting," Aeribela said. "Now it will make me nervous and wondering if someone is always looking over my shoulder."

Steigan stopped Aeribela from moving toward it. He ran his fingers over the dried oil paint, feeling the peaks and ridges beneath. It held no magic now. "I'm not sure I would worry about it," he told Aeribela. "Galault hasn't needed doorways to bring things to me. It's possible this was a one-time event. It took a lot of magic and I don't know if he's got enough to power it again."

"I'd still feel better if it wasn't there."

"Then you'd have a hole in your wall and feel like something was missing." He tried to say it with light, joking tones.

But her face darkened. "Something already is missing, Steigan." She looked toward the bed and he knew she was thinking about the man who normally slept there: her father.

Somehow, he needed to make this all end for her soon.

A golden glow emanated from the book. Steigan might not have noticed it if Aeribela gasped and pointed at it. He nearly dropped it when he looked down.

"What's happening?" he asked, flipping it over in his

hands to find the source of the light. He opened it to near the middle and pressed the pages of the book as far apart as he could. "It's coming from the binding."

The book was actually held together by a thread of delicately twined gold, silver, and white strings. He pulled out his dagger.

"Don't cut it," Aeribela warned. "That might break the magic."

"I won't," he promised. "But I'll need a needle or a pin if you have one."

Aeribela nodded, then rushed over to a wall where she pressed a concealed panel open to reveal a wardrobe behind. She began digging through the clothes hanging within.

As she searched, Steigan began to dismantle the book. He tore off the cover and the end paper. He had to significantly rip the spine off along with the protective ribbon that covered the thread because of how strong the glue holding it was, but soon he got down to just the stitching holding the pages of the book together.

Aeribela handed him a long pin from a broach and Steigan started undoing the knots between each stitch and dragging it from the pages. "I need more light," he said, moving toward the window. His eyes soon watered from staring at the glowing thread. He wanted to rub the moisture away from his eyes.

"Maybe an oil lamp," Aeribela suggested, lighting one and placing it on the table for him. He returned and sat back, glad that he didn't have to hold against the resistance of the book's light weight wanting to slip from his hands.

After a few moments, he pulled the oil lamp closer to him, hoping that more light would actually negate the shine of the thread. He remembered knotting together so many pages in the books he had created in his prior life and wished his fingers had only been so nimble them. Still, this was slow work and after a time, he had to set the pin down to give himself time to close and rest his eyes.

"We can take turns at it," Aeribela said. She held out her hands to offer her help, but didn't try to forcefully take the task from him.

Steigan nodded, slid the book to her, and handed her the pin. She sat down at the table and leaned forward over the project. Steigan walked away, choosing to go to the window and let his gaze look out over the distance, hoping it would be a nice change from the up-close work. He found himself looking toward Dubinshire Park. The sight of it brought back the ache of memories with Keteria. He let his thoughts drift to those, rather than into worry over what was happening to her now. As Laurient had reminded him, she was a powerful maege and capable of handling herself.

He thought of her smile as he'd handed her the roll on the way to the park, her bright eyes as she watched him fighting in the tournament. A lifetime ago. Then, her tears as she cast the spell that would place her in a slumber of a thousand cycles. Along the way, his feelings for her had changed.

Now he was no longer the man he'd been.

...what you are becoming... Alityka's words played in his head.

Aeribela sniffled and Steigan turned to see her massaging her irritated eyes now. "My turn," he said, heading back toward the table. She vacated the seat and went to the window as he resumed where she had left off. It didn't take long until his eyes began watering again.

They traded off a couple more times. Aeribela left the room at one point while he worked to gather a fresh pile of books which now sat on the table. She flipped through them looking for something. Time after time, she discarded them into a secondary pile.

After another switch of slowly taking out the knots in the

binding and freeing the thread, she got up and went to dig under the bed for yet another book. Steigan wondered how she kept track of all of these tomes. This one she read while sitting on the bed, but Steigan recognized it as the one Ithanes' mother had given to her while they were down with the Guardian.

Steigan finally loosened the last knot and pulled the thread free. "Got it," he announced, picking the twinkling thread up between his fingers. But now that he had it, he wasn't sure what to do with it. Or even what it was.

Day had faded to late afternoon, but the thread alone held back the notice of the diminishing light in the room until Steigan glanced toward the window.

Aeribela slammed closed the latest book she'd been reading and returned to the table. "We probably should have left it there. At least we knew where it was."

"What's wrong?" he asked.

She shook her head. Twice she tried to speak, letting only a puff of air escape before she pursed her lips together. Finally, she managed, "I've confirmed that this is an aspect thread. I've found lots of spells for removing an aspect out of a person, but I don't know how to put them back."

"Wouldn't you just reverse the spell?" Steigan asked, not sure why she was trying to make this more complicated.

"This is very delicate magic because it concerns meddling with the bloodwave. It's got to line up with every single one of your markers. This thread is a partial and it needs to merge into the strings which make up your magic as well. They should all twine together. I don't have the skill to do this, even if I did have the healing spells I needed."

"What's the repercussions if we try and fail?"

"You won't have any power at all. You could go blind." She looked at the floor. "You could die."

"How do you know that much if you don't know how to put the thread back in me?"

"Because it's just as dangerous if someone takes a thread out of you incorrectly."

"Okay." He sighed. "Ithanes' father knew how to take a thread out of an unborn child. Ithanes understands the bloodwave spells. Is it possible he can put the thread back in me?"

"I don't know." Now as she pressed her lips tightly together and looked away. "What if I don't want him to be able to do is to put that thread back in you. I don't want you to become a Winctonicht. I've failed my mission to keep magic from returning and I want to stop hurting the people around me."

"Hurting? How have you hurt me?"

"I started you on this mission. Everything that has happened to you is because of me. You've grown powerful, almost as strong as Ithanes. But this power in the thread, it scares me. This is part of your magic, taken right out of the bloodwave. It shines so brightly because of the capacity it holds. When you – if you, take it back, the magic you have will be enormous. Enough to rival a Necroatheling."

"Would it help for you to know that I'm scared too?" He pushed himself up far enough to put his head against hers.

"I had a vision of you and I'm scared of it coming to pass." She reached out for him and pushed her fingers into his hair, clutching him to her. "Your parents took this out of you for a reason. They were frightened of the power. What would they think if they found out you had gone against their wishes?"

Her words were enough to make him want to pull away, but she held him tightly.

"I don't have the luxury of getting into fears," Steigan said, gently sitting back down in the chair. "I have always trained to develop myself. If I don't better myself better as a warrior, people I'm supposed to protect with my sword die. If I don't improve my magic, I can't overcome the enemies that seek to destroy us with their powers. This thread is a part of me. I have to believe that it will only enhance me. Without this, I'm not a complete person."

"And that is precisely the way we'd like to keep it."

Steigan turned at the familiar but harsh voice beside him. He couldn't say he was completely surprised by who he saw. Martias closed the distance between them, the laces of his white shirt swinging with each stride. He looked so different in his human form without the purple Necroatheling cloak, pleasant and unthreatening like Laurient. Martias snatched the thread from Steigan's fingers and dropped it into a vial.

"Dominari Steigan has lost his thread," Martias sang at him with a tune that struck Steigan as familiar and made the cycles between them tumble away.

In the next instant, Martias vanished, leaving the room singed with ancient magicks.

CHAPTER 18

*T*he room around Steigan felt cold as he sat at the table with his hands empty. He glanced at his palms, normal like everyone else's without the lineage mark, helpless even, as the door to Aeribela's room crashed open. He had a vague, numb awareness of people approaching and of shouts and hollers, but none seemed to reach his ears in a fashion that made any sense.

He felt someone shaking him. The motion made him drop his vacant hands to his sides.

He'd been holding it, the aspect thread he needed to make himself whole.

Now it was gone again. It might as well be as lost to him as it had been in the book before Galault had given it to him.

Steigan stared at the dark stained pinewood paneling between the pictures. There wasn't much space between the frames, but in his vision now, in this dull world where his mind retreated seemed vast enough for his thoughts to stay for cycles. The long, striated grain of the wood were like valleys to be explored, crevasses in-between the boards were great canyons that got lost to the darkness, and the cool smoothness of the polished wood reached out to call him to sleep.

The shuffle of movement around him kept him from sinking deeper into his stupor. He rose back to the surface as the initial shock subsided.

Why did Martias continue to take things from him? His ignorance behind the superstitions, his title and position at the Temple, Keteria, his aspect thread...

Steigan screamed with rage, breaking through his stoic imbalance and bringing the chaos of the whole room around him to silence. Nearly everyone had gathered. Laurient and Ithanes stood near Aeribela trying to get her view of what had just happened since Steigan seemed to be catatonic. Rivic stood near the window pointing toward Dubinshire Park. Alityka had been striding toward Rivic, but now stopped. Her foot dragged against the floor as she slowly moved to a balanced stance. Ellis stood in the doorway, Dragzel by his side.

As if searching the whole world, Steigan's magic surged outward to seek Martias. It didn't go far.

"We had the thread that had been removed from Steigan," he heard Aeribela mention to Ithanes.

"Is this the time, what you saw?" Ithanes asked. Aeribela shook her head.

"Enough." Steigan moved toward the window where Rivic still pointed out toward the park. Two people stood on the grass, the evening casting their long shadows over the grass among the trees. They seemed to be examining something which one of them held.

Martias wasn't wearing the Necroatheling cloak yet, which meant that he hadn't been changed. There might be time to prevent it. Even Martias-na had said events could be changed.

Steigan prepared to flash down there.

A hand rested on his shoulder. "I will go with you," Alityka said.

A dark shadow passed in front of the window. Steigan made out Azote's abdomen as it flexed in flight before them.

"They are here," Rivic confirmed to the rest of the group.

Steigan met Ithanes' gaze. "Alityka and I are going out there," Steigan told Ithanes. "Raise all your enchantments on the castle to keep them out. We will do our best to make sure they don't even make it this far."

"Once you're outside, you won't be able to get back in. You won't be able to retreat," Ithanes said.

Steigan dropped his hand on top of Alityka's. "I know. Talcor dun."

Steigan and Alityka appeared on the grassy lawn in Dubinshire Park right as a thunderous crash sounded behind them. Azote had started bombarding the castle tower. Steigan doubted Ithanes had managed to get a protective spell up that quickly.

The Destroyer of Civilizations smiled. "Oh, isn't this delightful. Two Dominari together, fighting back-to-back. We need a few more spectators than just your measly little friends. Alityka, have you told your new friends about The Playground? Your fights down there were legendary."

Steigan watched Martias, wondering how far his process to become a Necroatheling had come. Obviously, Martias and Cirvel had yet to encounter Martias-na for a significant length of time as they both were unaware of Steigan losing his Dominari powers. Steigan hoped Alityka realized this too and wouldn't tip their hand.

Cirvel looked curious and tilted his head slightly to the side as he once more cast his gaze toward the castle tower. "Where is Rivic-na? I sense my novibrother's presence, but he chooses to let you come down here alone. Why would that be?"

Alityka struggled against the question. Steigan felt certain that if Cirvel glanced at him, Cirvel would know that Steigan no longer possessed his Dominari powers. "She came with me. I want my thread back. And the two of us could do that on our own."

Cirvel chuckled. "You can't be serious."

Steigan stepped forward, holding an arm out before Alityka so she would stay back. "I am. And I'd like to do it without a fight. Certainly there is something we can negotiate."

"Steigan?" Alityka muttered behind him.

"Lord Cirvel," Martias protested.

Now Cirvel raised a hand to cast Martias to the background. "I'm listening. What do you propose?"

"I've seen the dragon you are trying to save this world from. I know where he sleeps."

Martias stepped around Cirvel's raised hand. "So do we. You think you're so special, that only you gained something when we went to the Palin Mountains together. I found the dragon and –"

"Enough," Cirvel snapped.

Martias seemed to choke on his next words. He spun around clutching at his throat.

"I want my thread. It was taken from me before I was born. I'm told that putting it back will be a dangerous procedure. I don't believe anyone around me is capable of such a feat, but you have studied magicks for far longer than anyone else. If you return the thread to me, I will aid you in your quest. Alityka will return to the others to let them know I've done this of my own free will. You know that I hold sway with Lord Ithanes and I might be able to further negotiate getting you into Gohaldinest."

Once again, Alityka muttered protests behind him, but

the blood pounding in Steigan's ears kept him from hearing her words. He had no other plan if Cirvel didn't accept.

"You speak the truth to me about all this?" Cirvel asked.

"Yes," Steigan said without hesitation. If Cirvel believed Steigan was still a Dominari, then Cirvel would believe he couldn't tell lies.

Cirvel turned to Martias, still choking, who delivered the vial to Cirvel's outstretched and awaiting hand. Long fingers turned the vial carefully as Cirvel examined it. "Onesong, astral, and pure bravery," he muttered. His gaze flickered to Steigan momentarily. As he returned his attention back to the thread, Martias inhaled a deep breath and began to cough.

Alityka moved alongside Steigan and touched his arm as her shoulder nudged him. He refused to look at her, knowing that she only meant to question his actions. He had enough doubts about what he was doing without hers as well.

Cirvel clicked, his head twitching as he did so. "You are right. This will be difficult to return. Something had to take its place."

"My mother gave her magic," Steigan said. His rapid reply would keep Cirvel's thoughts moving forward and keep Alityka's protests at bay.

"Interesting."

Alityka's fingers slid along Steigan's. "Please don't do this," she whispered as she grasped onto his hand.

Cirvel looked as if he could slap her and, for a brief moment, Steigan thought he might have to protect Alityka with his body and armor. But with a breath, Cirvel eased the ire away and his face softened with a smile. "There is no reason why we can't all get along. In truth, we all really are on the same side. There is a dragon out there who would see this world dissolve to chaos. It will take the magicks of all of us to prevent that."

"Not your way," Alityka said. Her skin took on a shade of green as if she might be sick from the thought. She shook her head "Not your way."

Azote struck the castle again with another barrage of stones. Alityka flinched with each crash, her grip on Steigan's fingers tightening. Cirvel noticed, evident from the smile growing on his lips and the wry twinkle shining in his dark eyes.

"Would you succumb to becoming one of my Necroathelings?" Cirvel asked to Steigan.

A chill surfaced through Steigan's arms and back. Even when he'd held the cold magic, his blood had never felt so frozen. "No," he answered. Then he pointed the vial Cirvel still held. "I do not believe that would permit me."

Cirvel's grin broadened. "How very right you are. It probably wouldn't. But I have promised to restore all the Necroathelings with their souls as soon as we have convinced Leschemal not to destroy this world. Side with me and see the mission through to completion and I will return the thread to you then." He turned to Martias. "What do you say? Take him along, shall we?"

"I wouldn't believe a word he says. He likes to twist things to his advantage," Martias said.

Turning back to Steigan with a shrug, Cirvel clucked his tongue. "There you have it. Dissension among the ranks. I just can't have that. We can't take you along."

"Royka piryeian," Alityka said.

Vines sprang up around Alityka and Steigan, swiveling around their legs before they could move away.

With disapproving tsks, Cirvel shook his head. "Very disappointing, Dominari Alityka. I think I shall return you to class and let this boy go with you. You both still have a lot to learn. Martias, take them back to Gohaldinest, and while you are there, find a cahaster."

"Yes, my lord," Martias said.

Cirvel walked around the vines entangling Steigan and Alityka while chanting a spell. The only word Steigan could make out was Gohaldinest. "I have locked your magic so it will only work outside of Gohaldinest. This should make a great little game of cat and mouse, don't you think? Come now, Dominari Alityka, how fast do you think you can outrun me? Can you outwit me?"

Cirvel turned swiftly, sending his black robes swishing over the ground and fluttering behind him as he walked away.

Martias moved before Steigan.

"Martias, don't do this." Steigan knew Martias would most likely ignore the pleading whisper, but he had to try anyway. "Alityka, get us out of these vines." Once they got to Gohaldinest, if they were still in this tangle, they'd be helpless.

"Don't you think I'm trying," she said, wiggling against them. "Can you dispel the magic?"

"Radin lukion," he said.

"Don't you think I tried that?"

Martias' brown eyes glared at Steigan for a long time and Steigan had a hard time keeping his own gaze soft and begging as Martias challenged him. Steigan wanted to stare sternly back at him, but knew that wouldn't do anything to get him very far with his friend. Meanwhile, he wished Alityka would come up with something to get them out of these vines.

"At least let us out," Steigan said to Martias. "Your master won't have any fun if there's no game of chase to play."

"If you can't figure this out, you're not worthy to play," Martias said.

As Martias spoke the spell to take them back in time, Martias placed his hands on Steigan's and Alityka's heads.

"Rokta toyia." It was the only other thing Steigan could think of.

The vines dropped away from them right as Martias' enchantment flow over Steigan.

The magic had only enough strength to lift them from their current time and place them two thousand cycles in the past. Steigan felt it drain fast. Martias must have seen the shocked look in Steigan's eyes over this revelation because Martias snarled and ran off down the hallway where they had landed.

Steigan drew his sword and looked around. The gray stone looked similar to Dubinshire, but the feel was nothing comparable. A chill grew along Steigan's spine, starting in the small of his back and crawling toward his neck. The hair at his nape stood on end and made its way toward his scalp.

He wanted to chase Martias and dashed to the inter-secting hallways where he'd seen Martias turn. There was no one. Before he started off in the direction, Alityka grabbed him.

"Where did he go?" Steigan asked, hoping Alityka could follow Martias' returning magic. "We've got to get him before he finds a cahaster."

Alityka slapped Steigan. Tears brimmed in her eyes. "Were you really going to betray your friends by switching sides?" Alityka had her hands on her hips, feet braced apart as if prepared to attack him again if she uncovered his treachery.

Why that mattered at this moment, he wasn't certain. Steigan grimaced as the unicorn magic worked over him, trying to coax the answer out of him. Alityka really wanted to know the truth. A sudden desire to know if he could lie to her came over him. If he no longer stood as a Dominari, was immune to their powers? "No, it was all part of a plan."

Her head tilted as if she examined the truth of his words.

After a moment, she decided to believe him.

He wouldn't have.

Alityka wrapped her fingers around his wrist and started pulling him in a different direction. "We can't follow him."

"We have to. We can't let him get a cahaster to store his soul."

"We have no magic to fight him. We couldn't stop him if we wanted. Unless you're willing to kill him. Are you prepared to do that?" Alityka asked. "I didn't think so. We can't let Cirvel find us either. We have no choice but to run. We've got to get outside of Gohaldinest. That's our only chance."

Alityka began to lead the way, yet something about all this bothered Steigan.

"Come on," Alityka called with a wave of her hand to urge him along. "Cirvel has probably already felt us here and sent Necroathelings out to see what's going on. We can't remain here."

"Like an alarm." Steigan stopped.

"Alarm? What are you talking about?" Alityka asked as returned to him.

"Martias teleported inside the castle and grabbed the thread."

"Yes, we know that"

"He shouldn't have been able to. Yes, Ithanes had enchantments he would cast once Cirvel got close in order to keep him from getting in, but Ithanes always has spells on the castle that will only let certain people teleport in. There always are. If anyone could get inside, then anyone could kill the ruling Lord of Dubinshire. It's simple protection."

Alityka struggled with understanding where he was going, but by the time he finished, her eyes grew wide. "Right. Which means that if Martias got through that initial layer of protection, someone had to let him in. Who?"

Steigan shook his head, half afraid that the answer might be that he had done it. Worse, he could have done it unconscious. Could he undermine Ithanes' magic without awareness of doing it?

He urged Alityka to continue down the hall because he really didn't want her seeing the emotions on his face. In the unicorns' absence, he saw that he was not a good man. He'd become evil if it meant getting what he wanted; his offer to join Cirvel proved that.

But what had stopped him from promising to become a Necroatheling then?

He slapped a hand against his thigh as he ran, fully angry at himself now. He had no proof that the thread would stop him from becoming a Necroatheling. It had been his chance and all he'd had to do was agree; he'd blown the opportunity.

Would Cirvel believe Steigan if he said he'd changed his mind? Doubtful.

Which meant Steigan had to get the thread back and find a new option.

"Steigan, what's wrong? What are you thinking about? We might not be able to use our magic here, but I can still tell that your energy is frantic."

"Strange place," he lied, knowing that part of him wanted Cirvel to find them. Steigan might be able to make the Lord of Gohaldinest in this time period a proposal to become a Necroatheling. Had a similar offering of power overcome Martias into deciding to become a Necroatheling? What temptations had Martias fought and lost? Would Steigan give in just as readily?

Alityka's eyes held a look of deep sadness. "I know how the magic can dig into your thoughts. Please, Steigan, we need to go. Now. Before he finds us. As long as we are in the city, Cirvel has us trapped."

CHAPTER 19

*N*ight pressed black against the windows Steigan and Alityka passed so that it seemed like everything outside meant to close in around them. Occasionally Steigan saw an orange light off in the distance, but rarely did it have the strength to shed any visibility on what was beyond these gray stone walls.

He soon stopped trying.

Steigan couldn't help small, sidelong glances at her as they rushed through the halls of Gohaldinest castle. She had such determination in her stride, but it was her reddish curls bouncing against her shoulders that he couldn't stop watching. He felt the strength of her magic, practically breathing it along with the fruity scent of her. She smelled like strickleberries.

"What?" she asked, finally having taken notice of his glimpses.

"Nothing," he lied.

"I can sense when someone is lying to me, you know? You of all people should be aware of that."

"But can you? Can you tell when I'm lying?"

Her blue eyes raised. "No."

What he'd suspected was true. His having been a Domi-nari freed him from the influence of her powers. "We'll have to figure out how to use that to our advantage then."

"As in us or just you?" she asked with a smile. Then she reached out her hand. "I'm sorry I slapped you earlier. I didn't know any other way to get your attention. We should keep in contact so that one of us can't be pulled away from the other and an illusion be put into place. We don't want to get separated."

Steigan allowed his fingers to entwine with hers. Her grip on him was light though he could solidly feel her fingers between his. Her delicacy reminded him of Tyana and, with a selfish twinge, he held onto what he could of the unicorns in this moment. As long as he held Alityka's hand, he possessed the unicorns too.

Maybe this had been a bad idea.

He almost shook her off him. "Alityka," he started, knowing that he had to tell her of his conflicting emotions. What he felt wasn't right. He had to let her know that her safety was in jeopardy. Maybe the unicorns hadn't removed the bond between them and him, but had indeed broken it. No one had ever said how long it would take for him to become a monster, a senseless killer sent out to right the world at any cost. Maybe this desire to get the bond back was just the beginning of what would happen to him.

"Call me Ali," she said, her tone soft behind a gracious smile and backed by a feather touch of her gaze upon his face.

"Ali," he started again, preparing himself to say the words.

But she took a deep breath and turned toward him as she came to a complete stop. She inhaled and exhaled through parted lips, her gaze desperately searching him. "I feel it too. You're vacant and pulling on my power, magic that was once yours. I want nothing more than for it to fill you, but can that ever be sated."

Her statement echoed through him for a long moment. "No. It can't." Steigan looked away. He should release her hand.

The fingers of her free hand forced him to look back at her. "Then do not concern yourself with emotions that impede what we're doing here. Take it. Take what you need. I am not less for it."

"But I—"

She squeezed his hand. "Let me fill that lack and let yourself be whole. We need that if we're going to get out of here."

"What am I becoming, Ali?" he asked. "When you started me on this whole mission, you said that I needed to learn what I was becoming. You knew. I hope you know now because I need the answer. I don't want to become like Cirvel, but I fear I might be on that path. I want to go find him, learn from him."

"You are most definitely a relation to Rivic. But I don't have an answer to your question because I don't know yet. I hope that by the time I am to make that time jump to send you on this quest, I know the answer. For now, you are in the middle of that becoming. Magic, as it is in the middle of gathering for a spell, does not know what shape it will take and whether its purpose will be good or bad. It merely molds itself to the spell. Be like magic and allow the flow." She squeezed his hand and Steigan appreciated the physical reassurance. He nodded before they continued on.

"I swear these hallways are shifting. I feel like I'm walking through an illusion, don't you?"

Steigan felt like this whole city was unreal. While the odd sensations had diminished, they hadn't disappeared completely. He wasn't certain he could answer her question and suspected that she didn't really require one.

"This is not where we want to be," she said, her voice inching higher as if she were growing frantic. "We should turn here."

Alityka reached out and clicked the latch on a door, hurrying into a hallway with white and black tiles on the floor. Huge lattice windows faced out from the hallway. She slid to a halt, Steigan bumping into her. "No, no. This is not where we want to be." She turned to flee, but the door behind them had vanished.

She raised a finger to her lips, hushing his impending questions. Then, softly, she spoke, "These are Cirvel's quarters. I don't think he's here right now. There's no Necroathelings standing guard, but a Dominus will probably be along shortly. We should be able to go out the other way." She indicated the door at the other end of the hallway.

They started tiptoeing across the tile floor. But the sight out the window made Steigan stop for a look.

One of the moons hung just above the castle wall, shedding pale white light upon the many rooms and towers below. It cast highlight bursts along rooftops and edges of stone. Orange-yellow lights burned in several windows.

It took Steigan a moment to realize that he wasn't looking at Gohaldinest as a buried city, but as it once had been. He grappled with the reality of its beauty against the superstitions of Gohaldinest he'd been told during his upbringing.

Alityka pointed off to the far left. "That was my dormitory."

He had to inch her over to get a view of what she was indicating. He could barely make out a window from the faint light coming from inside. A form moved in front of the window and, for a brief moment, Steigan swore that it was Alityka herself.

A strange idea forming in Steigan's mind. "When we were

in the shadow room, before you woke up in this timeline, you knew Galault. Is he here in this timeline? Did you know him when you were an acolyte?"

"I don't understand how that can help us."

"He can shift things. If he's here, he can get us out of the castle without us actually needing to find a way out."

Alityka's eyes grew wide. "Right. Brilliant. Follow me."

They left the tiled hallway and went down a long staircase separated into several platforms. It felt familiar to Steigan and he thought about asking. But, as far as he knew, she'd never been in the ruins of Gohaldinest beneath Dubinshire save for their one teleported trip to the shadow room. She wouldn't know if this staircase still existed in the ruins, yet it must. Steigan remembered going with Ithanes to retrieve a staff from Cirvel's quarters. How strange to constantly have two sets of memories in his head. Yet, everything looked so similar too. How did one tell one hallway apart from another?

Alityka threw out her hand, forcing Steigan to a stop. "Necroathelings," she whispered, then indicated that they go another direction. They headed back the way they came, but the Necroathelings didn't follow. Steigan swore that Alityka didn't breathe until they had gone by and their footsteps faded.

Little blue ribbons of magic reached off the walls for Steigan as they went. "How come they don't go for you?" he asked.

"They're familiar with my magic, but they always reach for Rivic too. I figured it was because he was a noviho-midrak, but maybe your family has sweet blood or something."

Once again, Alityka led them through the castle, off in a different direction from the Necroathelings.

"Do you love him?" Steigan asked, the words blurting

unfathomably from out his mouth. He couldn't believe he'd just asked the question.

"Who?"

"Rivic."

"No," Alityka answered with sadness touching her face. "Rivic loves my sister, Ellonia. Or loved her, I guess I should say. But he is my best friend. Oh, he used to make me so angry. He was so afraid of his magic. But if I ever needed anything, he was right there. He knew what to say to make me reach beyond my own limitations. Much like you, he could see alternatives to situations that I couldn't."

Steigan glanced down at the spot where the lineage mark had once been on his palm. It felt strange, these feelings he felt growing for Alityka, his woman in white, his Goddess. Yet, if Rivic had produced children with Ellonia, then Alityka would be some sort of great aunt. It seemed as if his relationships got weirder with each one and he knew he had to stake this one before it developed any further.

"You get distant in the same way too," she said.

"Focusing on getting us out of here," Steigan lied, relieved that she wouldn't know it. Besides, she had never done anything that had indicated her feelings for him, so maybe these were only in his mind, much like the creation of this illusion. He would do well to quit feeling dreamy over her. He'd had his chance at a family, and, while some parts of it had been good, he'd messed up more than he could ever repair. It served him better to stay on the path of a warrior and give his life in defeating Cirvel. That was how it was always meant to be.

"Let's just hope that I've brought Galault here by now."

"You mean, Galault wasn't always with you?"

"No," Alityka said as she started for a doorway at the end of the hall. "I brought him…" She almost stopped. "I brought him from the future, your future. Now, don't ask me any more questions about it."

He knew why she made this request: with the Dominari magic, she would be forced to answer. Had she learned to skate around the truth without actually divulging everything as he had when he'd been a Dominari?

"Let's hurry," she said as she started down a staircase. Once at the bottom, she began to run faster through the halls as if being chased by demons. Steigan suspected it was his questions and her memories she wished to escape. But which scared her more?

CHAPTER 20

The hallways of Gohaldinest had an old, earthy smell to them as if the rocks used to build the castle had never quite lost the ground from which they'd been pulled. Wall sconces spaced between tapestry hangings lit the way, the flaming candles adding a touch of fatty oil odor to the air.

Steigan and Alityka stopped at a door made of very dark wood and Alityka opened it with a spell. Inside was a small, dark library with a round table in the middle. Between bookshelves hung a gloomy painting of city in rain. "This is the painting Galault came out of," Steigan said.

Alityka touched the frame. "Galault? Galault, can you hear me? It's me, Alityka. I need a favor."

Steigan nearly laughed. "Really? You walk up and ask the painting?"

"How would you do it?"

"Vocha chia cada'dada," he said.

The paint rippled and a Galault much younger than the last one Steigan had seen appeared. The watcher of worlds seemed very surprised to see both of them.

"Galault, we need to get back to Dubinshire, two thousand cycles from now," Steigan said.

"I cannot aid the passage of any length of time for it to be faster than it is."

"Yes, but you can open a door, can't you?"

Galault seemed to suddenly realize that he was speaking in the modern language rather than ancient. "You mean you've already come from there, but you need to get safely back."

"Yes. We've been brought back in time and our magic locked so we can only use it outside of Gohaldinest."

"That I can help with. Come up here."

Steigan knelt and let Alityka use his leg to help her step up to the painting while Galault helped to lift her. Then Steigan jumped through. He turned just in time to see a patch of light cut into the library as someone opened the door. Galault resealed the painting's portal behind them.

"That was close," Galault said.

Steigan realized this was an ordinary room with a small bed beneath a window. Beside the bed sat a stand with an unlit lantern and a closed book. But more than that, Galault looked so young that Steigan stood there staring at him for a long time.

Galault tried to pass it off with a smile. "I have always had the white hair," he said with a chuckle. "But you did not come here to see me. You need to get back. There is a battle coming. Let me see what I can find."

He opened the door to the room, but Steigan felt the wave of magic leave Galault as he took the handle. Rather than a straight doorway into another room, this way was blocked by a myriad of pictures suspended in what looked to be black netting.

His fingers began flicking on each picture as he chanted, "No, no, no, no, no," over and over. Much like in the column in the West Tower of Lilinar, the images changed at his touch. "Dubinshire," Galault screamed at it. Then he settled a bit and explained, "Ordinarily, watchers of worlds can shift time as well, but since this world is twisted from the Onesong, I can only go a few cycles on either side of my present moment. I might as well be a Drifter for all the good it does."

Steigan didn't understand half of Galault's rant. "Won't any of these places do?"

"No, not unless you can also travel through dimensions as well as time... which you can't, so don't even ask."

Steigan heard Alityka laugh while trying hard to contain the sound. She covered her mouth with the side of her curled index finger.

Galault continued, "But I figure if I can get you to the Dubinshire side of the timeline, then you can time jump back. If you can tell me when you were, an event that was going on which I could watch for or when you last saw me, then I can possibly snag you and shift you somewhere else. Obviously for you to make the journey all the way back here to go back there, something catastrophic had to happen."

Steigan knew what to say, but then he'd have to admit his failure to Galault. As hard as it was for him to speak the words, he had to. "You had just given me back a life aspect thread that had been taken from me before I was born."

"Oh." Galault thought about this for a moment. "Interesting. A little strange too. I have to admit that I never considered that this is all a time before you were born. For me, you've always been alive."

As tears started to gather in his eyes, Alityka stepped forward. "Please focus. Someone came in and stole the thread from Steigan just moments after you gave it to him. We were trying to get it back, but we ran into Cirvel. We're going through all this because we're outside the castle and we can't get back inside. We need you to get us back inside to help our friends."

Galault nodded his understanding. "Well, that certainly does give me an exact time." He muttered a spell and touched his temple. "Very well, I will meet with you when you time jump back. Shifting back into the castle should be no problem."

"Ithanes will have enchantments protecting the castle from dimensional magicks. You might have to talk to him and get him to break one of his spells temporarily," Steigan said.

Galault gave him a dubious look, but went back to finding the image he searched for. "Ah, here we go. It's not ideal, but it should do."

Smoke gathered across the image, making it very hard to see what was going on in the background. Galault touched it and the image expanded to full size to fit in the doorway frame. Steigan stepped back as if expecting the smoke to start filling the room. Alityka put a hand on his back, noticeable only by the light pressure against his backplate.

"Gohaldinest has just fallen and this looks to be outside the castle walls," Galault explained. "Cirvel is trapped away, but there may still be members of Krithstand's army about."

"Krithstand… does he make it through the battle?" Alityka asked.

Galault gave a broad smile and nodded happily. "Yes, he does. He goes on to build Dubinshire and rules for many cycles."

"Ellonia?"

"She goes with Rivic and together they build Lilinar."

A sense of relief swept through Alityka's shoulders. "Thank you." She looked at Steigan. "I haven't had the courage to ask Rivic about what happened to my father and sister. Silly, right?"

"No," Steigan replied. "You didn't want bad news. I understand." He thought of Sim and Lucinia, who last he heard were in Cove. He'd not sought out anything about them after that, for this same fear that he'd learn something about them which he didn't want to have to accept. Knowing Sim had lost the family inn was hard enough.

Galault stuck his head through the doorway and looked in both directions. When he returned, he said, "The way looks clear. Go now and perform the time jump quickly. If your magic doesn't work, return to the doorway and we will try another pathway. Otherwise, I will see you back in Dubinshire."

"Thank you, Galault," Alityka said before she went through.

Steigan saluted Galault with a fist of his heart. "I look forward to seeing you again shortly. Thank you."

Galault reached out and touched Steigan's arm. "I have much to do before then."

Steigan turned and headed through the door, emerging into a landscape filled with flames, smoke, and stray magic. Rubble lay all along the cobblestone streets, making it hard to walk. Alityka had climbed up on the remains of a stone wall and was looking around. In her white dress and gold armor, she seemed like a target. He reached up and pulled her down.

"What are you doing?" he asked.

"Looking for my father."

"We need to go. This isn't a family reunion."

"I know, but this might be my last chance to see him. We said our goodbyes before I went off to trap Azote, but if I could visit with him and let him know that I made it through all right, I know it would relieve his mind. He doesn't know that I survive. Right now, I'm dead to him."

"Ali, he will still never be able to see you again. Knowing

you're alive won't help. In fact, it might bring him more suffering." Steigan said the words, feeling the ramifications of his own speech being something he'd done himself. Hadn't he left Centhya and Annae in exactly the same fashion? He had walked right from their lives to live in another time. It had brought Annae chasing him, though she could never cross the span of time, only to be poisoned. Maybe if he'd been able to tell Annae that he was all right, she would have stayed safely in Dubinshire where she belonged.

Maybe letting Alityka speak to her father now would keep him from living with her ghost.

He wondered if Galault was still watching them. Had Galault's warning been because he knew that Alityka would try to see her father?

"Ali, we should go," he said, knowing he had to make a decision and stick firmly to it.

Alityka struggled. "He wins. He builds Dubinshire. When I'm walking through the city or in the castle, I'm echoing his victory."

"Yes, you are."

"I need to let him know."

At first, Steigan thought he might have to intensify his argument, but Alityka walked a short distance away to gather the remains of some black material from where it had become trapped beneath a rock. She shook a cloud of dust free from it, then lay it flat on the wall where she'd been standing. At her spell, golden writing poured over the cloth. Steigan recognized the ancient, but didn't read it. This was her personal note to her father.

Then she dug out a long shaft of wood and tied the cloth to it, sinking the other end into the ground so that it hung like a flag.

"Someone will find this and take it to my father," she said with a smile. "He'll know I've made the journey."

For a moment probably far too long, they stood watching the flag flutter in the breeze as smoke drifted by it. Then Alityka turned to Steigan. "We should go now."

Steigan summoned the magic and, with his arm around Alityka, brought them back to Dubinshire in the far future. As they appeared on the grass of Dubinshire Park, Steigan had a moment of dread, knowing that he still didn't have the thread. They literally were right back where they started, minus being stuck in a genie lamp.

Galault stepped seemingly out of thin air toward them. Both Steigan and Alityka reacted by reaching for their swords until they saw who approached. Rather than appearing fearful about two warriors nearly drawing a sword on him, Galault only chuckled. "Let's get you two back into the castle," he said.

A doorway appeared on the lawn behind him and Galault urged Steigan and Alityka through. Once on the other side, they were back in the castle. Galault didn't come through the doorway with them, but he did call out to Steigan.

When Steigan turned back, he saw that Galault had a vial in his outstretched hand. "Try not to lose it this time," Galault said.

"You got it back? How?"

"I gather the things you lose," Galault answered with a grin.

Steigan took the vial, wrapping it against his palm in a tight fist. "Thank you."

"Might I suggest, if I may, that you see if Lord Epious could put it back?"

Steigan had the suspicion that Galault had already seen this happen. "When do I need to go?"

"At a time when you know Ithanes is with his mother and she is distracted. It will help keep her from sensing you again." After Galault's cryptic answer, the doorway faded from view.

Yet Steigan knew the precise moment to which Galault referred; the day Steigan was born to King Cirello and Queen Corina. Ithanes' mother had been in attendance. With vial still in hand and determined to not let anything else separate him from it again, he time jumped.

CHAPTER 21

*S*teigan woke, the room around him dark at first until his eyes adjusted to the low amber light coming from the fire burning in the fireplace. Water boiled, probably from the pot held on a tripod over the fire, and the scent of a thick broth nudged at his hunger to remind him it had been a while since he'd last eaten

"*Hungry?*" a deep, stern voice asked.

As much as Steigan wanted to roll over on the cot, pull the blankets up further around his shoulders, and return to sleep, he knew he should wake. Despite the fire, he felt cold and wanted to nestle longer with the blanket. Someone called out his name. He blinked his eyes again, willing them to open further and bring him to full attention. With that came the awareness that he wasn't in a familiar room. It took Steigan a moment to remember his time jump to restore his aspect thread.

Lord Epious moved into view with a bowl in his hands. Steigan had found Epious similar to Ithanes in many ways, but with a harsher edge which Steigan associated more with

Greytas. Of course, he suspected that Epious had been waiting for Steigan when he'd appeared.

"*Sit. Eat,*" Epious instructed. "*Your body needs it after what it's been through.*"

Steigan tried to push himself upright on the cot, but found his body aching and weak. Perhaps a little nauseous too. He closed his eyes, trying to focus but the smell of the soup no longer seemed welcomed by his nose. He gagged.

"*Bucket,*" Epious said, pressing something cold and hard against Steigan's arm.

Steigan grabbed it, losing the contents of his stomach into the metal bucket as he heard Epious set the bowl aside.

"*My fault,*" Epious said as Steigan continued to purge. "*'Twas too soon. Perhaps I rushed a bit much.*"

Steigan wiped his mouth on a rag Epious offered. The bucket left his hands and Epious next offered a glass of water. "*The dizziness should pass soon,*" Epious said. "*Perhaps we should have you walk a bit, get your bearings.*"

As much as Steigan wanted to lie back down and return to sleep, Epious drew back the blankets and urged Steigan to stand.

The wood floor felt sharply cold beneath Steigan's feet. He'd reach for his boots if they weren't all the way on the other side of the room along with his armor.

Steigan remembered this room from when Ithanes had healed the gargax bites with a little help from the Destroyer of Civilizations, when Cirvel had been trapped in the painting. Little in the room itself had changed, but it seemed darker and less friendly.

He caught sight of young girl huddled with her knees up to her chest sitting in a chair off in a corner. She'd been asleep when Steigan had first come in. Now, she seemed afraid. As Steigan looked at her, Ithanes' older sister, Brendalyn, turned her head away.

"*He sees me as old,*" she said to her father, who hushed her.

"*Slowly,*" Epious said as Steigan started to rise. The Lord of Dubinshire didn't offer any assistance.

Steigan's knees felt weak and he wasn't certain his legs would hold him, but he found himself standing with more staccato urgings from Epious. Then there was one step, then two, and finally several more until Steigan made it to the window. Outside, Dubinshire lay in darkness. The glass reflected his image back at him. Steigan expected himself to look different, but he appeared the same. Other than being a touch sick, Steigan didn't feel any differently either. Except maybe colder. He couldn't shake this chill.

"*Was it a success?*" Steigan asked, his mind thinking back over Epious holding the bloodwave knife and the glittering thread over Steigan.

"*Aye. Your mother's magic, which filled in the gap you were missing, was irremovable though. I thought it might cause an issue, but it melded around the thread. Consider it your mother's love.*" While Epious sounded a little sarcastic about it, the thought gave Steigan great comfort, especially in light of how Epious' wife treated their son, Ithanes. That might also be why Epious sounded as he did.

Steigan found the glass of water still in his hand and he took another sip. His stomach was beginning to settle.

"*You should eat and then depart,*" Epious said, sounding as if he were ready to get rid of Steigan soon. Did Epious realize how much Steigan wanted to leave here as well?

Brendalyn scuttled out of the chair. "*Sit here,*" she said, sliding along the cabinets and wall out of Steigan's way. As Steigan took the offered chair, he noticed Brendalyn scooting over to examine the vomited contents in the bucket. She knelt down with curiosity, leaned closed, and sniffed it. The thought nearly made Steigan sick again.

"*Brendalyn,*" Epious whispered sharply as he picked up the bowl and brought it to Steigan.

Brendalyn ignored her father, continuing to take in the smell of the bucket. Then she said, "*He should have some ginger and...*" She took another whiff. "*...fennel. Tea with rosehip and wild orange as well.*"

Epious considered her for a moment. "*Very well. I will add the ginger and fennel. Will you fetch the tea from the shop?*"

Brendalyn curtsied, then flashed from the room. Steigan felt her magic leave the castle.

Returning from the cabinet, Epious carried two containers with him. He sprinkled some of their contents onto Steigan's soup. "*Fennel. Ginger. Stir that into your soup. 'Twill help to calm your nausea.*" Seeing that Steigan was about to say something, Epious stopped him with a raised hand. "*Please, say nothing. The less I know, the better off I am.*"

Steigan realized he'd been about to tell Epious that Brendalyn had always been a great healer and that Ithanes trusted only her to attend him when he was ill. But Epious was probably correct; the less he knew about what would happen with Brendalyn and Ithanes, the happier Epious would be for the remainder of his life.

Instead, Steigan asked, "*Is there anything I can do for you to repay you for restoring my thread to me?*"

"*Use it wisely. Your parents had their reasons for wanting to remove it from you. I'm not certain I agree with returning it to you, but are a man with a lifetime behind you, not the foolish child of my original visions. So I ask that you use your acquired wisdom and your mother's sacrificed magic to remember what you can and cannot change.*"

Steigan thought about Martias. Was that one of the things which he could not change? "*How will I know the difference?*"

"*If you have to ask that question, then 'tis something you cannot change.*"

Brendalyn returned with a mug filled with steaming liquid and brought it to Steigan. *"Rosehip and wild orange,"* she said as she handed it over.

The cup felt warm to his chilly fingers, a pleasing sensation. *"I am sure it will be delicious. Thank you for your suggestions,"* Steigan said. The tea had a delightful fruity smell, but certainly not like strickleberries. He drank and finished both the soup and the tea, noticing Brendalyn's dark eyes watching him.

"Better now," she said. *"Your strength is returning fast now."*

That seemed true enough. Steigan felt the magic gathering around him, filling him even deeper than before. *"Thank you,"* he said, handing her the dishes when she requested them from him. Then she disappeared again.

"I hope she doesn't put you off too much. She loves healing people and she comes by her talent naturally," Epious said.

"She will make a great healer. I feel much better already." This seemed to please Epious and Steigan wondered how much honest praise, if any, the ruler of Dubinshire received.

"You must continue to take it easy. You have made it through the procedure, but your body may still reject this piece which has been returned to you," Epious said. *"Only time will tell. You have been without that aspect thread for a long time. It may not merge back into you without consequences."*

With an understanding nod, Steigan stood, glad that his world remained stable. *"I must be returning now. Again, I appreciate your help and your words of wisdom."*

As Steigan started to gather the magic to return back to Dubinshire in his own time, Lord Epious reached out and grasped Steigan's arm.

"Wait," he said. *"I believe I have something else that belongs in your hands."*

Epious gathered supplies from the cabinets and, in a hurried fashion, slid them out on the counters. *"I apologize. I have been debating about this since you first appeared and returning your thread to you disrupted my future-sight enough that I couldn't trust what I was seeing. But then you accepted her prescribing without question, doubt, or hesitation, followed by words spoken so kindly to Brendalyn. I am afraid that too many people only see her mother's madness when they look at Brendalyn. They distain her attempts at soothing and healing them, afraid that she would rather poison people. But you were different. You looked beyond that. Whether that is because you knew her in the future or because you have a deep trust of Ithanes, I do not know. However, it reveals much about who you are. Knowing what I told your parents about your future that made them come to the decision to remove your thread, I believe you are the person who is meant to have... well, you'll understand when you see it."*

By the time he finished, Epious had everything out on the counter and leaned against it as if it supported his weight while he prepared himself. With one last check that he had everything, he began combining the ingredients for a powerful spell.

Steigan remembered Keteria in her workroom, mixing and blending components as she worked magic, but it had always seemed like something meant for High Maeges and not for anyone else. He'd never considered that this might be a level of magic above him.

Epious spoke the complex words to a spell as he worked. Every now and then, he moved his hands through fumes as if he were unfolding a paper from within the curling wisps. Steigan didn't think he'd ever witnessed a spell so diversified.

Then Epious slapped a hand on the counter and called for something to rise beneath his palm. At first, nothing seemed to happen, then a rusting metal box lifted right out of the wood as if it had been buried beneath it. Long, as long as Steigan's arms if he raised them out to his sides, yet only a few inches in depth, Steigan suspected a box of that size had to hold either a sword or a bow. He hoped for the former, knowing his skills with the latter were extremely lacking.

"*My family fetched this from the cave where Alityka had been turned to stone. Azote had knocked it from her hands and it lay several feet from where Alityka cast the spell. They were unable to recover her body at that time, and when they searched for it later, they found her gone, but they did bring back a very special weapon from that first expedition,*" Epious said. "*We have kept it guarded since then, knowing that one day it would need to be put into the hands of someone who could kill Azote and vanquish the Destroyer of Civilizations.*"

Epious said one more spell and the lid raised slightly, allowing him to remove it and set it aside. While the outside of the box had been rusty and dingy, the inside was padded in black velvet with golden cloth. As Epious removed the material, Steigan saw an incredible, shiny, almost black sword lying within the box.

Steigan wanted to seize the sword and run off with it. It smelled of forged metal as if it had just been created. That didn't even encompass the power he felt which called to him to touch it. He started to reach for it. The weapon wanted it too much. He drew back. "*This belongs in your family, or at least to Alityka. If it was her blade, she should wield it.*"

"*Alityka has neither the strength nor the heart to kill Azote. Twice she has been pitted directly against him. She told her father about her shortcomings in the first match, and the second...*" Epious gave a knowing smile which reminded Steigan so much of Ithanes' typical smirk. "*Well, be both know the result of that; Azote still lives.*"

"*So, you're telling me that with this sword, I am to take down Azote?*"

"*That is one potential.*" Now Ithanes was reflected in Epious' voice. "*Everyone is still given free will, but you all have a part to play in the coming battle, one that filled a different capacity*

213

than I saw before your parents had that very special thread removed from you."

Steigan sensed the many layers upon Epious' words, but his hands still yearned to receive the sword. He gave into the urge and reached out to possess the weapon.

"It speaks to you. It will come to your call," Epious said, watching now while referring to Steigan's abilities to bring his weapon and armor to him.

Steigan turned the sword, his hands warming. The magic of the blade seemed to seep under his skin and into his veins, merging with his blood, and sending a powerful feeling melding through all of him like an extra set of armor being forged for him.

Epious' smile broadened. *"Welcome, Winctonicht."*

The icy dread which first reached out to Steigan shattered against the strength of this new truth.

"Realize that if you had kept your thread," Epious began, *"you would have been a prince, not a warrior, though you would have been trained with a sword. Recall that Cirello nearly lost in the battle on the turret. Remember that Keteria wouldn't have been there to cast a spell, pressing all magic back down into the earth for a thousand cycles. These enemies would have come sooner and harder. Do not blame your parents for removing Winctonicht aspect from you. While they didn't want you to take part, all they did was rearrange the occurrence of events based on your actions. Though this has made a delay, you have been cast in the exact person you need to be. Even when events seem to be out of your control, you have already changed destiny."*

Steigan saw the exposed reality of Epious' words. Steigan nodded.

Epious bowed. *"'Tis been a pleasure to have my part in your creation."*

"I don't suppose there is any way I can convince you to tell us how we win this? The Destroyer seems too strong for us. If you will

not give us a hint, can I at least have your assurance that we are victorious?"

"Why would you want that? If you knew the answer and the outcome to a game, you wouldn't bother to play, certainly not with all your incentive to win. Would what you lose and what you must sacrifice be choices you could willingly make? In battle, both sides have casualties. Victory is but a moveable finish line declaring the mark when one side decides to take no more losses. If you decided to choose defeat right when you went back, might that be more of a win?"

Steigan again felt himself dancing in the layers of what Epious was telling him. *"Are you saying we should let the Destroyer into Gohaldinest?"*

Epious began to sweep the ingredients from the counter and place them back in the cabinets. His dark eyes twinkled while his mouth held a knowing smirk. *"You want evidence here in Dubinshire of Cirvel's defeat, but nowhere are the signs of someone else's victory clearer than in the ruins of Gohaldinest."*

"But Gohaldinest is where he gets his power."

"Sure of that are you? Did the armor you forged hold your power? Does Searn's armor which you wear contain your power? The sword you hold? Or perhaps your Winctonicht aspect? Did you do nothing before you had that armor, that sword, that thread merged back with you?"

Steigan grew uncomfortable with Epious' questions and Steigan found himself shifting from foot to foot. *"Are you saying there might be another reason he wants inside of Gohaldinest?"*

"I believe you begin to see the lesson," Epious said. *"Return. Your friends need the Winctonicht."*

CHAPTER 22

*T*he first snow of the season blanketed the ground outside of huge stone castle of Dubinshire. A chill had settled with in the walls and the fireplaces couldn't keep up, though eight out of nine of the castle's occupants drew in around them for closer, warmer conversation.

Steigan remained in bed, his body aching and shivering. No matter how many blankets his friends covered him in or pans of hot coals they shoved under the bed, he couldn't get be rid of the cold seeped deeply into his bones. They'd tried, even while he insisted that they stop, until they had thoroughly exhausted themselves and went once more to the fireplace in the great hall.

At first, the quiet had been welcoming. He'd slept, waking at various times of day and night, until he lost count of the days. Now Steigan wished for companionship. That, and maybe another attempt with the coals.

He grew tired of looking at the gray stone walls and ceiling. Red curtains hung in the windows, the sheer fabric letting plenty of daylight through, especially when the sun came through the triangular shaped crack about mid-afternoon and landed a bright spot of light across the floor.

Steigan wished he had the energy to get up and go to the wooden desk a mere few strides across the room from the bed, but he hadn't had the strength for days. The thought of reading usually sent him right into another nap.

His metal drinking cup, which he could barely lift from the stand beside him, was nearly drained. Stale bread had hardened on a plate beside the cup. Countless days had passed, it seemed, since his friends had tried to get him to eat.

"Goddess," he said, "if it is your plan to let me die, please let it happen." It had been a long time since he'd prayed, and a shorter time since he'd discovered that his former religion was based on a young woman, the true Dominari, who now resided in the castle along with all the rest of Steigan's friends. Yet with the way he felt, he really didn't care who he prayed to and just hoped that some being greater than himself heard.

He reached up for the cup. Clumsy fingers knocked against the metal, tipping it over and spilling the remaining water down over the sides of the table in a slow drip. He noticed a second cup and reached for it. The metal seemed to land against his hand. He slid it from the table and took a sip of the cold tea inside. It took nearly all his effort to raise it back up on the table.

Steigan retracted his hand and pulled it back under the blankets like a dragon returning to its cave. He refocused his gaze toward the ceiling. If only he could close his eyes and never open them again.

His thoughts drifted to Sim and Lucinia and he wondered what his adoptive parents were doing. Goddess, he missed them so much.

There he was praying again.

Steigan hoped that She had taken Arlyn in with welcoming arms.

If a dragon wanted to destroy the world, why wasn't he dead already?

His delirious thoughts cycled again. He wondered why he was still breathing. He ached so badly that he just wanted it to stop. What was happening to him?

Rejection. Epious had mentioned it to him. Was his body rejecting the thread he'd taken back? Why would he deny something that was part of himself?

Lucinia would know what to do to make him feel better. How many sicknesses had she gotten him through? He missed her so terribly. Sim too. He hoped they were safe.

Arlyn rested safely in the arms of the Goddess.

But what was happening to him? Steigan came back to one inevitable conclusion: his true parents had tried to make him different than he was supposed to be when they removed the Winctonicht aspect from him. They had wanted a different future for him than the one shown to them. In doing so, they had tossed a stone into a still lake and Steigan now rode the ripples of their actions.

He couldn't hate them, yet he was certain that they wouldn't want him to be living this life either.

Who would want to be here? In this life?

No wonder Steigan felt so sick. Everything had gone wrong. Nothing was as it should be. So many people were scattered into times different than their own, including himself. They had all come together to champion for the world and save it from the Destroyer of Civilizations, but were any of them being any more effective than riding the ripples which carried them further from the center of main cause?

Why was Steigan lying here sick and wishing for death instead of already enjoying the comforts of the Goddess' arms?

He felt an answer right there but hidden behind a thick, dark blue veil. He couldn't press through to get to it.

It had to be revealed, the curtain pulled to the side but not pressed through.

With another bout of shivering and nausea, Steigan felt himself ride another wave of sickness. He closed his eyes. Goddess, please…

With a gasp dragging into his chest, he opened his eyes and nearly sat up. Only the current tumble of dizziness over him kept him back on the bed as the new realization swept over him.

Sim's Inn and Tavern would need to be rebuilt.

But that wasn't it. Steigan knew that. But it was similar.

The dark blue veil swayed.

"Come on, Steigan," he heard a whisper behind him.

He didn't know anyone had come into the room.

Water pressed against his mouth, flowing down his throat.

He swallowed but he didn't want to.

Steigan tried to open his eyes. He only saw a faint crack of light. Sunlight streaming through the curtain and spilling across the floor. Darkness drowned him.

Someone crawled into bed beside him.

The Goddess' arms.

Death was coming for him. All he could see was a bright gold line running through black. A shaft of light.

More water. Warmth beside him.

The dark blue curtain.

Then, stillness.

Steigan felt the Goddess' arms around him.

Dark blue warmed in the rising daylight. The curtain parted.

Steigan realized that he'd lost everything from his old lives, both of them. Nothing he'd once held so dear remained. Not his title, not friendships, not his home, not religion. Yet he had his training, gathered friends, a new life waiting for him to become comfortable in it, and he had faith and hope. While it felt like he'd lost so much, his life had filled with emotions and experiences that couldn't be take away from him.

He'd become a Winctonicht.

Steigan felt consciousness returning and he opened his eyes, leaving the residue of these thoughts and dreams behind. He realized that he lay naked beneath the blankets and that someone curled against his back. He shifted, trying to look back over his shoulder.

"Are you awake?" Alityka asked.

He didn't really want to move even to settle back, yet his body demanded that he did. "Yes."

She gave a grateful sigh. Her forehead touched his back between his shoulder blades. He could feel her breathing deeply against him, then her arms squeezed him. "I'm glad. Do you feel better?"

He felt awkward.

"Um, no." His voice was shaky. "How did we get like this?"

Alityka moved, but her body didn't leave his. "I'm sorry. I kind of thought that I'd be able to leave before you completely woke."

"That didn't answer my question," he said, realizing that her unicorn magic forced Alityka to make her answer.

"I came in to check on you and you were pale like ice. I tried to warm you and give you water. We tried to fill the room with as much heat as we could, but you became fitful.

The only thing that seemed to help was when someone got close to warmed you with body heat, but it wasn't enough."

Body heat, remember that survival tactic?

She continued, "We had Ithanes and Laurient remove your clothes and give you a warm bath while Valic changed your sheets. They were awfully ripe." She gave a light chuckle. "Surprisingly, none of them wanted to crawl into bed with you."

Steigan choked. "But you did?"

He felt Alityka giggle behind him. Her cheek pressed against his back. "That came out wrong, I see now. Sorry if I embarrassed you. But yes, someone did need to volunteer. I figured it might as well be me."

Her hair slid along him as she rose. "Let me get my cloak. I want to leave you with the blankets."

Steigan turned his head as he felt her draw away. He could see her sitting up on the edge of the bed, her long hair falling her soft golden red curls over her back. She wore a sheer, white gown that silhouetted her body as she stood.

He rolled onto his back and into the warm place she'd left on the bed. Did she realize that he watched her get up and stride across the room to the chair tucked in at the desk where her cloak lay? She moved like a unicorn and the gossamer fabric did little to hide her body, round hips, powerful legs. Her hair swayed with each step. He had indeed been sleeping in the arms of the Goddess.

Alityka flung the cloak around her and once her body disappeared from his sight, he shifted his gaze toward the ceiling he'd become so familiar with. He heard her turn toward him.

"You look much better. Your color has returned," she said.

He let his gaze flicker back to her. More specifically to the cloak concealing the body which had just been up against him.

She clutched the robe closed where she thought it might open again as she leaned forward and put a hand to his forehead. "And you are feeling much warmer. Let's hope you are on the mend."

So many thoughts scurried through his brain at once and all seemed to slam into each other as if they were all mad. He released each crazy thought and merely nodded. The simple action reminded him how tired his body was and he nestled back down into the sheets. She pulled the blankets up over his shoulders and tucked them in for good measure.

"Let me go get dressed and tell the others know you are awake. Then I'll bring back food and water for you. Are you hungry at all?"

His tongue felt thick as he checked in with himself. "Thirsty, mostly." He reached up for the tea he'd been drinking earlier while Alityka fetched the metal cup that had fallen. He finished the remainder of the tea while leaves stuck to the bottom and sides of the glass. He handed the container to Alityka as well.

"Okay. I'll bring plenty of liquids for you." Then she strode out the door, leaving Steigan to wonder what he would do in the silence once more.

He drifted back to sleep, waking the moment the door opened again. He instinctively reached for his sword only to find it not there. Then he remembered Alityka curled up against him. He reached back to see if she was still there. Perhaps her leaving had all been a wild dream.

She was gone.

Footsteps moved across the floor. "Steigan?" Laurient asked in a whisper.

Steigan moved, letting Laurient know he was awake. Laurient dragged the chair noisily from the desk over beside the bed and sat down. "Hi, mate. How you doing?"

"Better days," Steigan croaked.

Laurient reached to the stand for a glass of water. The metal cup Steigan had been using was now gone. Laurient helped Steigan to sip some. "Alityka came back in, but you were asleep again. She didn't want to wake you. Ithanes has been by too. He's disappointed that you always seem to sleep through his visits. You know, he believes himself important enough for everyone to rise up and salute whenever he walks into a room." Laurient waited to see if he'd get a response from Steigan. "All right, not well enough for humor yet."

"How long have I been sick?" Steigan asked, fully expecting Laurient to confess that Steigan had been out of it for a month or two.

"A week."

"Surely it has been longer than that." Steigan tried to push himself up on his elbow.

Laurient shook his head.

As Steigan tried to come to terms with it, he asked, "And what's been going on in that time?" He came up on his elbows. "We've had the first snow. Cirvel, Martias-na, they were to attack after the first snow."

"Didn't happen. We don't even know where they are. Everything seems to be quiet. It's too quiet if you ask me. I can't shake the feeling that something big is about to happen."

Steigan recalled one of his more lucid thoughts. "If the dragon wants to destroy this world, why aren't we dead already?"

"You were that sick then? Wishing for death?"

Steigan thought of his prayers to be in the Goddess' arms and then waking up to just that.

"You blush. What's that for?" Laurient asked with a laugh.

Steigan shook his head. "Nothing. Must just be my color

returning." He was so glad that he no longer had to tell the truth, but skirting it had become such a habit. "Will you help me get dressed, get some leggings on at the very least?"

Laurient looked about to make a smart, goading remark, but stopped. His head bobbed in a very wobbly nod. "Sure." Then he got up to fetch clothes and Steigan noticed they were freshly laundered.

Steigan's body resisted being positioned to sit up and it took all of Steigan's might to keep himself there.

"This was almost easier when you were a rag doll," Laurient said. He hefted Steigan to his feet, braced against Laurient's shoulder while hoisting the leggings over Steigan's hips and tying the laces. "All good?" Laurient asked, setting Steigan back on the bed.

"Thank you."

"Shirt?"

"No, I think this was enough for now."

The door opened once again and Alityka came in carrying a steaming bowl before her. She looked surprised to see Steigan sitting up with his feet on the floor. He was glad she hadn't come in a moment earlier to see him dangling from Laurient's shoulder. Her face brightened. "I'm glad you're awake."

"He's even had a little bit of water and pulled on some clothes," Laurient said.

Alityka seemed to deflate a little with disappointment. "I see that."

An awkward pause lengthened while Alityka remained by the door. Finally, Laurient slapped his thigh and started for the door. "I think two visitors might be a bit much for Steigan to handle right now. I'll leave and come back later to see you, all right, mate?"

"Thank you, Laurient," Steigan said.

"Right." Laurient skirted by Alityka and went out the door.

Steigan felt his heartbeat quickening while Alityka remained where she stood. Then she seemed to remember the bowl in her hands. "I brought you some porridge. I wish I had some cream for it. I had to thin it with water. But I wanted to get some food and liquid into you. Laurient says our long-term supplies will get the few of us through the winter, but the perishables, like cream, had to be thrown out."

She took to the chair. "Are you ready to try some food?"

"I think so."

"We'll take this slow." She stirred the white mush within the bowl with the spoon. Her entire concentration was on the action, her thoughts seeming to have swallowed her. Finally, she added, "My sister was the healer, not me. If she were here, she'd know exactly what to put in this to restore your energy to you."

Steigan wanted to reach out and touch her hand, but he couldn't find the strength. "This is working wonders already." How was he to explain that having the Goddess feed him was more than he'd ever imagined? How many times had he bowed before the statues of the Goddess in New Lilinar and Whalston? Every day. To the point of Dominus Brynne mocking him and calling him too pious. None of the statues in the various Temples were exact replicas of Alityka, who stood encased in stone on the third floor in the grand Temple at New Lilinar, but the artists who had made them had indeed captured the sweet, round youthfulness of her face.

He took the first bite and it felt like his reward for all his years of devotion.

Would he dedicate himself to being a dominus once more?

"What?" she asked suddenly as their eyes met.

He felt the left side of his mouth tick up with a smile. She watched his smirk with curiosity.

"Ali." His hand came to her face, cupping her cheek against his palm. The strength he'd just found surprised him, though he guessed it shouldn't have.

Alityka closed her eyes and pressed against him.

He let his hand drop back to his leg. "I'm sorry. That was uncalled for."

There was the look of disappointment again. She tucked it away, then stirred the porridge once more. "Say nothing more."

He took the next bite offered to him and the next three while trying not to look up in her eyes. It was hard, especially when he knew that she was watching where she was placing the spoon. If she wasn't watching, he'd end up with a nose full of porridge, or maybe with the spoon in his eye. But he could make it easier by not staring back at her. Especially since he couldn't keep his thoughts off of her being his Goddess.

Dedication. That seemed to be what he needed. Somewhere along the journey, he'd lost the devotion he'd always known. Devotion to the Goddess, devotion to the mission, the dedication to helping people.

The spoon stopped on its way to him and Steigan made the mistake of looking up into her blue eyes. "Did you feel that?" she asked.

"A wave as if everything in the world was suddenly right again?" he asked.

She nodded.

"Feels good, doesn't it?"

She smiled and issued a slight chuckle. A tinge of red entered her cheeks. "Yes, but what was it?"

He wanted to tell her that it was him remembering his

place in the world, but he couldn't speak those words for fear of sounding egotistical no matter how much he believed in the truth of them. "That is the sign that everything's going to be all right."

For the first time in a long time, he felt like himself again.

CHAPTER 23

*M*aybe because Steigan had recently spent a moment in Gohaldinest before it had fallen, or because of Epious' offered advice, the hallways of Dubinshire seemed warmer, brighter, and gentler than the very same castle from a thousand cycles ago. Even the gray clouds amassing outside the windows didn't dampen this sensation. Steigan wondered, immediately after his return from seeing Lord Epious, if the ancient magicks of Gohaldinest had completely faded. Dubinshire had been built from and on the ruins of the former city. As Epious had pointed out, nothing remained the same and there were always possibilities.

If the magic had faded this much from Dubinshire, would Gohaldinest be equally barren?

Steigan tried to imagine standing in Cirvel's place and thought of how he would view Gohaldinest now. Steigan instantly thought of the Temple after the fire. He'd felt so defeated. When Martias had brought Steigan back to the Temple after he'd returned to this time, the walls had seemed so different, yet also possessed the scars of The Breaking.

Searching the castle for the others, Steigan figured that

Ithanes was probably reenforcing the enchantments on the castle to keep Cirvel and Martias out. That meant everyone was most likely gathered in the library where Ithanes would have access to all the spells while others fetched books for him.

The guess appeared correct, with everyone in the exact positions that Steigan figured. Except for Rivic and Alityka, who were absent.

Aeribela glanced up from the table where she was sitting at Steigan's entrance. Her gasp pulled Ithanes from the concentration for his next spell. Both were wearing robes of black, but Ithanes had silver swirls and jewelry while Aeribela's were gold, the circlet with the blue teardrop gemstone around her head. A Lord of Gohaldinest and a Lady of Dubinshire. Dragzel sat on the table, his head lowering to give Steigan a sly glance. Ellis moved between the shelves, his back to Steigan while Ellis gathered a stack of books in his arms. Valic, though extremely pale, sat at the table with pillows propping him up. Laurient was in the middle of returning books back.

Steigan felt himself break from the pause in his step and he moved toward the table too. "Lord Ithanes, a moment?"

Aeribela's mouth opened wider and her eyes grew in size. Finally, she took in the air she needed to speak. "Look at you. Your eyes." As if it were all too intense for her, she glanced away for a second, then back. She fought back her overwhelm to find the words to continue, "You are so bright I can barely look at you."

Even Ithanes seemed to struggle with it.

Valic just looked confused, as did Laurient.

Ithanes set the book he held down on the table and let it slide from his fingers. "A moment, my friend, though I suspect I am not going to like what you are going to tell me."

Steigan let Ithanes walk back out the door into the

hallway first, then followed. Ithanes travelled a slight ways down, then turned to face Steigan. But after looking directly at Steigan, Ithanes had to glance to the wall beside Steigan. Someone else might not have noticed the misdirected gaze.

"Am I really that different?" Steigan asked.

"Your aura is different. It used to be a shade of purple with blue being dominant and red a bare tone, both of which spoke to your bravery and courage. Now it's like the slate had been wiped clean. For those of us with sight like ours, you are hard to look at."

"Okay," Steigan said, "it's not what we need to talk about anyway. I think we should let Cirvel into Gohaldinest."

"Are you mad?"

"Possibly. I've felt funny since the aspect thread was returned, but I also see the possibilities with this suggestion."

Ithanes scoffed. "See the possibilities? Just what would those be?"

"He, Cirvel, goes down there into Gohaldinest and sees those dark ruins. How demoralizing is that, to come face-to-face with your own defeat? To see everything you once had in shambles?" Steigan had a brief flash of Sim and Lucinia standing beside the destroyed inn. He almost faltered in his next words, sensing them choke in his throat. "Everything you worked for, gone. I can think of nothing worse."

Along with that flood of emotion, Steigan also recalled losing his title as dominus. Yes, he knew exactly how humiliating, deep personal losses like that could devastate someone.

"I believe I understand where you are going with this, but the risk is just too great. We can't take it," Ithanes said.

"If he thinks he has hope down there, he is going to keep trying. Besides, what could possibly be down that that motivates him to go?"

Ithanes reflected on Steigan's words.

"We both know he will keep striking until he gets what he

came for," Steigan said. "If we just decide that this is not worth our loss of magic and possibly lives, then we remove his victory. He sees that he has nothing left, that there is no great city to rise back to the surface, and that his civilization is destroyed. Let us show him he has nothing left."

Ithanes' eyes narrowed, rapidly shifting between slits trying to focus on Steigan and Ithanes' normal face. "Except what he really wants from down there. You said it yourself, there has to be something. If we let him go in and he gets it, we've let him take it."

"At least then we know his purpose."

"If he's willing to show his hand. Were it me, I wouldn't taunt it in front of your face and let you see what I was holding."

Steigan firmed his stance, knowing that Ithanes was probing and seeking answers. For as often as Steigan was reminded that Ithanes' future-sight didn't work on him, Steigan wondered if that might be different now. With the Winctonicht thread replaced, might Steigan be whole once more and his fate determinable within the myriad of possibilities?

"Ithanes, you either need to get back to the spells or we need to concede. Either way, the choice is yours. I've spoken my thoughts. You need to decide our course."

A look of disappointment came over Ithanes' face as he looked back at Steigan. He glanced away up toward the ceiling of the hallway as if part of the stone was more worthy of his attention. "You're going to walk with them, Cirvel and your friend already at the Destroyer's side?"

Steigan's arms suddenly felt heavy at his sides. "No." How was he to tell Ithanes that he'd already offered himself to them and they had rejected him? "I'm here."

Ithanes' lips pulled upward as he scoffed and shook his head. "You don't get it, do you?"

"Obviously not, Ithanes. Why don't you enlighten me?"

With a step back, Ithanes raised his hands and motioned up and down as if gesturing over Steigan. "Look at you. This is what Cirvel needed. This was his focus."

"I don't understand."

"You never have."

"Ithanes?"

"I might as well lower the spells." Ithanes turned and started to walk away.

"Why? Ithanes, are you doing this because of my suggestion, or something else?" Steigan sprinted the short distance between them and seized Ithanes' arm, whirling him around. "Ithanes?"

"You…" Ithanes' looked tired as he shook his head. "We've already lost."

Aeribela burst from the library, her index finger raised as she shook it at Ithanes. "How dare you?" She stopped before Ithanes and stuck her finger right up to his face. She reached out with her other hand and grabbed Steigan's tunic sleeve, tugging Steigan toward her. "Steigan, he's afraid."

"Afraid of what?" He asked the question to Aeribela, but turned his look to Ithanes. When Ithanes continued his disdainful scorn down at Aeribela, Steigan returned to Aeribela. "What's going on?"

Aeribela took a firm stance with her hands on her hips. "Tell him, Ithanes, or I will."

The flaming glares lasted between them for but a moment while Ithanes must have judged Aeribela serious. "You've always been the wild card," Ithanes said slowly. "The one I couldn't see."

Yes, Steigan knew this, had heard Ithanes complain about it often enough. Why had it come to a head now? He stood silent, waiting for someone to explain.

Fortunately, Aeribela spoke, "He's afraid to trust you."

"Seriously?" Yet Steigan knew if Alityka were here, she might tell them of the bargain Steigan had tried to make with Ithanes. Maybe Ithanes was right not to trust him.

Aeribela put a hand on his arm. "I told him of my vision. I saw you going into Gohaldinest to welcome Cirvel and Martias after you had suggested that we let them in to avoid battle. Then, you leave with them. After that, Cirvel has all he needs to win."

"I have nothing to contradict what she sees," Ithanes admitted with a tremble vibrating through his shoulders.

"So you all are willing to believe that I betray my friends, those as close to me as family?" Steigan asked.

Both of them looked ashamed.

Yet Steigan knew they had no right to be. He would have gone with Cirvel if the Destroyer had promised to return the aspect thread. It left him feeling despicable. Ever since he'd become St. Steigan and destroyed the Temple, it seemed like everything he'd done was horrible. Was he so willing to side with Cirvel because he felt like a wretched traitor? Who was he? What had he become?

"Steigan, we're sorry." Aeribela reached out toward him. "Our visions... you know that future-sight is hard and comes with extreme responsibilities.... Are you all right?"

No, he couldn't say he was. Did this strange feeling setting through him come from tumultuous emotions?

"She's right," Ithanes added. "You're not looking well. Maybe you need to go to your quarters and get some rest."

"I'll be fine. Where are Rivic and Alityka?" Steigan asked.

"In Gohaldinest. They are going to free the Guardian. She might be our only defense if Cirvel gets in," Alityka said.

"You'll release the Guardian, knowing she is loyal to Cirvel as his dragon mother? What are you afraid of?" Steigan asked, practically shouting the words in Ithanes' face. "Your father gave me this suggestion after he returned my aspect thread to me. Why would he have said anything that would put his son in danger?"

But the look was there in Ithanes' blue eyes before he turned his head away.

"Your mother," Steigan said slowly. In his peripheral vision, he saw Aeribela break away from them and start back toward the library where Laurient had stepped out into the hallway. This left Steigan and Ithanes alone. "She always said that Cirvel would return to Gohaldinest. You feel that if he gets in, she was right all along and she wins. And that makes you wrong. You aren't a Lord of Gohaldinest then."

It took several moments before Ithanes could speak, let alone look Steigan in the eyes. When Ithanes finally managed it, Steigan thought there were tears in Ithanes' eyes. "Strangely enough, that is part of the reason. But only part. The taunts with my mother, with us trying to harm each other, go as far back as I can remember. She would always tell me, 'I am Madame Orcee. Your visions are pathetic compared to mine. I see beyond the span into realms you cannot imagine.' She would drink her tea and make me drink mine. She splattered the walls with both of our tea leaves. Hers were huge, elaborate pictures that shifted. Mine were small, stationary. When you told me to see the possibilities with your suggestion, I already knew that I had none. In conjunction with Aeribela's vision, the only thing I see is me losing the only true friend I've ever had."

Ithanes turned and walked over to a wall. He threw up his arm, bracing himself as he leaned against it, then put his head on his forearm. His long, black hair hung down along the sides of his face, shielding his expressions.

"You were surrounded by people who care about you. Leloran, Keteria…" Steigan said. So those were the only people that Steigan could really think of immediately who weren't part of Ithanes' family who would stand by Ithanes if any other choice were possible. Steigan was pretty certain that Aeribela and Laurient weren't here for Ithanes, but rather for their own motivations. It made Steigan wonder if he would stay around if Ithanes wasn't always the one making the choice to surround himself with Steigan. Or did Steigan care as much for his own self-interests as the others did?

Still, the last thing they needed was Ithanes in an emotional funk.

"Come on, Ithanes."

"No," Ithanes said as he raised his head and pushed away from the wall. "I will not let the Destroyer into Gohaldinest."

"Let him see he is already defeated."

"No!"

Ithanes started back toward the library, throwing another seething glance at Steigan before putting his head down bullishly into his determined stride.

Steigan knew he should follow and help Ithanes with the spells if this was their course of action, but Epious' words about defeat lingered in Steigan's mind. He reached out for Alityka's magic and found it. Using it as an anchor, he said, "Talcor dun."

He half expected to slam into the doorway where Dubinshire led into Gohaldinest. Instead, he found himself in dank blackness. The air smelled wet with mildew and off in a short distance he heard the sounds of water dripping. "Laza-'pre ren."

As the small, floating orb flickered with light, Steigan realized he was down in tunnels which had the look of being man-made but weren't smooth or braced with supports to keep it from collapsing. The rock looked melted as if extreme heat had bonded them together to form these tunnels.

Alityka wasn't here. Once again, he felt out for her magic

and found it nearby. Grabbing onto the orb, Steigan hurried toward where he sensed Alityka.

This area looked nothing like any of Gohaldinest Steigan had ever seen. It had a feel like the cave where the Guardian was chained, but it was different as well. The Guardian's cave was naturally formed, whereas only parts of this winding structure didn't seem man-made. It felt like a maze and Steigan quickly wished he'd thought to mark his trail.

Where was Alityka going? She seemed to be moving along very fast, but not by magical means. It almost seemed as if she knew the way she was going. If she didn't, then maybe Rivic did.

Concentrating again, Steigan flashed toward their location. He teetered, feeling himself land with his back against the wall.

"You're up and about," Alityka said with a smile. She nudged Rivic. "Doesn't he look incredible?"

Rivic didn't seem impressed, even at Alityka's urging. "Teleporting into unknown areas can be very dangerous, especially down here," Rivic chided.

"I had to catch up," Steigan explained.

"Well, you're here now. Why was it so important?"

"Is Cirvel in Gohaldinest?" Alityka asked.

Steigan looked at both of them in turn, knowing he could trust Alityka but didn't feel so sure about Rivic. Steigan reminded himself that Rivic was family; some of the very blood coursing through Steigan's veins came from Rivic. "No, but I think we should let Cirvel into Gohaldinest to see the remains of his defeated city."

"Are you crazy?" Rivic asked.

"You're the ones going down to let the Guardian out. Who's to say that she won't just go flying back to him?"

"She won't." Rivic looked away as if weren't going to add anything more about the Guardian.

"Have you never felt crushing, overwhelming defeat and then been reminded of it?" Steigan snapped back.

Rivic and Alityka shared a glance. Rivic emerged from the wordless conversation still looking uncertain. "If Cirvel gets in here, he'll be able to call upon things this world has forgotten. I understand where you're going with this, and with anyone else, that might be a very good plan, but this is Cirvel we're talking about and he's had thousands upon thousands of years to learn—"

"Years? What's that?" Steigan interrupted, unfamiliar with the word.

Rivic gestured with his hands. "I don't have time to explain that right now, but let it show you that Cirvel knows things about this planet and other worlds out there that we have no idea about. All of our knowledge," Rivic made a circle between the three of them, "barely scratches the surface of what Cirvel understands. We can't play simple mind games with him."

"But Rivic, there's got to be something," Alityka said. "Think about how long you held onto your fear of magic after your accidents."

"Cirvel isn't going to take one look around the ruins and crumble just because Krithstand threw a few good shots and I managed to shove Cirvel into a painting. He's going to want vengeance and he's going to gather all the magic of Gohaldinest remaining back into himself so he can do that. Letting Cirvel walk into Gohaldinest without a fight is a bad option."

"Everyone fears something," Steigan said.

"Well, I tell you this: Cirvel fears nothing. Why should he? I'm the only one that has a hope of killing him and I assure you that he is not afraid of me. His magic is unrivaled. Even his novimather is no match for him."

"But that's what I'm saying. The city does not hold his

power. He already has all the magic and knowledge he needs, yet we still manage to hold him at bay. We're missing something."

Rivic's eyes widened. "I was always saying that."

"Yes, you were," Alityka said.

Steigan took Rivic's reaction as incentive to continue. "Cirvel built up this belief that he will make Gohaldinest rise from the rubble and ruins, keeping us focused on the city, making us believe that his power is here. But there is something else, his true purpose. He misdirects us so we don't see what is in his heart."

"His real motivations," Rivic said with surprised realization entering his voice.

"Right. We won't know what that is unless we let him show us."

"I wonder if it's Dek'tae."

Steigan gave Rivic a questioning look before glancing at Alityka to see if the word was just as foreign to her.

"Dek'tae," Rivic repeated. "Cirvel's plan might include Dek'tae."

"That horrible monster which makes people reveal what they want most?" Alityka asked, her face going ashen white. "How could it possibly be involved in Cirvel's plans?"

"I don't know, but here's my thought: The Playground would be large enough to hold a dragon, and he has all those Necroathelings. He might be thinking of using them to trap Leschemal and with their combined power, take the dragon to the Playground, where Dek'tae is waiting. He might be hoping Dek'tae is strong enough to convince the dragon not to destroy this world."

"That's a sad plan," Alityka said. "Even more than some I've heard."

Rivic shrugged. "Just a thought. I think we should go see if Dek'tae is still alive in the Playground. You know, Cirvel could get to the Playground from anywhere. He's been training a Necroatheling." Rivic spoke quickly as several connections came to him at once. "What better place to do it? That's practically a backdoor to Gohaldinest. Ithanes can't keep him out."

"The Playground?" Steigan asked, mostly to Alityka. "Cirvel said that your fights there were legendary. What is this place?"

Alityka gave a quick shake of her head and started following Rivic as he led the way. "A battleground," she muttered, her head down as if she were talking to the ground rather than to him.

Steigan realized, with guilt, that she'd only answered because of the unicorn magic. He understood, without words, that she never wished for him to find out.

Yet, they obviously had no choice but to go there.

CHAPTER 24

*R*ivic and Alityka called this place The Playground, but Steigan had yet to see anything here he liked. There had been the lion-head knocker, which when Rivic spoke a word to admit them, had teleported them to the other side. Yet to Steigan, he felt like it was an entirely different dimension. They had assured him it was safe, but Steigan felt like hundreds of eyes watched them out of the shadows.

They walked through tunnels much smoother than the ones Steigan had originally found himself in when he'd flashed into Gohaldinest. If he'd done it with such ease, then why couldn't Cirvel do the same? Ithanes was powerful, but Rivic was right; Cirvel's power was unmatched on this world. If they thought for one second that they could keep Cirvel out, they were woefully wrong.

In a round room, Steigan found chains and cuffs hanging from the walls as if they were meant to secure someone against the wall in a standing position. Neither Rivic nor Alityka seemed to pay the chains much attention, which told

Steigan that they were familiar with the surroundings and had been down here a number of times.

Soon, they were out in a large circular arena with seating that rose up far around it. Steigan tried to imagine someone fighting down here while cheering, or booing, spectators watched from above.

"Look," Rivic said in a hushed whisper as he pointed toward some of the lower benches. On one, Lord Cirvel seemed to be in a deep sleep. In a deep purple robe, Martiasna rested on another with his feet pointing toward Cirvel. "What are they doing?"

"They are in a timelock," Steigan answered. "Probably training."

That seemed as foreign to Rivic and Alityka as the Playground was to Steigan.

"Is this part of Gohaldinest?" Steigan asked, finding it hard to believe that Ithanes would not know about something like this. "Has Cirvel been down here this whole time and none of us knew it?"

Rivic answered, "This space is outside of the world we know and that makes it hard to sense what's down here."

"Like another dimension?"

"Not quite. It's hard to explain, but it's more like a pocket." Rivic resumed his study of Cirvel and the Necroatheling sleeping. "Can they hear us? Do they know we are here?"

"No. Usually you have someone standing guard."

"Cirvel would never leave himself unprotected. If we try something against them, chances are good it would rebound on ourselves. But, maybe if we call Dek'tae, we could set up a trap for when they come out of their spell. Potentially, it could make Cirvel would reveal his motivations."

"All right, how do we call forth this Dek'tae?" Alityka asked.

Not answering her, Rivic moved into the arena where

something caught his attention. He stared upwards at something above their heads. Steigan glanced in that direction, but couldn't see whatever Rivic did.

Rivic, noticing Steigan, moved closer. "There's a glass cage up there. I think there's someone in it."

The sounds of heavy thumps like someone knocking drifted down over them. Steigan thought he heard someone shouting as well, but couldn't make out the sounds.

"Wait here," Rivic said, then he began to rise straight up into the air.

"Goddess," Steigan said. He watched until the shadows engulfed Rivic. Then, to Alityka, he asked, "Do you see him?"

She shook her head.

With her head tilted back, her golden red hair cascaded in gentle waves down her back. Her face relaxed with soft curves as if she wasn't worried about her friend levitating up there in the darkness, though Steigan knew she had to be concerned.

"While I was with Lord Epious, he gave me a sword that once belonged to you," Steigan said.

"To me?"

"Vochey." At his summons, the sword appeared across his palms. "I feel it should go back to you."

Alityka quit looking up after Rivic and saw the sword in Steigan's palms. She gave a little snicker. "The sword Rivic gave me." Her hands reached down to the sword at her side. "I appreciate the offer, but that sword was forged for a man to wield. It was meant for my father. It felt so wrong in my hands that I made two slashes with it and tossed it aside. I prefer my sword."

Her eyes grew sad as she touched her scabbard. "You never had one of these, did you?"

Steigan didn't understand. "A sword? Yes, I forged my own."

"Then you didn't have one of these." She pulled the blade, then offered it in exchange for the one he held. "Examine this one."

While he'd fought side-by-side with her, he'd never taken a good look at her weapon. Of course, he may have been too jealous at the time, he thought as he recalled his emotions when he lost his Dominari powers. Steigan swapped swords with her and looked at her blade in the scant light. He saw an etching of a unicorn horn along the blade. The twists of the horn were lined with sparkly, golden flecks.

"That is the blade of a Dominari, a bone sword," she explained. "It is infused with horn of a unicorn. My armor also possesses their horns within this forging to give it added strength and protections."

Steigan knew the depth of the weapon was not enough to encompass even the horn of the youngest unicorn, so he didn't know how a horn was infused with it, yet he felt the truth of it in his hands. With this, he realized that her words about him merely being a placeholder was absolutely correct.

She reached to take back her sword. "But I see now that the unicorns did what they could to protect you. That is why they made you a Dominari. Without your aspect thread," she said, raising her eyes, "you were powerless. But they could help you, channel their magic through you because you would be capable of holding it."

Steigan nodded his understanding. He still felt the sting from the memory of his lost powers, but it no longer gripped him with a sensation for revenge like he had first felt. No, now he had acceptance within the truth of Alityka's words.

"There is someone up here," Rivic called from above.

"Put that on your sword belt," Alityka said. "Epious gave it to you, so that is now where it belongs."

Steigan unfastened his belt and slipped the new scabbard on it so that he now had a sword on each side while Alityka resumed her upward stare. The fond memory of Searn teaching Steigan to fight with dual blades came to him and he felt a smile on his lips. It would be good to put that training to use with two of his own swords. If only Arlyn could see him.

"It's Keteria," Rivic shouted from the shadows. "I'm coming down with her. She's weak."

By now, they could see Rivic's legs coming into view as he slowly dropped back to the ground.

"Has she been here since Martias-na took her?" Steigan whispered the words, not really intending on anyone else hearing them.

"You can't think like that," Rivic said, obviously hearing Steigan. His feet touched down on the ground and his whole body seemed to settle with the gravity. Rivic turned and Steigan saw Keteria drooping in his arms. Her face looked pale, especially against the brown curls that fell over her cheeks. Her cracked lips looked more like scales. Steigan brushed the hair out of her face and called her name. She responded with a grunt of air that disturbed the broken skin on her mouth. Flakes of skin moved with the breath and blood oozed from beneath.

"Has she been up there without food or water?" Steigan asked, his voice nearly breaking on the words.

Rivic started moving off toward the sides of the arena and then the walls beyond. "No, it looks like she was left with some and that she rationed it, but her supplies ran out a day or so ago. They probably thought they'd be out of their time-lock by now. Don't beat yourself up about it. There was no way you could have known any of them were down here."

Rivic's words didn't help. Steigan still felt his rage growing. He had no idea how, but he would make Martias-na pay for this.

Rivic looked uncertain about what to do. Keteria needed

to be taken back to Dubinshire and her situation given attention to. And yet, there was their mission which needed to be completed. Especially if they could set a trap here and now for Cirvel and Martias-na.

Instead of Rivic needing to decide, Steigan asked the question, "How long will it take to get this Dek'tae?"

"I don't know. I've only seen it summoned once and there may have been another spell involved other than the chant calling it forth."

Steigan knew they might not have another opportunity. He'd already forced his way into Gohaldinest to catch up to Rivic and Alityka when Ithanes protested. Surely if Keteria had lasted this long already, a few more moments weren't going to make that much of a difference.

"I say we summon Dek'tae. If we fail, we try to destroy this place," Steigan said, thinking back on how he'd destroyed the Cauldron of Life. This place was big, but with their combined powers, he felt they stood a chance.

Settling Keteria upon the bench seats, Rivic turned and headed back for the arena. "It'll take all of us to trap Dek'tae within a magical sphere. I'm hoping that we can then move it over to where they sleep. We'll set the sphere to break when their magic dissipates."

Rivic gestured to the walls. "We should probably stand against these in a triangular formation. I have no idea how big this creature is." He looked a little nervous. "I'm not even sure this creature is visible on our plane."

"Then how will we know one we've summoned it?" Alityka asked.

"We'll know. Trust me."

Steigan bit back the response where he wanted to declare that he didn't trust Rivic, but he held back, choosing instead to take a bracing stance with his feet apart and his hands out as if ready to catch magic.

"Dek'tae," Rivic called out. He started a slow chant of the name over and over, encouraging Steigan and Alityka to join him. "Dek'tae, Dek'tae."

Nothing seemed to be happening.

Steigan looked to Alityka, half hoping that she would interrupt Rivic and tell him that it wasn't working. She sent him a look with about the same message.

Then, a strong serpent slid around Steigan's leg. He looked down, but didn't see anything there. "Something grabbed me."

"Dek'tae," Rivic continued to chant.

Alityka went to break their formation, but Rivic stopped her.

The long, round tentacle-like sensation rolled over Steigan, crawling up to his belly. He felt it pry at his armor and part of him longed to tear it off.

"What is in your heart? What do you want? What do you long for?" a slurred, nasally, voice with a slightly accented twist on the words asked Steigan. He was pretty sure the sound was only in his mind, but he couldn't prove it. "Let me see."

"I want a family," Steigan found himself saying.

"What will you do with this family? What keeps you from it? What would you give for it?"

"I want to belong to a family. I want a wife, children who are my own, people who love me as much as I love them."

"It's Dek'tae," Rivic confirmed.

"But it's on Steigan," Alityka said. "How do we free him?"

Two men, one in black and the other in robes of deep purple, stepped into the arena. Cirvel and Martias-na were awake from their timelock.

"You always have been pathetic in your desires, Steigan," the Necroatheling said. Then he started to mock, "I want a family, people who love me, blah, blah, blah."

"Hush," Cirvel said to the Necroatheling.

But Dek'tae's questions demanded an answer from Steigan. "I will protect my family. I would die for them."

"Steigan, no," Rivic yelled.

"Then die," Dek'tae responded.

"Dek'tae, not yet," Cirvel commanded. "It is not time for your feast."

"Hungry," the monster said, and this time Steigan knew it had spoken aloud.

"I just said to wait. You will get your feast." Cirvel continued toward the center of the arena and looked between Rivic and Alityka. "But maybe one of these other two would like to take your friend's place. He might just go on to live and have that family." Even Cirvel had issues keeping the sneer out of his tone.

Steigan felt his feet lift off the ground as Dek'tae insured that his prey wouldn't get away.

Martias-na moved toward Steigan while Cirvel faced off with Rivic and Alityka.

"Found a cahaster, did you?" Steigan asked. "Your soul all stored nice and safely away?"

Martias-na sneered. "Much more than yours." He turned then and started heading for the benches where they had rested Keteria.

"He's going for Keteria," Steigan shouted, struggling against the monster's grip. He felt the toes of his boots slide against the ground, but he gained no footing.

Rivic and Alityka didn't move from their positions.

"Don't let them go," Steigan said, trying to encourage Rivic and Alityka into action.

Cirvel pivoted toward him. "They won't make a move against me, lad. Rivic holds too much respect for me still and Alityka knows that she cannot hurt me in the slightest. Both understand their disadvantage. You on the other hand..."

Cirvel approached. "You have cleverly become the Winctonicht. I am afraid though, that your magical advantage still holds none against me."

The Lord of Gohaldinest's dark eyes searched over Steigan. "This, however…" His gaze landed on the sword, then flickered back to meet Steigan's face with an expression of surprise.

"Don't let him get the sword," Alityka shouted.

Steigan saw Cirvel reaching for it. "Vochey, sword."

Cirvel's lips twisted with amusement as he stepped back. "The only reason you have any ability to do that is because you have novihomidrak blood running through your veins." He held up his hands. "Vochey, sword of Rivic-na."

The sword appeared in Cirvel's hands. He appraised it as he turned toward Rivic. "Very well done. Too bad you created this when you were my apprentice and my Necroatheling. The power you imbued within it contained my magic as well, making this my weapon. Do you know what that does to it as a novihomidrak weapon?"

Cirvel slid his long fingers around the hilt, then ran the blade against this other hand. After he went the length of the sword, he turned his hand to show everyone. "Useless."

Rivic went pale and he couldn't keep the emotions off his face. Anger, disgust, loathing, hatred, respect, fury, awe, they were all there. "No."

Cirvel tossed the sword to the ground beside Martias-na. "Finish your friend and the Dominari; we have no use for them. Let Rivic watch his friend and family die. Dek'tae, you may feast."

"Hey, Cirvel," Steigan called out. "Have you seen your city? Gohaldinest is in ruin. You have nothing but rubble."

Cirvel gave him a dark, amused sidelong glance but said nothing. He turned then and started heading for the benches where they had rested Keteria. He took one look at her, then stepped away and teleported.

Steigan realized that Rivic and Alityka hadn't moved all this time because they couldn't. Only after Cirvel disappeared did his spell fall, allowing Rivic and Alityka to stagger forward. Martias-na reached down for the sword.

It vanished at his touch.

"What?" Martias-na asked, staring at the space where the sword had been.

Rivic charged, jumping and slashing downward with his sword. Alityka rushed in behind Rivic.

Martias-na didn't have time to draw a weapon and Steigan wondered how proficient the former sapere would be with it. If Cirvel had only trained Martias with magic, Martias-na might not be as lethal as other Necroathelings, such as Rivic.

The blow swept the Necroatheling off his feet, knocking him back just beneath Steigan.

Rivic switched his hands that held his weapon and he called a second sword to his primary hand. He stormed over before Martias-na recovered and Rivic, his eyes gone yellow, slashed at the monster holding Steigan.

Steigan dropped toward the ground, but Alityka said, "Shi'baten to'a helcord." The casting pushed Steigan sideways, nearly blasting him into the wall.

Martias-na started to scream.

Rivic circled toward Steigan, passing the sword off. Steigan realized it was the sword Rivic had forged. "How?" Steigan asked.

"Cirvel wasn't the only one who could call that sword."

Their attention went back to Martias who scrambled around, kicking randomly at the ground as he tried to pry something off him.

"I want to belong, to be accepted," Martias shouted. "I want to return to the centaurs."

"Dek'tae?" Steigan asked.

Rivic nodded. "Dek'tae."

Martias clawed at the fastening of the dark purple cloak and tore it open. He shed the Necroatheling cloak, leaving himself dressed in black leggings and a billowy white shirt which laced up the front.

"This is our chance," Rivic said as he motioned Steigan and Alityka back to their places. "Let's get the sphere around Dek'tae. Then I can then collapse the energy with dragon magic."

"What about Steigan's friend?" Alityka asked. "You'll trap him in too."

"We leave him with Dek'tae."

Steigan moved to position himself. He kept his eyes on the ground. As much as he wanted to save his friend, he wasn't certain that Martias actually existed inside that body anymore. For a long time, Martias hadn't even been himself in his thoughts. Steigan needed this to end. The best thing to do was not to look.

"Steigan, I'm sorry. I never meant to betray you," Martias shrieked. "Steigan!"

He made the mistake of turning a bit prematurely and saw in his peripheral vision that Martias reached out toward him. It brought a choking breath to his throat. A memory of him and Martias running from the gargaxes during the Sacred Knight ceremonies flashed through his thoughts. His stomach felt a similar sickness. When had their lives gotten so twisted?

"Steigan, I had to do it. Please understand. Please! I had to stay secure. What would happen to me if the Temple turned me away? I would have had no one."

His heart felt like it might burst from his chest. Feeling

himself on the verge of tears, Steigan looked up. "You would have had me. I was always your friend." Steigan raised his hands and summoned the magic around him.

"You still are, right? Please. I'm so sorry. Don't leave me."

"We have Dek'tae," Rivic announced. "Put a sphere around them."

Steigan saw Rivic give him a nod. It might as well have been a sword stroke severing his heart in two. "Miex'calidori."

Hearing Rivic begin speaking in a rapid, foreign language, Steigan turned away and faced the wall, unable to watch. He wondered what Martias was going through. Was Martias feeling any pain as the sphere collapsed around him? Steigan bent over and rested his head against the rock while he tried to get a hold of his turbulent emotions. He'd lost so much. When would he actually get a victory?

A hand touched his arm and Steigan flinched. As he spun around, he felt tears spring forth. They dribbled down his cheeks.

Alityka studied him, her face twisted in the pain he felt. Then she wrapped her warm arms around him and drew him as close as their armor allowed. Steigan shivered. He didn't know if he'd ever stop.

CHAPTER 25

Steigan sat in a chair near a window in the library. The others were gathered around the table behind him. He preferred to look out as the sun rose on this new day. Everything inside him felt beyond numb. A part felt dead.

The sky already had a brilliant blue cast to it with soft clouds. He knew from the condensation creeping along the edges of the glass that it was colder outside than it looked. He could see the tops of some leafless trees and watched a set of finches chase each other around the bare branches.

"How much of Dek'tae influenced what Martias said?" Steigan had asked to Rivic as they made their way back to Dubinshire.

"I don't know, but I do suspect that it changes a person," Rivic answered.

Steigan tried to focus on drawing in each breath. As he exhaled, he wasn't certain he'd ever be able to draw in more air again.

"Is he all right?" Laurient asked in a whisper over at the table.

"I don't think so," Alityka answered.

"He's not wearing his armor," Aeribela added.

"He doesn't need to. He can call it to him in a moment," Ithanes told them.

"Not if he feels that he's lost everything," Rivic said. "He might not want the protection."

"Is there anything we can do?" Ellis asked.

"Leave him be. He needs time. He's been through a lot," Valic stated.

Steigan turned his focus back to the world beyond the glass even though there wasn't much more to see than a few stark branches, blue sky, and the stone to part of the castle to his right.

The sun's rays touched his hand, letting a warm sensation crawl over his chilled skin. He watched the patch of light elongate over his hand.

The magic had failed him. Time after time since he'd arrived back in Dubinshire, he'd met with defeat. As if he were cursed.

"Steigan," came a softly familiar, yet unexpected whisper beside him. When he turned to look, he saw Keteria standing near a stack of books shrouded in darkness. She barely had any illumination on her, but he saw her beckon him.

Seeing that the others were paying him no attention, Steigan silently rose and slipped into the shadows to follow her. "Keteria?" he whispered back, having lost her to the blackness of the library.

A hand reached out to his. "Here."

So many questions filled him as he felt himself draw close to her. He picked his top two and asked them. "Are you all right? Are you feeling better?"

She'd been unconscious when they'd returned from the Playground. He'd heard that she had come around and was eating and drinking, but he hadn't had the nerve to go visit.

He'd felt too much shame about Martias-na taking her and his failed attempt at rescuing her.

She pulled him around to where a small shaft of sunlight brought faint light through the rows of books, but they stood a good distance from the others. "I'm fine, much better. Thank you. I had to see you one last time."

"One last time?"

She took both of his hands in hers. "We don't have long for me to explain it all. I'm not staying."

"Why not? We need you."

"Steigan, please, let me explain. The Martias-na who took me from Dubinshire and left you in the hole is later than the one you currently have trapped away. He told me this before he put me in a timelock to hold me, knowing that Cirvel wouldn't take me, and I'd end up back in the castle. Cirvel doesn't know I'm his daughter. But Cirvel knows about Tanold. When I tried to ask about all this, future Martias-na hushed me and said it was vital when I saw you again that I let you know."

"But Tanold is dead."

"No," she said with a small shake of her head, "he's not. But I don't know where he is, so don't ask."

She paused with a breath, the began again. "After turning Martias into a Necroatheling, he sent Martias-na out in search for Lihn... Matoline. I don't know why, and Martias-na didn't know either, but Ma-Mat is very important to Cirvel's plans. Steigan, you are the only one who has ever been able to keep her safe. Please, you've got to protect her."

"You told me she died when you were young."

"I never saw the body. I was only told she died. What if she didn't?"

Steigan saw the fear in her eyes which spoke of her fear that Martias-na had found her Ma-Mat.

"As much as it hurt me to lose Ma-Mat then, if you were

to go get her and bring her here, then I might have a chance to reunite with my mother. I want that more than anything."

"But she's in more danger here."

"Is she? Right now, she is alone and unprotected in the past. It could put all of us in danger if Martias-na finds us. What happens if Martias-na takes her back to Cirvel? All I know is that I lose her, but I don't know if she's safe or not."

"Okay, I will do what I can."

"Thank you."

She started to move away, but Steigan held tightly onto her. "Where are you going? Why aren't you staying here? You still need time to recover."

He saw her shake her head in the dim light. "No. We will meet again with the time is right. Until then, there are a lot of people out there in the world who need me. It has always been my mission to help people understand the magic. Right now, they need me more than ever."

"Keteria." He practically choked on her name. It felt like the day in the clearing when she'd cast her spell to suppress magic and fallen into her deep sleep. He wasn't certain he could lose her again. And yet, he also knew he had to let her go. She was right. He had to keep Matoline safe, and the people of the world needed her to teach them about magic.

"Goodbye, until we can meet again." She stretched up on her toes and kissed his cheek. Then she moved off toward the beam of sunlight and vanished as if carried out on the rays.

After standing there for a moment to see if anyone had sensed the magic and come to check it out, he lumbered back to his chair unnoticed and sat down once more. Get Matoline. Do it before Martias-na found her. Martias-na had been too close when he'd tortured Steigan in the Temple, but still cycles off. Had the Necroatheling been close to realizing that? Did Steigan have a way to slide in there undetected before Martias-na did?

More importantly, what did Cirvel want with Matoline and why wasn't he making the jumps himself if she were so crucial to his plans?

He wanted to reach out with his magic, to feel for where Keteria had gone. Instead, the familiar essence receded inside him like a child hiding beneath the bed from a thunderstorm. Once again he had to remind himself to breathe. His chest felt so tight. The sensation of being enclosed had been the reason he couldn't put on his armor. His rib cage felt confining enough.

He caught sight of a creature flying in circles through the blue sky. He rose off the back of the chair and leaned forward to watch the white dragon making loops. Interesting that a dragon who wanted to destroy the world would be having so much fun. Maybe Leschemal did rejoice in Steigan's defeat. Was the dragon aware of what had happened?

Someone moved up alongside him. "Hey," Alityka said, "Ithanes thinks that we should finish out time jumps. You still need to go back and retrieve Laurient to bring him back to this time and I have several times to visit you. Afterwards, Ithanes has a spell which will prevent what he calls 'time displacement' for the span of thirty cycles."

"Is that wise?" Steigan asked. He really didn't care if Alityka gave an answer or not. He was merely responding to her statement so that she thought he was agreeing with her.

"Yes, we have to keep Cirvel from making some time jump. He could go back and kill Krithstand the night before the battle, making it so that Gohaldinest never falls."

Considering that Cirvel had made no move like that, Steigan thought that maybe the Lord of Gohaldinest had more sense than the rest of them. Instead, Cirvel had always sent Martias-na on the time jumps.

Steigan felt a little lighter as he looked at Alityka. "Martias-na went back about a thousand cycles ago to look for Cirvel's mistress, Lihn Harvestendale. Why would Martias know to look there, and why wouldn't Cirvel have come himself?"

Alityka only shook her head.

Perhaps someday they would understand the reason.

Silence drifted between them and Steigan returned his gaze out the window. The dragon no longer circled in the air above. Maybe it had never truly been there to begin with.

"Steigan, the spells?" Alityka touched his hand.

"All right." He gripped the round ends of the chair's arms and started to push himself from the seat. Duty and his friends called.

As Steigan approached the table, he found himself looking around at everyone gathered there. Laurient and Aeribela had their heads close together as they spoke and shared a tender moment. Dragzel sat curled up on the wood table, asleep near Ellis. Ithanes poured over his books. Valic and Rivic engaged in talk about battle strategies.

Alityka came to stand beside Steigan and he slid his hand around hers, waiting in the blissful moment of peace with the others.

If Martias were here, Martias would have felt himself among people who cared for him. He wouldn't have felt alone. Steigan certainly didn't anymore. He was surrounded by friends from three timelines all coming together to stop Cirvel's plans.

Magic may have failed for Steigan, but he had powerful support.

"Steigan and I want to make the final series of time jumps," Alityka announced to the group.

"There's one more that wasn't on your list before," Steigan said to Alityka. "I'm going to get Lihn Harvestendale."

"My lady Lihn," Dragzel said excitedly as Alityka smiled back at Steigan. "You're going to bring her back?"

"She's part of our group and she's missing."

Even Ithanes seemed to approve. "One can never have too many allies."

Steigan reflected on the journey and those he'd gathered around him. They had a lot to do still in order to stop Cirvel's plans, but at least they were on their way.

"Well, a few time travel spells and then one to cease them all. What a lovely way to start the day," Steigan said.

"Are you going to complain about doing what you do best?" Ithanes asked.

"There is something to be said about coming home, especially when you know your friends are waiting for you." He sat down at the table with the others. He definitely felt like himself again. And never before had he ever felt so much like he was right where he belonged.

THE ADVENTURE ENDS

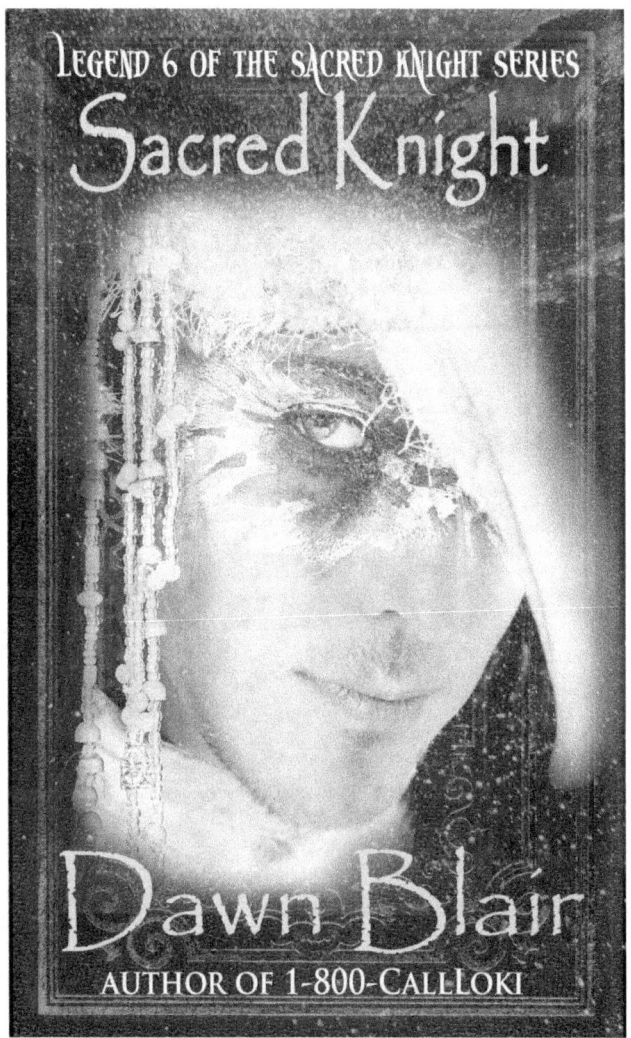

LEGEND 6 OF THE SACRED KNIGHT SERIES

Sacred Knight

Dawn Blair

AUTHOR OF 1-800-CALLLOKI

COMING SOON

A ONESONG NOVEL
BOOK 1
Tangled Magic

DAWN BLAIR
AUTHOR OF THE SACRED KNIGHT SERIES

With all his might, Rivic
hated Gohaldinest.

Find now at your favorite bookstore or visit us online at
www.morningskystudios.com

READY FOR ANOTHER QUEST?

Sign up for Dawn Blair's newsletter to learn about new releases, get access to fun and free stuff, hear about events, and more!

It's easy.

Go to **www.dawnblair.com/newsletter** to join the adventure and get a free PDF of the reading order to Dawn's books.

About the Author

Dawn Blair grew up on a ranch in a rural Nevada town. The old buildings provided inspiration for her imagination as she thrived on stories of unicorns, princesses, heroic knights, and hidden doors to other dimensions.

For as long as she can remember, Dawn has had a passion for storytelling. Though she started out writing, her creative life expanded into painting and illustration.

She loves creating worlds and spinning tales for people to enjoy. The best ones are the stories that surprise her as she's writing. She loves her characters doing the unexpected. She'll gladly tell you that the most exciting part about being a writer is being the first one on the journey.

Thank you for taking the time to join her on these adventures.

Find more about Dawn and her work at:
www.dawnblair.com

facebook.com/dawnblairbooks
twitter.com/dawnblair
instagram.com/dawn.blair

www.ingramcontent.com/pod-product-compliance
Lightning Source LLC
Chambersburg PA
CBHW070328260626
47160CB00003B/980